The Last Shades of
Scarlet

WOLVES OF LACONIA

WILLIAM A. LAMON

PAGE PUBLISHING, INC.
New York, NY

First originally published by Page Publishing, Inc. 2019

ISBN 978-1-68456-536-8 (Paperback)
ISBN 978-1-68456-537-5 (Digital)

Printed in the United States of America

For Caroline Hupp

Acknowledgments

While recreating moments in history, an author must be careful in the liberties he or she decides to take with the real individuals and events that once took place. Scholars and historical-fiction writers will often portray people and events differently or debate details regarding specific dates, locations, battles, or even the personalities of characters depicted. An author will never be able to satisfy the opinions of everyone. However, I made a conscious attempt to keep the story within the realm of "what could have happened" by focusing my research around the works of the historians closest to the events, Thucydides and Plutarch. Plato and Socrates were also products of the time, and their philosophy was extremely useful in the formation of individual characters. I don't believe one can have an opinion regarding the lives and minds of ancient Greeks without having examined their words.

I want to thank my former professor at Southern Methodist University, Melissa Dowling. She was able to take my interest in history and turn it into something more akin to an obsession. Her ability to provide a window into the lives of those who lived in that time period made the topics she taught in class much more than just a collection of significant dates. Melissa bridged the gap between her students and the historical events that took place by making you feel a connection with those who lived through it. Without her ability in the classroom to bring that period of history to life, this story would have never materialized.

Current historical-fiction authors like Steven Pressfield, Michael Curtis Ford, and Bernard Cornwell also have left notable footprints on my writing style. Their brilliant and unique craftsmanship of stories within the context of history and the incredible attention to detail enabled me to realize the importance of painting a vivid mental picture for the reader.

To my family, thank you for all your love and support. Although we often differ in our affections for specific time periods, we all share a passion for history. My cousin, Ben Gurley, has been an example for me of strength and self-control. Like Julius Caesar, he never appears fazed by his epileptic condition, nor does he let it diminish his intense love for people or deter his quest for greater knowledge. Thank you to my brother, Hunter. A man of few words despite his many opinions. His quality as a leader, combined with his strength and stubbornness, provided a current example of Plutarch's stereotypical Spartan. My father and mother, Hollis and Jane Lamon, have been constant inspirations in my life. Like mentors in this book, my father gave me the tools to be a good man, offering guidance and support while also allowing me to figure out my path on my own. As for my mother, she is an uncanny representation of how sources like Plutarch and Herodotus describe Spartan women—incredibly supportive, caring, intelligent, but tough as nails. There is no doubt she would have fared well in that society.

I also want to show my appreciation for all my friends. Our lives and relationships are what crafted this story. Furthermore, thank you to everyone who gave me their thoughts, opinions, and suggestions. Some of the best advice I received was the unfiltered criticism. The only reason this novel is no longer in the form of a word document is because of my friend, Caroline Dallas. Her preliminary edits and the extra set of eyes were invaluable.

There are also many dear friends and loved ones that are no longer with us who are also responsible for the conception of this novel. Following my time at SMU, I often spoke of wanting to write a novel about this time period, but Caroline Hupp was the first person to tell me to "shut up and write a book," and that is one of many reasons why this novel is dedicated to her. I admired her wit, cunning, depth as an individual, and loyalty as a friend and companion during the interesting stages of early adulthood. Her personality will bring to life many of the female characters throughout this series.

Kevin Baker's influence on this work can be seen in the way in which Spartan youths admired, honored, and looked up to exceptional young men who were slightly older. As a boy, I remember looking up to Kevin in a similar way. Handsome, athletic, and an exceptional man in all his undertakings. However, he always made an effort to make others feel appreciated. The quality of his character and that dynamic between young men is an important element in this story.

Whitner Milner certainly left a significant impression on this story. The love and friendship, combined with the rivalry and physical altercations, created an important bond between us that I believe was common between Spartan boys during their upbringing. We held each other to a certain standard, and he was a real-world example in my life of the kind of tough-love theme that I try to illustrate in the novel.

Whitney Boyer, along with other friends and family, was present during my first trip to Greece. Her wonderful sense of humor, combined with her kind and selfless persona, was a testament to her internal strength and self-control. She always appeared impervious to the melodramatic, and her love for everyone was a subtle reminder of my own demerits as an individual and were important lessons in humility. All this I attempt to communicate in some of the softer moments in the novel as characters grapple with the realities of the war, while also attempting to exemplify the traditional virtues they were taught to honor.

I also want to mention Matthew Olsen, Tyler Cross, Brice King, James Green, Jim Glasser, Kendrick Reusch, as well as Wink, and Mark Wynne. They, their families, and many others had their own unique influence on this story. Unfortunately, it would take over a hundred pages to adequately acknowledge their contribution. Still, words cannot express how much I appreciate all the inspiration, assistance, and support from my friends and family. Please enjoy *The Last Shades of Scarlet: Wolves of Laconia*.

Historical Context

This is a novel about the Peloponnesian War between Athens and Sparta (431–404 BC). The Peloponnesian War took place in the aftermath of the Greco-Persian Wars, known for notable battles like Marathon, Thermopylae, and Salamis. The Persian Wars forced many city-states in Greece to either fall under the yolk of the Persian Empire or unite to resist the invaders. Under the leadership of Athens and Sparta, Greece was able to win significant battles on land and sea, forcing Persia to withdraw. Following the Persian Wars, Sparta and Athens remained the dominant powers in the Greek world.

While Athens and Sparta were both Greek, their different political and military philosophies led them to develop very different societal structures. These ideologies are significant because it was how Athens and Sparta projected their influence over other Greek city-states. States that allied with Athens were expected to embrace democratic political principles while those that allied with Sparta adopted an oligarchic political system.

Sparta

Sparta had a small but specialized land army that was known for its elite hoplite warriors that did nothing but train for battle following their seventh birthday. Throughout Greece, Sparta was admired for its discipline, austerity, and the professionalism of their land army. The Spartans were able to train for battle their whole lives because of the helots and perioikoi that fulfilled the other demands of the state.

The perioikoi or "the dwellers around" lived in communities in the territory adjacent to Sparta, following Sparta's lead both politically and militarily. They were farmers, traders, and blacksmiths by trade. Their population greatly outnumbered the Spartans; as a result, their hoplites actually made up the bulk of Sparta's military force.

The *helots* were a community of Messenians forced into servitude by the Spartans. Their population also dwarfed that of Sparta, which was why much of the Spartan military's time was spent managing their subjugation. Spartans did not own *helots* as slaves; meaning, they could not buy them or sell them. Nevertheless, they were forced to serve Spartans in a variety of ways. *Helot* farmers were required to allocate a significant percentage of their harvest to a specific Spartan master. Female members of *helot* families often served in Spartan households while young males accompanied their Spartan counterparts into battle as squires.

By not having to take up other trades, the small Spartan population was able to focus on nothing but the art of warfare. However, the subjugation of the *helots* was a continuous source of instability. Many Messenians resented their Spartan masters, resulting in occasional uprisings that continually threatened the stability of Sparta.

Spartan government was a form of oligarchy, consisting of a congress of Spartan equals (*Gerousia*), a council of elders (*ephors*), and two kings. By having two kings and three different branches of government, the political system had a variety of checks and balances designed to keep any king or group of elites from becoming too powerful.

Athens

Athens, on the other hand, was a democratic republic and the premier naval power in the Mediterranean. Their naval power enabled them to secure vast trade networks, leading to an increase of wealth, influence, and manpower in the form of immigrants. The system of government allowed wealthy families, military leaders, and good orators to gain popularity and rise to political prominence. In the forum, these leaders would address the people with various matters of state, including matters of law and various political appeals or policy proposals. While admired for its inclusiveness, the Athenian democracy was extremely susceptible to corruption, with wealthy families often using their financial leverage to sway public opinion. After the Athenian population voted on different issues, enacted proposals would then translate into policies that the state would carry out.

The naval power of Athens, combined with its economic influence, allowed them to force many weaker city-states to comply with their demands. Often, these smaller states were forced to pay large tributes, allow Athenian garrisons within their territories, make trade agreements favorable to Athens, and/or put military forces under Athenian command.

Instability and War

With Athenian power and wealth growing, many turned to Sparta for assistance as they were seen as the only city-state in Greece capable of balancing Athenian power. The collection of city-states allied to Athens was known as the Delian League, and this consisted of many coastal and island city-states on the Aegean and Adriatic. Those allied with Sparta were known as the Peloponnesian League, the most significant members being Corinth, Boeotia, Elis, Melos, Pylos, Mantinea, and Epidaurus.

As communities all over Greece began choosing sides, an ideological rift developed within every Greek city-state. This division manifested itself in the form of violent political polarization, with Athens and Sparta both supporting opposing political movements within every city-state in Greece. Athens supported the democrats, while Sparta supported the oligarchs, all in an attempt to destabilize any government allied to their enemy. Instead of traditional pitched battles, the political aspect of this war led to a rise in siege warfare. Both sides used the threat of disease and starvation as a tactic to force occupants within a city to capitulate. Under this pressure, fierce internal battles erupted within the besieged city-states. This led to unspeakable atrocities and slaughter as citizens often betrayed their friends and family during shifts in political allegiance.

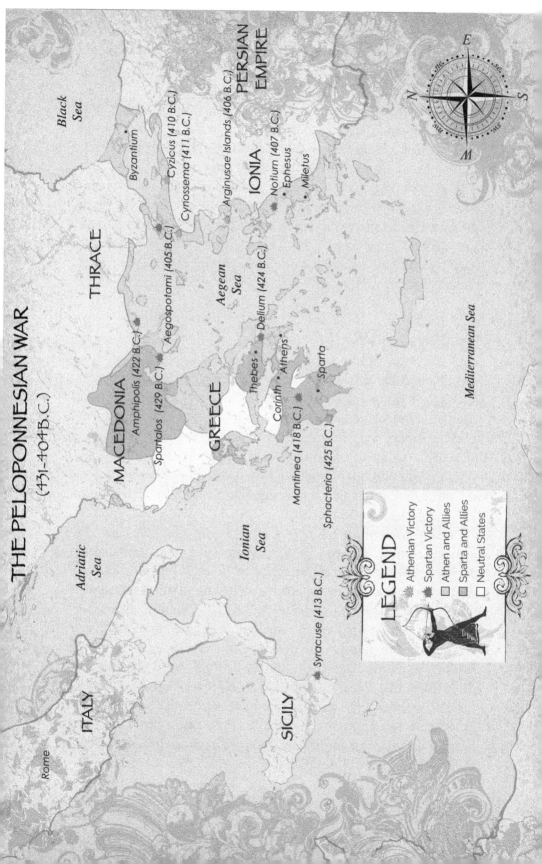

THE PELOPONNESIAN WAR
(431-404 B.C.)

Black
Sea

Byzantium

Cyzicus (410 B.C.)

Cynossema (411 B.C.)

THRACE

Aegospotami (405 B.C.)

Arginusae Islands (406 B.C.)

PERSIAN
EMPIRE

IONIA

Notium (407 B.C.)

Ephesus

Miletus

MACEDONIA

Amphipolis (422 B.C.)

Spartolos (429 B.C.)

Aegean
Sea

Delium (424 B.C.)

GREECE

Thebes

Corinth • Athens

Sparta

Mantinea (418 B.C.)

Sphacteria (425 B.C.)

Adriatic
Sea

ITALY

Rome

Ionian
Sea

Mediterranean Sea

Syracuse (413 B.C.)

SICILY

LEGEND

☀ Athenian Victory

☀ Spartan Victory

☐ Athen and Allies

☐ Sparta and Allies

☐ Neutral States

First Lesson

I feel nothing. My body is numb, and yet my senses are strangely acute. I can taste the salty air of the dark sea that lies calm before me. I know it is vast, but the cool fog that floats above it obscures any view of what lies beyond. Though ominous, it welcomes me with a mysterious gentleness. I glance over my shoulder and then turn back toward the fair lady that patiently awaits my exodus.

She knew all along that my road would lead me here. Her companion knew too. Both pass me a comforting smile as I prepare to depart. The lady places her hand into mine as I set a tender kiss upon it, her gray eyes gleaming as she smiles back at me. If I were the young man I used to be, I would say that I almost detect a delicate blush forming in her cheeks. I lean down and grab a fistful of sand and let the grains flow through my fingers, looking back on this land that I leave behind me. Hopefully, this will be a quick and peaceful journey. This war-torn soul is no Odysseus, but my armor still fits, and my hand can still grip a spear. My heart does long for this next adventure. The figure in the boat says nothing as I stare and grin at his empty face. The ugly bastard looks just as I imagined him. As I toss my kit aboard, I cannot help but think about where this journey all began…a feckless boy born in Sparta.

My eyes crack open as I awake to light flashing into my eyes. The blinding ray of sunlight hampers any attempt to assess what is happening. All I can make out is a dark form at the foot of my bed. His arm is extended, and the light that is blinding looks as if it is coming from the palm of his very hands. Is this a dream, or is this Apollo himself summoning me to the day?

"Get up, boy," the voice bellows as I rub my eyes once more, realizing now that the ray of light is not the hand of Apollo but rather a man who is manipulating the reflection of the sun with the blade of his *xiphos*.

He laughs, seeming amused as he guides his blade with his wrist until the beam of light hits his intended target.

"Rather gentle of you, Gylippus… I would have expected a more forceful approach from a man that is overseeing the training of my son," I hear my father comment mockingly as another dark outline enters the room, my eyes still recovering.

"Very well," the stranger says with a menacing grin as he grabs my ankles and pulls with such tremendous force that the next thing I know, my back lies not in my bed but rather in the dust.

Out of the corner of my eye, I see my mother in the other room. She is observing with attention all that is happening, and yet her own eyes do not stray from the urn she is polishing with a small cloth. I climb quickly to my feet and jab my fist toward the stranger's stomach, landing the blow with a thump. My arm recoils as the fist bounces off his hard abdomen. I pause, stunned by my reaction and the futileness of its result.

"Good, Andronikos!" the man cries, following his words with a quick backhand that lands across my face.

He strikes quickness and strength that my feet fly out from under me, and just like that, my back returns to the floor.

"Now, if we can just teach you how to duck!" he roars as both he and my father burst out in laughter.

He then reaches his hand out toward me, but I do not accept it. Instead, I pull myself off the ground again, my mouth dry with the taste of dust and blood. I can already tell that I am going to hate this man.

Before leaving the house, I reach to my mot'
However, she ignores my plea and says nothing
as the man grabs me by the neck and shoves me for
road.

"No more of that, son of Hippagretas," the man utters w
subtle laugh.

As I walk beside him, I look up at his face. His formidable
profile stares forward. It is as if he has suddenly recalled something
of significance. He has a beard that is dark black with the youth of a
young man and yet coarse like that of a seasoned soldier. Compared
to me, he looks like a giant, even though I know he is just out of the
agoge. He is likely ten years older than myself, give or take a couple.
I vaguely recall how my father spoke of him in the days leading up
to this. He told my mother about this man's progression through
the *agoge* and how it was most impressive. My father has always
preferred hands-on training. It was the same for my brother, and he
now believes this man's youth and vigor will work to my advantage
in the early stages of my instruction. I remember my father grabbing
this Gylippus by the shoulder, saying, "Who knows, maybe you'll
live long enough to fight by his side."

We continue down the road toward the agora, the swift breeze
creating a chorus of sounds as it hums through wheat and the branches
of the olive trees. My eyes look up into the empty bright-blue sky. I
follow the blue down until it meets the earth upon the rocks of the
mighty mountains. The smell of lavender and jasmine mix in the air
as we pass the many quaint households of the peers, made simple
and pleasant by the diligent work of the Spartan wives, mothers, and
daughters. On any other day, I would be doing the morning chores
and collecting wood for the small fire for my mother as she prepared
breakfast. Then, I'd be off down the road to join with the other boys
to race and wrestle, occasionally watching the torment of the older
boys as they drill in the hot sun. Just around dusk, I'd hurry down
the road to see my *helot* friend, Gorga, whom I meet in secret. She
often tends to my scratches and bruises, singing softly as she lightly
traces her fingers along my back. Sometimes, we lie in the tall grass,
her head against my chest as I run my hands through her dark hair.

Such pleasing thoughts fill my mind as my eyes stare into the vast landscape. Yet the resulting grin does not go unnoticed.

"Your mind wanders, Adronikos," Gylippus states as he sees my glance captured by the scene of young Spartan girls fetching water down by the stream. "Women…heh! Now is not the time to think of such things, young Adronikos. That instruction comes much later, and well, ha ha, I won't trouble you with those details quite yet," he states, shaking his head with a grin.

"I do not believe I have formally introduced myself. I am Gylippus, son of Cleondridas, and I am going to oversee your training. You will do as I say always. You will never question my demands," he orders, looking down at me for the first time. "You do not want to disappoint me, boy. I have been disappointed a time or two already in my youth, and I promise, you do not want to do that." He straightens his posture and looks down the road again.

I rub my head slightly. There is a lump where it had made contact with the floor during my first encounter with Gylippus. While I continue to probe, I feel a trace of wetness, followed by a small slit that is sensitive to the touch.

"Ahh." I grimace softly as I bring my fingers down in front of my face to inspect them. On my fingertips, a small trace of crimson-red blood glistens in the morning sunlight.

"Head hurt?" He takes a quick glance at me out of the corner of his eye before looking back toward the road. *Whack!*

I must have only blinked as I failed to see his clenched fist fly through the air and make contact with the back of my skull. The unexpected impact causes me to stumble and fall forward. Once again, I find myself on the dusty earth. My body goes numb as I slowly lift my face from the dirt. I can make out the distant chuckle of a group of Spartan girls watching this display from outside one of the dwellings that line the road.

Anger boils within me. I pause, taking one deep defiant breath as I try to plan my response. With haste, I rise with all the speed and determination I can muster, running back toward my foe without any consideration about what to do when I get there. Gylippus reaches out with his long muscular arm, straight as a spear, his large hand catching me by the throat before I can even get within striking range.

"Still hurt?" he says quizzically, looking directly into my eyes. Something tells me that I need to choose my words wisely. Instead, I decide to ignore the question entirely, not wanting to give him the satisfaction of a response. All I can think about is my desire to be rid of this man.

"I'd like to kill you," I snap, surprising myself.

The words quickly slip from my tongue, but there is no use trying to retract them.

"You may get that chance, little one. One day, you might just be the end of me," he says in a more serious tone, his face peering curiously again toward the mountains as if they had just whispered something to him. Then, he abruptly snaps out of the trance.

"But not this day, you little piece of horseshit," he exclaims as he slaps me hard on the back. "You have a lot to learn before then, and I fear we all are running out of time."

I can sense that the playful sarcasm in his voice is forced. There is a sad truth that is betrayed as the words roll off his lips. Although I hardly know him, I can see that this man is very calculating, and there is something on his mind that is troubling him. Still, there is a great strength radiating from his presence as I watch him peer with fortitude down the path ahead. He is a combination of handsome and terrifying. I want to be like this man.

"You are feeling no more pain, are you, son of Hippagretas? Not until…this moment," he states, delivering the sentence gradually as if he is summoning the pain back to my skull.

It is strange; only with that revelation does my head begin to throb once more. Puzzled, I probe my bloody gash with my fingers. I can see him smile in the corner of my eye. Then, he steps in front of me and kneels down, placing both of his hands upon my shoulders. Again, his face and his tone become serious.

"Pain and love, anger and fear, every man feels these. But these feelings are wild as beasts, young Adronikos. Within every man, they manifest all that can make a great warrior, a coward, and everything in between. Your father has given me the charge of instructing you, to teach you how to harness these beasts. Harness, not control, for such an ambition is folly. Even the gods themselves are not immune to the power of the beasts. In fact, it is where they draw their strength.

"What keeps the gods supreme and makes mortal men wise are the skills to guide or manipulate this internal savagery. It is not tact or brute strength which makes us superior to our foes, son of Hippagretas. Rather, it is because we have learned to respect the beasts who reside within us, and such respect can make them powerful allies to the warrior that is able to recognize their influence and authority."

Agoge

I kneel to grab another fistful of sand and glance over to the lady and her companion as we wait for my ride to reach the shore. Before the small craft arrived, their strong faces just peered off into the distance, as if they could see through the fog. During that time, it felt like we were standing here for hours. Yet they stood there tall and triumphant, as if to anticipate the sudden arrival of a magnificent fleet, not this lonely craft that has come to carry me across this still sea.

I continue to run the damp sand through my fingers over and over again as the gentle ripples of the water barely push themselves against the shore. One after another, the waves softly splash up the desolate beach before retreating again into the black water. I take my time gathering myself before I board the boat, watching the repetition of each small swell folding over into a break. The simple scene reminds me of the years of my youth in the agoge. Gylippus came and plucked me out of early childhood, introducing me into the barracks that would be my home until it was time for me to marry. The memories of those years all seem to run together, even though they were some of the longest of my life. Like each swell, we rose every day, rolling forward through constant pain, blood, sweat, dirt, and fatigue.

Simple scenes like this one never escape memory. One might think, the mind, like the rest of our bodies, seems to consume what it needs while discarding the rest. It commits important instructions on footwork, formations, and spear thrusts to memory. Intertwining with the impulses of instinct, the mind and body retain and engage these proficiencies as if they had been bestowed upon us at birth.

In reality, the mind develops these attributes only through recognition, anticipating the consequences of every situation and summoning the necessary reaction. Significant moments of virtue are also retained, as they validate the hardships of training, the wisdom of experience, as well as the presence of the gods. These moments lie at the intersection of all that we have seen with all that we have been told.

The rest of our mind, however, seems to be filled with moments of no real significance. Recollections of festivals, a woman's smile, the smell of lavender. I often wonder why our mind discards certain instants we wish we could recall while filling itself with random glimpses of a single rock, a flash of lightning, or a helot farmer's dog taking a shit. Why does memory choose to retain such things? Perhaps they are moments where we were unknowingly in the presence of the gods, our consciousness unable to recognize it, yet our mind subtly tucks it away like a young girl stumbling upon a precious stone.

I smile to myself briefly as the sand falls through my fingers, glimpses of my past running through my head. They are the events of my childhood as well as my early hatred for my dear friend and mentor. Then, I did not yet understand the intent of Gylippus's first lesson. Over time, I would learn many things from him, both the decent and the corrupt.

Many said that he had a talent for turning average men into adept warriors, a skill they said he acquired while fighting with the great Brasidas in Thrace. In preparation for that campaign, Gylippus was tasked with the training of helots and ordinary men from all over the Peloponnese, turning them into a semblance of proper hoplites before departing to Thrace out of Corinth.

Later, I would see my mentor apply his talent many times in our exploits together. Although Gylippus was gone for several months over the course of my years in the agoge, he built his reputation on those campaigns. One year in particular, toward the end of my education, I recall well. The memory is as clear as glass. It was when the rivalry between Athens and Sparta became more than just an intangible tale and where the gods started to weave the threads of this war into the story of my life.

Word has reached me of Gylippus's return with Brasidas, as the thickly clouded sky grows faintly red in the east. Daybreak will soon be upon us. Perhaps I will be tested again today, and Gylippus will have an opportunity to see the progress I have made since he left last campaign season and what I have become over the past several years since he brought me here.

I live with my troop in the *paidiskoi* quarters, which are on the far side of the village next to the gymnasium. Our barracks consist of six different troops of youths in their late teens. This is our first year here. Once in these barracks, you are eligible for recruitment into a *sussitia* after completing a yearlong initiation ritual that requires us to survive on our own in the wild on the outskirts of Sparta.

Many boys older than the rest of my troop still live here. A few come from either disgraced families while most have just failed to be recruited for one perceived weakness or another. This shame causes them to be spiteful, and they hardly ever let us sleep. Their higher rank, combined with their shortfalls as individuals, makes them bitterly authoritative. They constantly force us to wrestle with one another for their nightly entertainment.

When we are fortunate, they only make us recite random verses, either lines from Homer or various laws passed down by Lycurgus. However, any lapses in memory are punished with heckling or a well-thrown pebble in the direction of one's face. For them, only quick and quality recitation is acceptable.

Often, they pose questions designed to produce an unsatisfactory response and follow up with a variety of punishments. One such punishment involves the singling out of a boy among us who will be issued personal beatings in response to mistakes made by another.

On moonless nights, our instructors will interrupt these sessions and force our troop to run for miles up the Aphetaid Road, around the gymnasium, across the Laconian plain, down along the Eurotas River, and back down through the Hyakinthian Way. All is done in total darkness. The route takes several hours, and our elders let none retire until every member of the troop returns.

On occasion, a member of the troop falls behind either because of an ankle sprain or broken toe. Those who recognize their absence often double back to find their comrades, only to discover another already supporting the weight of an injured companion. However, this makes us vulnerable to the older boys who will sometimes lay in ambush. If discovered, they will hurl small stones from out of the darkness, and if they are able, they will tackle you on the road and pummel any who fall into their trap.

The instructors test us by offering various rewards to those who finish first. Often, these come in the form of additional rations of bread with our black soup. The last to finish is refused bread the next meal. Gylippus says this is done to encourage competition and discourage the temptation to fall behind to aid our weaker companions. If one is discovered helping a fallen comrade, he is issued ten lashings. The same is delivered to any victor caught splitting their extra rations. Occasionally, instructors get creative with the punishment, forcing the slow or injured to lash their comrades. In this way, others in the group have to suffer for the misfortune or carelessness of another.

I don't believe that the instructors' intent is to discourage giving our companions aid but rather to shame the weaker among us. Gylippus told me that they do this so no Spartan becomes content with failure, and that these unfortunate older boys and their torments are a necessary part of the *agoge*. The lesson being, that in battle, the mistakes we make rarely affect our own fate. Instead, they can lead to the demise of others, sometimes our kin, mentors, or friends. We must be aware that our own shortcomings have greater consequences than damage to personal pride.

As I lie awake here in bed, I try to recall these lessons by marking each point from the instructor, dissecting its meaning, and thinking of situations where I can apply them. I have gone through this routine each night since I entered the *agoge*, testing myself so I could avoid scorn the next day in training. Now, however, there is a new motivation for these meditations: war.

"Learn something new every day," I tell myself, recalling Father's words.

Sparta has always boasted about being cut off from the rest of the world. Pure. Disciplined. Superior. Yet words of war still land on eager ears among the youth. Each day, we hear that appeals to Sparta are arriving from political allies within each Greek city-state. Diplomats usually stick to the usual pleas for assistance, while refugees, wanderers, merchants, and mercenaries spill gossip that spreads through Sparta like a wildfire.

One might think other Greeks would choose a more hospitable or familiar destination than Sparta, and yet they still come. Their arrival often coincides with horrible tales of internal political squabbles that escalated into violent civil conflicts. Each story tells a common tale: a dominant political class declaring for either Athens or Sparta, while those in opposition bide their time to plot revolt and massacre. Even our own messengers bring news of city-states revolting and switching allegiances. However, these stories are deemed as less reliable as agents being paid by Sparta always tend to embellish favorable news while communicating the unfavorable in as few words as possible.

So far, pitched battles in this war have been few, and yet, the wounded still return with tales of one skirmish or another. Seems all that is needed to take a city is to show up with an army, lay siege, and wait for the citizens inside to tear each other apart. When the armies retire, seasons pass, and the previously disposed citizens return to act on their plots for revenge. Just the winter before last, my brother's mentor returned from the three-year siege at Plataea. I've never spoken to him about it directly, but we've all heard it was nasty business.

From what I have gathered, it was the dead of night when some among the Plataeans invited our Theban allies into the city. After occupying it, the commanders gathered the population into the agora the next morning to communicate their intention to remain peaceful. However, shortly after, they were ambushed and slaughtered by the citizens of city.

A detachment of Spartans accompanied a small Peloponnesian force to respond to the incident in support of the Thebans. The siege lasted two winters. The conditions of squalor became such that men were getting diseased, either from the water, the cold, or from the whores that wandered from tent to tent in numbers greater than the rats. Many among our allies deserted, and the thinned ranks had to be swollen by spears for hire.

Morale on both sides was apparently piss-poor when the starving Plataeans tried their luck, sallying out in an attempt to break through the siege and flee. Only a few brave souls had the courage to stand and fight. These were easily cut down before the Spartans ordered an assault in retaliation.

After the walls were breached, a herald ordered Plataea to surrender. Once we reoccupied the city, a trial was held. Most of the Plataean men were executed while the women were sold as slaves. The city, we razed to the ground.

With such events taking place, constant banter is everywhere. Somehow, our commanders continue to display an air of confidence and calm. They measure their words to friends and foe while the outsiders speak of the destruction of Greece. To add to the commotion, detachments from Sparta come and go. Many are being sent to reinforce Brasidas in Thrace, while others are dispatched to ravage farmstead and orchards in Attica or aid our allies in Boeotia. The elders say Spartans have not left our borders with such frequency since the times before Lycurgus, when our forefathers sailed across the sea to retrieve Helen under the banners of Agamemnon.

The sound of soft rain outside is making my eyelids grow heavy as I think about my father and brother out there. Hippagretas is a good man and has always been a great father. He chose Gylippus to oversee my training because he knew where this war would take him. For the first seven years of my life, Father would visit home at night. He would kiss and hug our mother, make sure our chores were done, and ask us one thing that we learned that day. He does not mind failure so long as we learn from our mistakes. He takes great joy in our achievements and any efforts we make to improve ourselves. Fatigue is what he abhors. He does not tolerate it as an excuse to neglect responsibility and duty. He always says that if we can discover one piece of additional knowledge each day, my brother and I would be wiser than he by the time we've seen twenty summers. I miss those times with Father, but he knew the world we were going to be thrust into. With everything we go through in the barracks, I am thankful that he prepared me in his own way.

I wonder what he and my brother are doing tonight. Is it even raining where they are, or are they joking with comrades by a campfire? Do they accompany some of the younger men on watch, or are they staring into a starlit sky, wondering what news will come tomorrow? For all I know, they could be part of the same garrison or hundreds of miles apart. I wonder what adventures and sights this war will bring me, or will it all be over before I have a chance to fight?

I wish I were still in my bed, pondering various thoughts before succumbing to sleep. Instead, this. Shortly after we awake, heavy clouds begin to settle over the city as our instructors muster us into rank and file outside the barracks. The rain has been falling all day now as I glance up at the Aphetaid Road, almost invisible through the downpour. Part of me is hoping there will be no forced sprint along that route tonight. We have been drilling for hours in the mud, and now we all are covered in it. While the wrestling exercise likely resembles just an unorganized mass of bodies, our betters tell us that the lack of secure footing helps us become more familiar with the nature of balance and leverage.

"Now, let's see if you can keep your feet in formation. Phalanxes!" the instructor belts out loudly.

We scramble to our feet and stumble through the mud to retrieve our wooden spears and shields. The "spears" are more closely akin to sticks, and the shields are just a rounded arrangement of three blanks nailed together.

Anticipating the instructor's demands, we arrange ourselves in a formation of three shields deep and five across. We are all familiar with this exercise and keep our spear arms raised throughout the drilling so that we get accustomed to having our arm in the thrust position.

"Shields port!" the instructor shouts.

He places a practice shield a few yards behind us and another behind the formation opposite of our own.

"This is your *polis*, you fucking shitworms!" he yells, kicking the shield behind us. "If those sons of whores retrieve your shield, then you've lost your city. Oh, and let me remind you that Spartans have never witnessed such defeat, and by the gods, neither will any pupil of mine." His voice sprays drops of rain and spit as he points to the formation opposing us.

The group of boys on the other side include many that are perioikoi, sons of *proxenus* (guest friends to the state), *mothax* (Spartan half-breeds), and other bastard youths that have been sponsored by a peer. Once sponsored, boys of these classes are allowed to train among the Spartan youth. While their use is primarily for our instruction, every season, a few within their ranks are taken into a mess and allowed to become Spartan peers.

A few of the boys are those from the last troop that were not invited into a mess. One among them, Pidytes, disdains me. I best him in almost everything, and for this reason, I do not even recognize him as a rival. His older brother was labeled a coward and a deserter. Some say he fled to Persia while others swear to have seen him recently, drunk in some brothel in Corinth. Either way, his shame follows their family.

To make matters worse, Pidytes left a comrade behind on the road one night during exercise after being ambushed by older boys. So eager to finish first and advance himself, he abandoned his partner. His companion was my cousin, and while left alone, he took a stone to the head and died shortly after. It was a freak accident, and everyone acknowledges this, for no one desired his death. Yet I believe Pidytes still feels the weight of that night on his heart, suspecting that I blame him for the death of my cousin.

Once, he asked me why I deem myself to be better than he. In response, I said that I do not concern myself with what others believe me to think. The only thing that drives me is love for my friends, respect for the gods, and the honor of my family.

I don't exactly understand why he asked that of me, but still, I pity Pidytes. Perhaps it is a combination of my pity and his pride that have made me his target. Now, he stands in the opposite formation. I cannot be sure through the rain, but I feel his stare upon me.

The entire formation of the opposing boys is at least twice the size of our own, so retrieving their shield seems highly unlikely.

"How are we supposed to get through that?" I hear from the shield behind me. It's Diokles, son of Epitadas.

Diokles and I grew up close to each other, and he is one of a handful of companions I knew prior to our lives in the *agoge*. His timorousness makes me smile to myself just as our instructor sounds the advance. Suddenly, the older boys charge toward us, trying to pick up some speed as their feet attempt to gain traction in the mud. As I dig my own into the sludge, I realize a lack of pressure being applied to our front line. My stomach sinks. I know that if they hit us now, our formation will falter.

"Rear ranks! Brace!" I yell, but I fear the downpour has muffled my voice because there is still no pressure being applied by my companions behind.

Without the weight of our subsequent ranks, we are unable to apply the pressure needed to withstand their advance. I lean forward anxiously, posting my shoulder deep into the bowl of my shield, but my efforts are to no avail. Their front line smashes into our own, sending us backward into the mud. On my back, I squint through the rain and mud to see rank after rank of the older boys trying to pass us as they advance into our second line. However, our slick bodies squirming under their feet cause many of them to stumble. For a moment, I sense a chance for us to recover, until their consecutive ranks kick us and start smashing their wooden shields into our faces or ribs. Through the chaos, I can still hear the muffled voice of our instructor yelling in outrage.

Then, I see a muddy figure above me raise his shield. Just as he attempts to strike me, I roll away, just avoiding a blow to my chest. Quickly I roll back into him and manage to grab his shield. With one sudden twist and jerk, I cause my opponent to lose his footing and fall to the ground beside me, both of us still clutching the shield as he hits the mud. Still screaming, I cannot determine the content of my instructor's speech. As the melee ensues, I am able to rip the shield from my rival's grasp and throw it off to the side. Now, all I can see is the muddy face of my enemy and the rain pouring down around us. The boy and I continue to struggle for the upper hand, exchanging blows while trying to gain a position on top of the other.

The ground is full of bodies as other boys appear to be engaged in similar brawls on either side of us. A few stand frozen, perhaps transfixed by the chaos or unsure what the instructor's stifled shouts are trying to communicate. Finally, I regain my footing and feel three of my comrades fall in behind me.

Encouraged by their presence, I pick up the discarded shield and prepare for a final assault, but I am too late. Time seems to slow as my opponent pulls himself up off the ground. As he brings himself to one knee, I glimpse a charging figure behind him appear faintly through the rain. With speed and determination, the boy vaults off the back of my opponent and uses this momentum to crash, shield first, into our line. The force of the clash causes my own shield to smash into my face as both my comrades and I are once again thrown backward into the mud.

My right eye throbs, but through my blurred vision, I see the figure use his momentum to roll through the impact and continue in the direction of our shield. The rear ranks of my troop scramble to reform before the figure slams into them in full stride. With the slick ground, their line also fails to withstand the jolt.

"Shield! Don't let him get the shield!" I hear Estathios, our troop leader, bellow.

The opposing boy wavers only briefly from the second impact, granting me just enough time for me to gather my footing. However, as I turn toward him, I catch a glimpse of his mates beginning to rally behind me. They are obviously inspired by their young Achilles, who is now shield to shield with the last of my mates. I gain ground quickly as they all seek to find their balance on the slick ground. I see one member of my troop slip and fall away as the boy finds a foothold and surges into him. The push causes my opponent to turn ever so slightly, revealing his spear side. I lunge forward, smashing my forehead into his exposed rib cage, sending both of our bodies to the ground with a loud crack. The impact causes us to slide several feet across the mud.

"Reform! Reform the line!" I hear Estathios say before turning his head down toward me. "Take care of him!" he hollers through the rain before falling back into the overlapping shields.

I wrap my legs around my victim's waist and throw my right bicep around his throat. The more he fights and squirms for air, the more his body grows limp in my arms. Then, I hear a roar erupt from a small crowd that has gathered around our spectacle. Thunder? My eyes search through the rain, looking at the muddy figures either side of me. I can no longer recognize friend from foe as we all are covered so thickly in mud. There, I spot Estathios and see him wipe the muck from the front of his shield. Our troop lets out a howl of triumph as he reveals that it is the shield of our enemy.

"Enough! Fall into order!" the instructor yells as the two troops scramble into formation.

I squirm from beneath the boy as he rolls motionless into the mud beside me. I look down at my victim triumphantly until, under the layer of muck, I see a face I recognize. It is Messulius, a *helot* boy I have grown up with. His father serves my own as physician and battle squire. I did not recognize Messulius in the rain.

The whole time, I had envisioned Pidytes as my adversary. My heart races as I realize whom it is that I have just incapacitated. I also feel shame for wanting to put Pidytes down in such a pitiless fashion. Abruptly the instructor walks over and shoves me out of the way.

"Is he going to be okay?" I ask, trying to hold back any emotion.

A knot is forming in my throat, and although there are no tears welling up in my eyes, it takes all my strength to hold them back.

"That should be the least of your concern, Nikos," the instructor states calmly, pushing the boy's limp body aside to reveal a shattered shield beneath it.

He then takes a handful of sludge and squeezes it through his fist until it oozes out the bottom and drops directly on Messulius's face. I let out a sigh of relief as he begins moving. After a brief moment of disorientation, he shakes the mud from his brow and then stumbles awkwardly back into his formation.

"Your foe is fine, Nikos… Your polis, however, is destroyed," he snarls, holding the split pieces of the shield in either hand.

"But…but we captured their shield, sir. We were victorious," Diokles chimes in from among the group of mud-soaked boys.

"What the fuck did you just say, cub?" the instructor snaps back, referencing the humiliating nickname given to him by the peers.

In the mess, other peers used to tease Diokles's father, Epitadas, about the small stature of his boy, as well as his overprotective wife. Many times, she was suspected of hiding olives and bread by the creek for Diokles in his early years of the *agoge*. Maybe six or seven summers ago. Now a fine size, many believe Diokles's healthy stature yet timid nature is a result of this coddling.

"You of all people should not be claiming victory," the instructor continues. "You were located in the second rank, which failed to brace to support your front line. Did you not see them buckle and break before the enemy's advance, or are you fucking blind? You may have been born into Sparta, but a cub suckling at the teat of a lioness does not make him a lion. What you claim is certainly not victory... Victory," he repeats sarcastically beneath his breath. Even through the rain, you can see the anger building in his eyes. "And what is victory, cub?" the instructor yells out in a mocking tone as he ominously walks over to Diokles.

"Success on the battlefield, sir," Diokles responds timidly as the instructor stands over him ominously, like a wolf about to feast on a carcass.

Unexpectedly, the instructor strikes Diokles across the face with half of the shattered shield.

"And what good is success in battle if the city you swore to protect lies in ruin upon your return? What is a Spartan peer without Sparta? Without her, we are no better than the *helots.*"

Through the torrent, I can see the faces of many other peers that have congregated to witness this instruction. My mentor, Gylippus, is there, as well as Diokles's mentor, Aristonike, and they are all looking on intently.

"Get back in formation! Course maneuvers!"

Diokles is mute. He is trying to get through the rest of the day's drills, but something is obviously wrong. Blood drips from his swollen face but is almost instantly washed away by the pouring rain. As we continue our marching drills and formation adjustments, Diokles begins to fall out of step. We push him toward the center of our formation in an attempt to hide the blunders, but it is no use. The instructor singles him out once again.

"Cub! You ass of a swine, get over here! You've been quite the example today, haven't you? All afternoon, your performance has been sloppier than an ass-puckering Athenian. Out here…in front… now!" The instructor waves four of the older boys out.

"Form up there!" the instructor orders.

They overlap shields as instructed, two across two deep.

"Cub, stand in front of me, shield up. Advance!" he shouts, and the four boys charge toward Diokles, the instructor taking position behind him.

As they ram into Diokles's shield, the instructor steps back, sending Diokles tumbling backward.

"See what happens to the man in front of you when you fail to support him? The formation is nothing if we do not apply pressure to the backs of our comrades in front of us. The strength of a phalanx lies in the collection of men, not in the individuals that make it up. Witnessing the front line of a phalanx being broken and trampled is enough to cause the whole damned army to break. Can you imagine what our allies might do if they saw this happen to a Spartan front? Do not shrug this off, youths, for this is no typical instruction," he cries out through the rain, turning back to address all of us.

"If you have not already noticed, we are at war. Right now, men from every nation of Greece are scheming, plotting, training, talking, fighting, bleeding, and dying. Every man and every nation jostle for some illusion of advantage. Friends, brothers, sons, many turn on one another, all too eager to sacrifice others in their personal pursuits of greater power and fortune!

"Many Athenians that would have otherwise fought against us rotted in their beds, cut down by infirmity rather than infantry. These are the realities of this war and the reasons why we are not out here just to go through the motions! I am not here for your entertainment. I am here because one day, the boys to either side of you will one day surround you in a phalanx!" he exclaims so that everyone can hear before he turns back toward Diokles.

"Again," he states sternly, grabbing Diokles by the shoulder to move him back into position.

This time, the older boys clash into Diokles, but as they do, the instructor shifts his weight and nestles his shield firmly into Diokles's back. With a sudden jolt, he times the application of additional pressure with the impact of the older boys. Diokles's legs hold true and his position firm. Of course, the forward momentum of the charge causes him to give just a bit, but with the support of the instructor, the recoil propels him forward. As a result, Diokles maintains balance while causing the attackers to falter and lose their footing in the mud.

Now, the instructor struts out in front of the troop. He knows that no words are required to describe the purpose of his instruction. Instead, he just holds his arms out to either side as if to say, "That is how it is done."

Despite the result, Diokles just stands there motionless. Even through the storm, I can see his eyes swell with the tears he has held back up to this point. As the instructor dismisses us, I run over to his side as he just begins to slowly walk off the field, not even acknowledging my arrival. Then, the instructor falls in beside us and places a hand on Diokles's shoulder. Diokles slowly looks up at him with a solemn face as the instructor leans down.

"Victory indeed, son of Epitadas," he whispers with a grin.

Night falls as all peers and youths eat in their mess. We youths are usually crowded around by fires, eating *zomos:* also known as black soup, the soup was a combination of boiled pig's blood, the pig's legs, vinegar, and salt. While those outside Sparta describe our fare as uneatable, I know little else, and my appetite is usually unquenchable at this hour. I gulp down the hot bloody broth while chatter of war once again spreads through the mess and around the fires. Rumors about recent events on the southwestern coast of the Peloponnese are spreading all over Sparta.

Word is, the Athenians dispatched a fleet shortly after the plague subsided, and their marines have now fortified Pylos on the southwestern coast of the Peloponnese. The Peloponnesian fleet at Corcyra recently departed to confront them. King Agis also returned to Sparta from his raids on Attica few weeks back and dispatched a land force to complement the fleet.

My father was called up for the deployment, with Messulius's father accompanying him. My father is second-in-command to his loyal friend Epitadas, Diokles's father. In earlier times, it may have been called peculiar for so many within one troop to have relatives deployed, but in truth, this war is different. Everyone has relatives deployed on the many fronts and garrisons across Greece.

The *agoge* is designed to be approximately thirteen years long; however, the demands of this war have led to many young Spartans being recruited into regiments early, sometimes by three years. The initiation ritual where Spartan boys are forced into the wilderness to survive on their own is now being abbreviated. With Athenian raiding parties frequenting the Peloponnesian coast and talk of war making the *helots* increasingly hostile, Gylippus said that the *ephors* came to the conclusion that the risk to Spartan youth is too great for a yearlong excursion. This, however, does not mean that the training curriculum of the *agoge* will become easier. The gaps in the ranks just need filling.

Clearly, Sparta needs all the warriors she has, and she needs them healthy and vigorous. The previous year, my brother, Theron, was not elected to a regiment. Instead, he was allotted another role entirely, the *kryptea*. The *kryptea is* a fraternity of assassins who hunt exceptional and insubordinate helots, both considered a threat to our stability. Any *helot* with exceptional skills wields influence, influence fuels ego, ego turns to ambition, and with ambition comes treachery.

Insubordination among helots can begin like a spark starting a fire. The *kryptea* is there to smother any flicker before it has a chance to flare. With Athenian agents trying to incite uprising among the Messenians, the *ephors* have made controlling the *helot* population a priority. Sparta cannot afford to fight a war within our own borders with so many peers on external deployments. Any such event could have dire consequences on the outcome of this conflict.

That is why the *kryptea* embarks on these campaigns of murder, sabotage, and infiltration. The goal is to spread paranoia and fear among their population by making an example of a few. The *kryptea* also use misinformation to pit influential *helot* families against one another, making them eager to incriminate their neighbor before the same is done to them.

While I eat my broth, I hear the rumors make their way around the mess. The constant gossip often leads to elaborate stories and exaggerations, each claiming to be from one reliable source or another. Gylippus tells me to be skeptical of a herald's words, hear them, but be mindful of their possible agenda. Make note of the city they hail from and what the interests of those cities might be. Weigh each word against the facts that you know, then look for patterns and consistencies between alternative stories to make your own conclusion about each event. Don't let the nonsense associated with rumors dilute your reason. As the *kryptea* have shown, misinterpreting information can have catastrophic consequences if it leads you down a path of your rival's choosing.

Despite all this talk of war, what truly is weighing heavy on my mind is the absence of my friend Diokles. I have not seen him since today's instructions. He said nothing to me afterward, nor did I bother to query. As I take the last mouthful of soup, I notice a boy off in the distance running down the hill toward us. I look around to see if anyone else in the mess notices him, but they all appear more focused on the meager meal before them. He looks to be dispatched on some important errand rather than someone being punished or in training. I rise to my feet and begin to walk toward the road. Just then, I hear Messulius's voice from out of the bushes behind me.

"Nikos," he whispers, motioning me forward. "You about killed me today."

"Messulius? That you? You fool, I thought I had. What news?"

"Gylippus wants to see you. He is at his mess and wants us to meet him there."

While Messulius leads me down the road, I look to the sky. The clouds have passed through, revealing the moon and the stars. Notwithstanding the saturated earth, it has turned out to be a very pleasant night. As I follow my friend, I briefly mark the other planets in the heavens, the ones my mother told me about. *They are bright tonight*, I think to myself, before my mind quickly turns back to the boy I saw running on the hill. Something about him seemed off. I can't help but feel that something is amiss.

The air hangs heavy from the rain. My father always said this is best weather for hunting. The scents of the earth are always more potent after a heavy rain, and this helps to mask our own stench. Furthermore, the wind will often lie still, and the soft earth makes it easy to sneak up on prey. Even as I think of these things, we forget ourselves as we approach the mess, carelessly bursting out of the darkness and into the presence of our elders.

"By Zeus! You little shitcakes, what are you doing here?" Clearchus jumps back as if startled by our unexpected appearance.

Pieces of meat are all over his face as he takes another swig of his wine sack, grinning with approval as he recollects some wisecrack he had just added to the conversation before we interrupted. The low chuckle among the peers dies down gradually as they continue to chew on their venison. In the corner of my eye, I see *helot* attendants still cutting meat from a carcass. Clearly, some peer has taken advantage of the favorable conditions this night and brought game to the table as a treat for the rest of his mess.

"Surprised you can sit down after that ass-pounding Lysander gave you wrestling today," Gylippus chimes in, obviously in reference to the story we had walked in on.

"Why, you son of *helot* swine!" Clearchus jumps up, playfully pulling out his *xiphos* as if to go after Gylippus's throat.

"Easy, friends," Lysander interrupts. "No need to remind us of Clearchus's embarrassment, or that Gylippus has a *helot* bitch of a mother."

Gylippus and Clearchus laugh as they chew full mouths of venison.

"But do tell me, youths, what errand gives you the authority to interrupt our mess? Lashes shall be dealt to each at daybreak," Lysander utters in a serious tone while he too fills his mouth with meat.

The revelation that we will be lashed tomorrow hardly brings me back to reality. I am too dumbstruck by the collection of the men before us, most in this mess being young men of significant prestige within our quarter. All the same, Messulius and I must check our eyes. It is seen as a sign of disrespect to look into the eyes of peers unless addressed directly. Both of us are frozen, hoping that Gylippus will stand up to our defense. After all, we are on his errand.

"Answer him, you insolent bastards!" Clearchus barks as he removes a bone from his mouth and throws it forcibly in our direction.

The bone hits me right in the forehead, and I feel a mix of his spit and the meat's juices slide down between my eyes. Still, I dare not move. The peers break into deep laughter while I try to find the appropriate response to excuse our intrusion.

"Reporting to Master Gylippus, sir," Messulius responds, beating me to it.

"Does the *helot* speak for you now, son of Hippagretas?"

"No, sir, but he speaks the truth. We are here on the request of Master Gylippus, sir."

"Even if this is so, why did you not wait until after our meal as is custom?" Lysander continues, prodding us both, his eyes focused on his meal as if to give the impression that we are insignificant to him.

"We were told it was urgent, sir."

"Is this so?"

"Indeed it is!" Gylippus responds loudly as he wipes the food from his beard and slowly begins to stand up. "I just wasn't finished chewing yet. Thought you all could keep these little bastards entertained. Besides, look how wily they are. Would you really expect me to have to go looking for these sons of whores in the dark?"

"Gylippus! I always took you for a lazy *helot* bastard," a voice emits from across the mess followed by the expected laughter.

"Let's go, boys," Gylippus says, laughing to himself while the crude comments still fly toward him as we depart.

"With your permission, Gylippus! Can we borrow son of Hippagretas for a moment!" Clearchus shouts toward us. Gylippus looks down at me and looks back at the mess.

"You know where Epitadas's house is, correct?" Gylippus whispers. "We will be there with your friend Diokles. Meet us after they are finished with you."

I nod to him in acknowledgment and approach the mess again. The feeling of awe that had first consumed me now manifests itself into something more akin to dread.

"Don't get in the habit of letting the *helot* speak for you, boy," Clearchus says with a serious but subtle tone as he picks his teeth with another bone.

"Yes, sir," I reply.

"You obviously know that you are supposed to speak before your companion, but do you ever ask why? Do you feel as if you are superior to him because he is a *helot*?" Lysander interjects.

Each head at the mess now turns slightly toward me, anticipating my response. I feel myself freezing up again. I have no appropriate answer at hand.

"No...I..." I fumble my words and nothing coherent flows from my mouth.

"Dammit, son, speak!" Clearchus screams, frustrated at my lack of response.

"Messulius is a loyal companion, sir. His family has always served mine well. His father has been a loyal squire to my own father on many campaigns long before I was born. His mother helped bring me into this world. I know he is not Spartan...and I know his blood may not be same as mine, sir, but..." I pause, gathering myself once more. "His loyalty is, and I feel his heart is as true to Sparta as my own. My father would not have sponsored him for training in the *agoge* if this were not so."

"You are not yet wise, Andronikos, but there is some wisdom in what you say. As you probably already know, your own mentor was a *mothax*. Gylippus is the spawn of a *helot* servant girl, but also the son of the Spartan peer Cleondridas."

Apparently, Lysander is already aware that I've heard of Gylippus's past, but he pauses anyway to indicate its relevance to the point he is about to make.

"Loyalty is a cruel bitch...and many in Sparta, even among the peers, have forgotten that lesson," Lysander grumbles.

I can feel an uneasy tension among the mess is growing, and while these men all belong to the same mess, their political loyalties vary. Some, like Lysander, support the Eurypontid royal family, represented by our present King Agis II. The others, Gylippus among them, favor the Agiad line of kings and the exiled King Pleistoanax.

While Sparta attempts to exhibit an image of unity to the rest of Greece, its factions have begun to polarize to a level that's potentially destabilizing. My father always told me not to flaunt our loyalties, of which we are obligated by blood. Instead, consider all sides, and determine the course that is the most prudent. Warriors follow leaders, not politicians. Lysander believes in forced obedience and that our allies must adopt the Spartan way of life or else be deemed untrustworthy. Warriors do follow Lysander, but Greece does not consist of only warriors. And while Lysander speaks, I begin to perceive what Gylippus and my father have spoken of with regard to the combined wisdom and fallacy of his philosophy.

"How loyalty influences the soul is different for every man. Your *helot* friend has a stout heart. There is no doubt of that. He may well serve you with honor in the future. One need not be an oracle to foresee this. The outcome of this war, however, none can foresee. It is a war the likes of which Greece has never seen.

"Already, Sparta has taken into consideration many courses of action that we have never had to before. No longer can we Spartans only rely on one another as we have always done. Instead, we must keep all our friends close and even consider those not of Dorian decent. It is clear now that Sparta will not be able to win this war alone. It is bigger than just you and me...and any among this mess.

"Greece lies upon a crossroads, and Sparta and Athens both vie over which road she is to take. The old ways of war are over, and a new age has begun. Sparta and a small collection of our allies are firm in their Dorian identity..., and identity just so happens to be the reason for this war.

"Freedom. Justice. Courage. Patriotism. In every city-state, the interpretation of these virtues and how to implement them politically is turning friends, neighbors, and even kin against one another. Many found that those they had come to rely upon suddenly became unreliable. The unfortunate ones caught in the middle have either been slaughtered in the streets or burned alive within temples dedicated to our gods.

"It seems loyalty is becoming an increasingly rare thing in these times, and the uncertainty of this war has even caused many to consider loyalty as foolhardy and dangerous.

"We must force our hand in this war, son of Hippagretas. We must make others live as we do. All of Greece must be shaken awake so that they may remember that the virtues we embody are what bind a *polis* together. Perhaps, it is time that they be forced to learn the will of the gods from us. Let us teach them the old Dorian way before Greece tears herself apart. However, if we are to be the example, we Spartans must maintain our bonds of loyalty. Because if all fails and Greece divides and descends into chaos around us, surrounded by our loyal mates, with shields overlapping, they will see us marching into Hades together.

"I know of Messulius and of his family. His parents are of good stock as you say. In the past, they surely would have been prime targets for our *kryptea*. Yet thus far, they have proven to be what you say, loyal. I know you care for him, that you love him as a brother. This much Gylippus has told me, but you must remind Messulius of humility.

"Word of his abilities has reached my ear and not just from your mentor. The boy appears to have good instincts and is showing exceptional skill in the art of hoplite warfare. He is progressing even faster than many of the Spartan youths in your troop, but he will need you, Nikos...and you him. Never forget where he comes from, and do not let him forget it either. His life depends upon it. Do you see? For him, it must always remain a privilege to fight by your side, not a given right. Do not let your feelings for him make you forget what he is. He must always seek to earn his place beside you, doing so through the silent virtues of service," Lysander concludes. "But enough talk about the *helot*, how is your troop holding up?"

"Not my troop, sir, command belongs to Estathios," I reply.

"Yes, I am aware, and do you approve of this?" Lysander continues.

"Yes, sir, he is a sound and steadfast leader. I rarely find fault with his decisions."

"Bahh, he's belligerent, like his father," Lysander says dismissively, licking meat scraps off his fingers.

I say nothing, sensing the hostility in his voice. Estathios's father, Epikrestes, was a friend and lieutenant of Brasidas and was one of the few who died in the extraordinary assault on the Athenians at Methone.

"And how is the troop responding to the last call up?"

"All appears well, sir," I answer quickly, obviously puzzled by the question.

Why would he ask me such a strange question? Most Spartan boys hardly know their fathers because of the frequency of their deployments. Of course, it is a point of pride for us all, although it is ill mannered to display it.

"Good. Report to me at sunrise. That is all," he declares as he takes another swig of the wine bowl and stands up.

As Lysander departs, I can't help but notice that all other conversation at the table has stopped. The other peers are all glaring at me, their faces glimmering in the firelight. The crackles of flames are the only sounds I hear as the men continue to probe for any sign of diffidence or lack of understanding. I nod to Lysander and depart, still confused by the conclusion of the instruction and the behavior of the other peers during its implementation.

Such sessions usually consist of yelling and defamation; this one, however, had a tone of seriousness and sincerity. Lysander has never even acknowledged my existence, much less revealed a concern for me or that of my troop. On any other night, I would feel relief. However, I was experiencing something quite the contrary. My stomach turns in the mix of confusion, dread, and adrenaline. Whatever this is, it is as unsettling as it is invigorating.

I arrive at Epitadas's dwelling; the sweet fragrance of lavender and thyme pierces my nostrils as I traverse the small path leading to the entrance. The comforting scents lighten my mood for a moment, causing me to slow my pace. A feeling tells me to savor this small pleasure before revealing my presence to the occupants inside.

I open the small gate and walk toward the lamplight within the door. Diokles's little sister greets me with a damp cloth for my hands and some cut wine. As I sip the bowl, I peer into the next room. There, I spot Gylippus's battle squire and field physician, Shrill. He is surrounded by a group of *helot* and perioikoi apprentices. Once, Gylippus spoke of his real name, but my head has discarded the memory. Shrill is the only title he is referred to.

He is a Rhodian man about Gylippus's age. Gylippus told me that he was an orphan boy who became a pirate and that his travels took him all over the Mediterranean. He only arrived in Sparta when the outlaws ran their boat ashore south of Argos while fleeing from an Athenian fleet of triremes.

While Shrill is an excellent physician, Gylippus primarily boasts about his skills with a sling. The lead bullets he crafts are carefully fashioned with ridges that he claims extend the speed and distance of the projectile. The finishing touch is a small hole that he drills in the middle. This is what he says "makes them scream." As a result, those in Gylippus's company took to calling him Shrill, an obvious reference to the loud and terrifying pitch that accompanies his bullets when he lets them fly.

As I stand in the doorway, Diokles's mother approaches me.

"Greetings, young Adronikos," she says lightly, nodding to her young daughters, a silent instruction for them to retire to the other room.

"Is he okay?" I ask calmly, referring to Diokles as I watch Shrill instructing his companions, explaining everything in detail as he sets Diokles's broken jaw.

"He'll be just fine," she says to me with a soft smile.

I see Gylippus standing in the corner of the room with my troop leader, Estathios, and his mentor, Chirisophus. All their eyes remain trained on the old Rhodian as they continue in profound conversation. My mentor catches my glance and soberly waves me over.

"You've arrived, good. I have already told the others. Your father's regiment at Pylos has run into some complications." He pauses as we all watch Shrill insert a mix of euphorbia and amber between Diokles's teeth, gently clamping his jaw down around the leafy resin.

"Our forces surrounded the Athenian fortification near Pylos by land and sea. A detachment of about four hundred men positioned themselves on the small island of Sphacteria to provide support in case of a naval engagement."

We continue watching Shrill as he places his fingers lightly around Diokles's head, holding it steady as he presses the other hand firmly under Diokles's chin.

"Brasidas led an amphibious assault on the fort, but given the rocky beachhead and the superior position of the Athenians, the attack was repelled. Brasidas himself was wounded in the assault. Thank the gods he'll live. Word of his deeds continue to spread, making him quite the thorn in the side of the Eurypontids, who will surely have to give him a command soon," Gylippus says with a small smile.

Knowing Gylippus's relationship with Brasidas, it will mean a reassignment and deployment for my mentor soon. Brasidas has become somewhat of a symbol to the supporters of Agiads and a hero to my companion and troop leader, Estathios. I recall his father, Epikreste, who died in Brasidas's service outside Pylos six summers past. Then, Gylippus turns back to me and continues, this time in a more serious tone.

"While Brasidas survived, the failed assault was followed by Athenian naval reinforcements, and our navy was forced to disengage." He turns his glance back to the physician.

I know immediately what this means. Diokles's father and my own are now cut off, their regiment stranded on a rocky deserted island, barren except for small trees and shrubs.

"You're doing fine, Diokles. Just lucky you are not on campaign. Men like Shrill are not so readily available, and those that are, are not quite as gentle, I assure you," Gylippus jeers before continuing to address me.

"In case you have not already discerned this, those men on the island are under the command of Epitadas and your father. Emissaries have been sent to Athens to negotiate terms for armistice. We do have our land forces encamped near Pylos, so perhaps this ordeal will be over soon," he concludes, trying to reassure me. However, his tone betrays more doubt than optimism.

"The island, have they fortified their position? What of food, water, and supplies?" I ask, probing Gylippus for any additional information that would help me assess the situation.

Not that I could do anything to influence their situation, but Gylippus has always taught me to envision such scenarios to deliberate what actions I might take if in such positions. I see Gylippus betray a slight grin of approval out of the corner of my eye.

"The island is shaped like a bone, wide at either end, gradually narrowing as it progresses towards the center. It is approximately twenty-five stades of maneuverable terrain in length and averages about four stades in width. Of course, a *stade* is only about six hundred and thirty feet. Their only source of water is a well about fifteen stades inland, just south of the northern tip. Epitadas and your father have fortified the high ground on the north end of the island. The northern face of cliffs rises out of the sea. The southern face ascends from the interior of the island, creating a backdrop of stone that forms like a bowl behind the fortification," Gylippus explains by making a U shape with his hands.

Estathios's and Chirisophus's eyes are still trained on Shrill and Diokles. I can tell they are listening intently, though they've already discussed the quandary prior to my arrival. I can see the dilemma is working on Estathios's mind. Like a child learning Homer, Estathios is committing the facts to memory and pondering his own conclusions about the situation.

"Due to the cliffs on the north side, an invasion is only possible from south of the fortification?"

"From what I know of the island, that would appear to be the case. The only viable landing sites on the island are at its core, where it narrows and the elevation drops."

"I suppose food and supplies are being rationed accordingly, but has there been any talk of resupply or maybe even evacuation?" I persist.

"*Helots* that claim to be exceptional swimmers are being recruited in the surrounding area. However, there is no guarantee of a successful journey from the mainland, especially while carrying supplies. As we speak, Aristonike, Lysander, and the rest of the assembly are meeting with the *ephors* and *Gerousia* to discuss the predicament," Gylippus concludes, switching the conversation back to Diokles as Shrill finishes the instruction of his craft, holding up his hands just off the cheeks of Diokles before looking back at us.

"All set."

"Well done, you skinny old man! Diokles looks as good as new."

Gylippus then switches his attention to Shrill's attendants and the crowd of *helot* children that have congregated to watch the Rhodian's work.

"All right, off with the goats," Gylippus exclaims as he kicks a few of the slow-moving boys in the ass to clear the floor as he approaches the physician.

"Should hold for a while," Shrill comments as he wipes the excess resin off his hands.

"How long?" I inquire.

"Could be twelve days, could be twenty, but that thing doesn't look like it's going to budge anytime soon," he replies, turning his head slightly as he inspects his work. "Just come to me if it gets loose, and I will reapply the resin until the bone is healed," he says with a grin as Diokles responds with a mumble and a nod. "Speak through your teeth instead of trying to move your mouth. You'll get the hang of it."

Then, Lady Leodamia, Diokles's mother, enters the room with another boy who looks about our age.

"Diokles, this is Protesias. He is the perioikoi that is to serve as your squire. Your father and your mentor, Aristonike, desired it so," she said frankly before departing the room.

Diokles rises from the chair to examine the boy even though we already know him well. He has been training alongside us with all the other non-Spartan boys. While perioikoi are the free citizens of Laconia, they are not Spartan equals. They are the locals that dwell in the territories that surround Sparta, and they rely upon her for their protection. They follow Sparta's lead and often make up much of her infantry force. Perioikoi are not required to serve an individual Spartan, but many choose to do so.

Estathios and I talk to him briefly just so Diokles doesn't have to. Gylippus ensures us that he has inherited his father's skill in craftsmanship and will make him very handy with weapon and armor upkeep. Shrill also informs us that he has been learning the basic trades of a physician. The boys among my troop already know that he is very capable with a javelin. Given these abilities, I would envy Diokles and the selection his mentor has made in Protesias if I did not already have Messulius.

The next morning, Messulius and I report to Lysander to receive our punishment for last night's carelessness. We arrive just before dawn and await Lysander outside his barracks. The dew glistens across the landscape as the sun rises over the mountains, its thin layer resting on the small leaves of the olive trees and atop the stalks of tall grass. If it weren't for the muddy areas of trampled soil, one could never have guessed it had rained so hard the day before.

Lysander shows no appreciation for our punctuality as he grabs the lash, walking past us as we follow in tow. Not a word is spoken as my companion and I brace consecutive olive trees and await our lashings. The lash makes a low whoosh through the air as Lysander swings it back with all his strength. Both of us cringe with anticipation for the crack. He hits Messulius first. I let out a quick sigh of relief. Such relief is short-lived, however, as the heavy weight of shame descends on my shoulders for allowing myself to feel such a selfish emotion. As the whip thunders heavily through the air again, I am almost begging for it. I want to erase the weakness I have displayed to myself, to share in the pain of my comrade. Redemption does not come. Again and again, Lysander continues to strike Messulius. I can see the blood streaming steadily down his back, then his calves, before it eventually mixes with the muddy earth.

Perhaps he is just working on Messulius first. I can see my friend holding himself up on the tree for what seems like eternity. Finally, his legs give way, then he goes unconscious. Not a word is spoken.

The air feels empty, and Lysander says nothing. Do I turn around? Where is Lysander? Why isn't he lashing me or calling upon me to see to Messulius? I slowly turn my head to see Lysander casually walking away. I promptly give chase, enraged by this injustice. I did not get the opportunity to shed my shame. My anger continues to grow as I treaded frantically after him.

"What justice is th—"

Before I can finish my sentence, he swiftly turns around. I catch only a glimpse of a whip unfurling furiously toward me before a loud crack accompanies what feels like a hammer hitting my chest. The blow knocks me to the ground and splits my skin diagonally from the base of my neck, across my chest, and down above my right nipple.

"Justice? Tell me, Adronikos, what the fuck would you know of justice?" Lysander stands over me now. "Is it just that your father and two hundred other peers are now abandoned on a barren island? In Athens, a plague consumes both the courageous and the cowardly. They go to their death without even the thrust of a spear or the clash of a shield. Ask them, Nikos, is such a death just? What about the Theban hoplites at Plataea? Invited into the city by its inhabitants under a flag of truce, only to be ambushed and butchered by their hosts. In turn, we arrived and slaughtered the treacherous bastards. Was that reprisal 'just'? Was it? Was it 'just,' son of Hippagretas!" Lysander kicks me in the kidney as if I were some unruly mutt.

"Shall I continue?" he says.

I just stare back at him, panting on the ground, my side aching and blood throbbing from the wound in my chest. I see Gylippus and Shrill watching from farther down the path. Lysander spits at my feet in disgust. He paces back and forth, peering up into the clear sky before looking back down at me to continue his instruction.

"I should not have to explain myself to you, you little shit. You should have already determined the purpose of my display, and yet you demand answers from me? From me? Like some aristocratic Athenian brat!

"I lashed the *helot* unconscious because he walks unnoticed and unchallenged among us. He might not be dangerous, but the confidence he displays in our presence is. The *helots* must know their place. If they forget, we all die. Our enemies surround your father on a deserted island. At this very hour, the morale of the city hangs on the tip of a spear. The army is stretched thin, and the survival of our people now lies on the shoulders of you, our youth. We equals all know it, and they look for strength within you and your companions, especially those akin to the peers trapped on the island.

"I cannot afford to have you sulking about, demoralized and in pain from the physical wounds that I could have inflicted. I thought it better to strike your pride rather than your flesh. I want you angry, Nikos, but I also want you to be able to harness that passion and use it effectively. Sparta needs you prepared, mentally and physically, for all the injustice you will witness in this war. Whatever fate is in store for your father and his regiment, I fear it will not be good for Sparta. If we come out of this looking weak or vulnerable, it will be up to our youth to strike forth and show Greece that they are mistaken."

As soon as Lysander appears to be finished, Gylippus approaches and kneels at my side before directing Shrill toward Messulius. Gylippus's eyes fill with rage as he inspects my wound.

"Lysander!" he yells as he lifts himself from my side, approaching the administrator of my punishment.

"What is it, little Cleandridas?"

Gylippus's lip begins to quiver like a cornered wolf, but just as quickly as it appears, it vanishes again as he regains his composure.

"Clever words, Lysander, slander me and my family if you wish, but mind your whip when instructing my pupil," Gylippus responds in a calm tone, trying to avoid the attention of nearby peers who are beginning to anticipate a confrontation.

"My whip strikes true, Gylippus. I meant no malice in my instruction. Would you rather I vent my dissatisfaction on a *helot* whore like your mother?"

"Ha! We have all heard the tales of what goes on in your bedchamber, Lysander, if only your dick could strike as true as your whip."

The growing congregation of peers nearby begin to laugh, but Gylippus grabs Lysander by the arm and pulls him off the road to gain some distance from the others.

"I know the intent of your instruction. By the gods, I agree with you! Bend them over and lash as you see fit, but I will not let you blind my pupil with an accidental strike to the face."

"These boys must learn the harsh lessons quick, Gylippus. Our youth are growing weak. We shorten their training and thrust them into regiments before they are truly our equals. Sparta needs not just our best warriors for this fight. She needs men worthy of Leonidas! And you know that we need a lot more than we are capable of mustering.

"Friend, the gods know that we have never sought empire, but if we win this war, all of Greece will look to our leadership. Look at these boys. These boys! Are they capable of ruling Greece when this war is over?"

"Ruling Greece? You speak, Lysander, as if you wish Sparta to become the very empire we seek to vanquish."

"Have you not heard a word I have spoken, Gylippus? Greece follows the lead of Athens or Sparta. They always have. It is not I who made this so."

Lysander tosses the whip to a nearby instructor and heads off in the direction of the gymnasium. Gylippus shakes his head in frustration, but instead of speaking, he just instructs us to report to our companions in the *agoge*.

"Following today's instruction, meet Shrill at your father's house so he can attend to your wounds properly!" he shouts from behind me as I stumble off.

Throughout the day's drills, my chest throbs, and I can feel the sticky wetness of my blood mixing with sweat. The dust and the heat cause my wound to dry into my scarlet cloak, only to crack and ooze all over again with every exertion. Messulius is not faring any better. He has hidden his wounds from our comrades as best he could; however, I can tell every move is agonizing. Diokles's injury, there is no concealing. He can barely speak as his face is growing more swollen as the day progresses. I almost laugh to myself as Diokles takes each blow, wondering how the hell that shit in his mouth is still holding his teeth together.

The three of us are a mess. Our troop is a mess. Drill after drill, the day passes by in a slow haze as we go through the motions. Not surprisingly, the instructor points out each imperfection and continues to push us accordingly. Surprisingly, however, he does not press. After our instruction, he deems it necessary to call us to assembly so that he can address us all.

"You all are lucky that my wife rode me well last night. She even had her little *helot* slut suck my cock after we were finished," he said, leaning back with his hips out with both hands gripping the belt around his cloak.

"We were not perfect today, youths, and even as peers, there are days when we aren't at our best. But in battle, we must be perfect. We must be composed and unwavering, even when wounded. The man beside you will not benefit from your shield if you are not able to bring it to port, and don't expect respite from the enemy once the battle lines clash. Had you found yourself in a life-or-death struggle today, most of you would lie dead," he says, starting to smile.

"Still, those of you who would have perished would have died well. Sometimes limbs fail, knees buckle, and shields shatter. In times like these, will alone can produce victory. If you can endure the suffering without being possessed by fear, then you need not worry about shame. Best to have a shitty day and all die together than to survive your friends and know that you could have done more. Now, get the hell out of here before I come to my senses and make you all run the Aphetaid loop!"

When we finally reach my father's house, Gorga and my mother have already prepared the table with cut wine and Shrill's surgeon kit. Protesias pours some wine down Diokles's throat and dabs his swollen face with a wet rag. Before walking outside to continue with her duties around the *oikos*, my mother orders Gorga to aid Shrill in whatever he needs.

"Nikos, come here, son," Shrill commands as he sets the kit at his feet and waves Gorga forward.

In her hands she holds a thin layer of soft sphagnum moss. Shrill carefully takes the moss from her hands and gently applies it to my wound. The soft moss feels surprisingly soothing as it begins to soak the discharge oozing from the crusty gash. My eyelids are heavy, so Gorga places a blanket under my head. I take a deep breath. She has folded lavender into the cloth, and the sweet aroma fills my nostrils as I feel myself falling asleep.

I come to after a short while as Shrill was pulling the moss from my wound. I watch as he unwraps a leaf, revealing a small portion of myrrh wax. Shrill explains that it is created from the resin of a special tree, and the trees produce this substance to heal their own wounds. He says that these trees lend the same healing properties to men, but the wax of this tree is a precious commodity that is not easy to obtain.

While Shrill continues to ramble on about trees, I see him place a tab of the wax onto Gorga's hand before motioning toward me. Shrill is still talking as he removes the moss from Messulius's back, but all I can focus on are Gorga's small fingers dipping into the sticky substance. Then she begins to gently apply it to my chest. Whether it is the light touch of Gorga, my intake of cut wine, or the power of the wax, the entire process is incredibly soothing despite my severed skin.

I notice Messulius watching with attention, knowing well that he will not receive the treasured ailment as Shrill places the wrapped leaf back into his surgeon's kit.

"Wine, another swallow of wine, please, thank you," Shrill asks Gorga.

She hops up to take the bowl from the table and pass it to him, but while the Rhodian turns around to receive the bowl, I slip my hand into his kit and grab the coiled leaf, placing it carefully beneath my cloak. Gorga catches the maneuver in the corner of her eye and looks at me wide-eyed in silent protest. I return her glance with a slight nod and small grin as I sip the wine, communicating my innocent intentions so that her surprised look will not reveal my ruse. Almost on cue, she gives me a light smile back and subtly rolls her eyes.

Those eyes. With the flicker of the lamps bouncing across the room, I can't help but notice their gentle glow. I hope death is as peaceful as this moment, for I would not argue with the gods if they told me that this was where I must spend eternity. Just then, Gylippus barges in the door, startling Gorga and disrupting my pleasant trance.

"Nikos, Messulius, gather round."

I hold out my hand and look at him as if to imply that he must be joking. Realizing the ridiculousness of his request, he decides to pull up a stool.

"I hope you understand what Lysander was doing to you this morning."

Gorga places a bowl filled with water, lavender, and rose petals on the table in front of him. He dips his dusty hands beneath the water and then looks to me for any response. I open my mouth as if to speak, but before I can conjure the words, he continues.

"He was testing you, Nikos, and you, Messulius."

I had never heard Gylippus acknowledge Messulius by name, and yet he had already done so twice since his arrival. "You both did well." He nods toward Messulius.

"The *helot* stood firm, and you—" he looks back at me—"you defended your honor and that of your companion. But, Nikos... Nikos, you overstepped. You disrespected his authority, and he reprimanded you accordingly. Now, I will get to the point.

"Lysander knows of the bond between your families. You are a Spartan youth, and he is a *helot*. Lysander wanted to exploit that connection, and he did so effectively. You broke, lost your composure, and challenged him, just as he knew you would. He chose to use this display as a metaphor for the realities of this dynamic and how it relates to this war. All of what he said about your family and what our city will require of you, every word is true. He wants you to understand this, not as an obligation but rather to recognize the dictates of necessity and what it will require of you.

"The old glories of pitched battle have vanished from this war. Nothing remains but corruption, treachery, disease, and murder. Lysander understands this and will use them all if it is required to obtain victory. Many among the *ephors* speak of undying traditions and reference the fortitude of our laws as an excuse for inaction. Lysander is a brilliant man, a rare breed in Laconia. He does not wish to change Sparta because he has lost faith in her laws and traditions.

He wants Sparta to change because he believes it necessary for her survival.

"Do you see? Sparta's vulnerability is the consistency of our discipline and the stubbornness of our laws. While it has made us unbreakable in battle, it has also made us predictable. The only way Sparta survives is by occasionally rearing a boy of audacity, innovation, and influence, one who can spring forth at Sparta's hour of need. This is Sparta's way of preserving itself, by occasionally adopting the very characteristics we have sought to suppress since the dawn of Lycurgus.

"The curse of such audacity is ambition. Lysander wants to expand Sparta's laws beyond her borders instead of restraining them within the confines of our territory. He wants to take our humble city and make all of Greece fall under her yoke. He will use any means at his disposal to make it so.

"That is why he points out the injustices and lack of virtue that taint this war. He wants you to learn, to become familiar with the torments of the mind and troubles of the soul. To understand what war is in truth, not what you hear in our histories.

"The point of the *agoge* is to condition the mind so that it will not be consumed by emotion when all appears lost. We must recognize the dangers that lie within both our head and our heart. Be able to command yourself, Nikos, or you will not survive very long in this war."

I pause to digest Gylippus's words while also trying to recall Lysander's instruction.

"Does Lysander not forget himself and the source of Greece's respect for our state?"

"Go on," Gylippus says, appearing intrigued with my query.

"Greeks fear us because of our military might and professionalism, but they only respect us because of our defensive posture. We only use our strength to protect our allies and preserve our laws. Will we not turn Greece against us if we take the offensive, if we impose our will on others, as Athens has done?

"I know we subjugate the Messenians, but this is the very source of our insecurity. Without them, our men could not prioritize the arts of war. While this may hone our skills for battle, our stability is hard fought. We have no true navy to extend our reach. The only force we can apply is the force we can put in the field, and that is barely adequate enough to balance Athens and the threats within our own territory. We simply do not have an army capable of empire. Nor do I think empire was the intent of Lycurgus."

Gylippus smiles. I can't tell if he thinks my answer is wise or naive as he takes the wine bowl from Gorga.

"You sound like the *ephors*, my dear Nikos. But what you fail to see is the present reality of Sparta's position. Our unwillingness to submit in the war against the Mede propelled us into history but also into a position of influence and power, regardless of whether or not it was our desire. Greece rallied to Athens and Sparta for leadership, two states that champion different virtues, which manifest themselves in different political philosophies.

"Lysander recognizes this, and while there are Greeks who look to us to ensure their freedom and security, we are obligated by our position to protect them. From this role, we cannot withdraw. This is not a conflict over disputed territories but over different ideals and the very definitions of freedom.

"We Spartans are not politicians. We are bred to value the laws of our forefathers rather than debate their validity. The Athenians trust in citizen rule. They devise, debate, and apply their laws according to the political fashion of the moment, and that is often determined by the amount of coin they can put in someone else's purse."

"A war over ideals?" Messulius says, perplexed. "How does one win such a war?"

"Only when one submits to the other, young *helot*," Gylippus utters.

"Or the arrogance and stubbornness of both cause them to bury one another. They become weak, the weak get conquered, and then both are forgotten by history," Shrill adds with a smile.

Gylippus nods his head slightly, acknowledging the unfortunate truth within the jest. Then Gylippus pats me on the shoulder as he and the Rhodian walk out the door.

All in the room are silent as I begin to rub the remaining myrrh wax onto Messulius's back and let the weight of Gylippus's somber words set in.

In the *agoge,* preparation for war is all we know. We are reminded constantly of the superiority of our ways and the important example we set for all of Greece to envy and strive to emulate. However, I am not certain that even the elders and peers understand this new kind of war or how they can end it without destroying the rest of Greece.

My stomach turns. I feel as if I am going to throw up. Wars of old were fought and won in a matter of days or even hours, decided by the army that occupied the field. Embassies were sent, and terms were dictated. This war goes beyond the field, into the very agora of each city, and at the doorstep of every Greek, and my father was stuck right in the middle of it. I feel unprepared. We Spartans have never trained for such a war, for occupying the cities and exposing and eliminating political dissidents.

Thoughts are racing through my head, and emotions fill my heart as I help Messulius up. While we walk out the door, I lock eyes with sweet Gorga, and without thinking, I grab her around her small waist and press my lips against hers. Obviously, the move surprises her because I feel her weight swiftly shift to her heels. Her first impulse is to step back, but then she relaxes, and I feel her hold the kiss, letting me decide when to conclude the engagement.

For me, it seems like it is over as quickly as it begins; however, it is long enough not to go unnoticed by my companions. Both Diokles and Messulius look at me puzzled after the exchange. Her warm and nurturing nature caused me to forget myself, and in doing so, I have possibly sacrificed the secrecy of my affection for her, Messulius's cousin. Once again, a feeling of shame and regret overtakes me as I reflect on the former sanctity of my secret.

I first noticed the blooming body of Gorga one afternoon when I was stealing cheese from their home, the layout of their dwelling known to me because her family's plot is under the charge of my father. Of course, my familiarity of their home made them an obvious choice for secretly procuring a meal.

This was in my early years in the *agoge*, and I entered their home as the sun was retreating over the mountains. After surveying their routine several days in a row, I knew that at this hour, the men of the household were finishing up in the field, while the females tended to the livestock before fetching the night's water from the stream.

As I quietly entered Gorga's home, I immediately noticed the wheel of cheese lying on the shelf by the kitchen. I grabbed the cheese and turned to run out the door. Before I was able to make my escape, Gorga appeared from the kitchen. In some hurry to finish whatever chore or errand she was on, she had turned the corner so quickly that we startled each other. She let out a quick scream before I was able to cover her mouth with my hand. I then peered out of the entrance of the dwelling to see if my presence had been compromised. Sure enough, her father and brothers were now advancing toward the house at a run. She squeezed my arm, and I turned back to her.

"Out the window with you, quickly now." I tossed the cheese back to her, and she calmly placed the wheel of cheese back on the shelf before grabbing the water jug and walking out the door. After crawling out the window, I pressed my body against the wall of the dwelling. I remember my heart beating furiously; I could hear the men arrive to inspect the suspected disturbance.

"You all right, Gorga? We heard you cry out."

"Sorry, Father, just a mouse caught in the water jug. Forgive me for causing such a fuss."

I smiled to myself, not the best lie, but I couldn't help but admire the convincing delivery.

Following that event, I began to steal small rations from her house more often, almost entirely for the purpose of catching a glimpse of her. Her long brown hair waving like grains in the wind and her tan legs glistening with sweat after a day of helping her family work the land. With every gentle breeze or ray of sunlight, there was another attribute revealed for me to lust over.

She must have been intrigued with the consistency of my visits and my willingness to expose my thievery to her. Like a hunter luring in a hungry fox, she would track my comings and goings before baiting me in. After discovering my intentional routine, I'd find small amounts of bread or cheese she'd left in convenient places, allowing me to evade the other members of her family while they conducted their daily business on the farmstead. Often, I'd watch her from afar as she found some excuse to run back to the house to see if I had found the bounty she left for me.

With time, I planned my approach not only to collect the bounty but also to catch her alone. It became a game of cat and mouse. Occasionally, I'd let her catch me, but most often, I would intentionally startle her. This would prompt a quiet laugh before she threw herself into my arms, wrapping her strong legs around my body as her dusty hair swung across my face. What a sappy little shit I was back then.

We would roll around on the ground, sweating and swirling up dust clouds that seemed to dance in the rays of sunlight that shone through the small windows. All this we did in secret. No one knew of our friendship, as the consequences of this game being discovered meant serious punishment or even death, depending on the timing of the situation and the matter of our discovery.

It is well-known that Spartan youth often seek to quench their sexual appetites on unsuspecting *helot* girls, a dangerous game to be sure. Brothers or fathers of exploited girls often try to exact justice by killing the youth. Then, they attempt to avoid reprisal by finding clever ways to dispose of the body.

By the time I had come of age, the affair had gone on for some time. I've found myself caring for her deeply. At times, I watch over her and her home with no other purpose but to be sure some other youth does not try to sneak in and violate her. During this time, Gylippus has also commenced my training in the tactics of courting women. The purpose, of course, is to make me capable of not only acquiring a wife but also how to keep one happy.

The instruction involves several lessons that involve Gylippus waking me in the night to accompany him to his dwelling. This is not a casual stroll in the dark but rather two men on a mission. Both of us have to sneak out of the barracks and stay out of sight. Any man caught outside the barracks in the middle of the night faces punishment.

After the caught individual receives their lashings, physical and verbal abuse follows. For in the *agoge*, the price of getting discovered is severe. Of course, lashings are administered as well as several creative forms of punishment that manifest themselves within the drills the following day. Older boys label the accused as cowards that would be prone to eventual desertion later in life. However, men of military age perceive such outings as a kind of war game, hoping to catch a careless comrade coming back from a happy reunion with the wife and/or *helot* mistress. Those who catch their friends not only are able to administer the lashing the next day but also obtain bragging rights that few in their mess ever let go.

On such nights, Gylippus places me in his wife's garden, right beneath their window. There, I can peer in with a perfect view into his wife's sleeping quarters. Before he enters his house, Gylippus instructs me to watch as he pleasures his wife. After the deed is done, the two of us have to slip back into the barracks unnoticed.

Now that I am a young man, I need no more instruction in such matters. However, Diokles and Messulius now know of my attraction to Gorga. Do they think I want her for my pleasure, or do they suspect my more intimate infatuation? Will they expect me to move on her? Will they follow me to her house and discover our game? I scorn myself for potentially ruining my secret passion for this girl with a single kiss.

I do not sleep at all that night. All I can think about is getting to Gorga, and yet I don't have a clue about what to do once I get there. Do I approach her, act like I meant to do it, as if it were part of some clever design that I had already worked out previously in my head? Or do I watch from a distance, take a couple of weeks to make sure others are not on to me?

After the day's drills, just before mess, I slip away. Racing across the countryside, I traverse fields of wheat and groves of olive trees toward the thicket just beyond the pasture adjacent to Gorga's home. I watch intently, trying to spot her before scanning the horizon for any sign of another.

"Ha, there you are!" Gylippus barks in what resembles a shouting whisper, the force of his sudden arrival almost knocking me over.

Both of us are sucking air as we take a minute to recover our breath under the cover of the brush. Obviously, he was running to keep pace with me on this little excursion. Trying to ignore his presence, I once again look across the terrain for any sign of Gorga. My body tenses up, and I lower to a crouch as she appears over the small hill's ridge.

"Good, good, you want that little *helot* bitch, don't you, my boy?" he scoffs, trying to catch his breath.

I watch as Gorga heads straight for the house. She will be expecting me, but with Gylippus present, the situation is much more dangerous.

"Best be careful now. Have you scouted her movements? If not, better wait—"

I cut him off.

"Her father is a squire, and he is currently trapped on the same damn island as my own. Her mother and sister usually tend to the goats at this hour. Her brothers are finishing their work in the field, and she is to fetch water and begin preparing supper."

"All right then," he says enthusiastically, like a spectator that just lucked into a spot on the front row before a big race. "She is alone then. Take her, I got you covered."

He has me covered? Shit. All I need is Gylippus cutting down one of Gorga's brothers. She would never speak to me again. I take a deep breath as I ponder my next move. I am going to have to choose my actions carefully.

As soon as she disappears inside the house, I make my move, darting from cover to cover before rushing into the dwelling. Gylippus follows, taking position just inside the front doorway. She turns around briskly; a smile is on her face as she anticipates our reunion. However, the smile turns to fright when she notices Gylippus.

With one swift movement, I grab her by the throat and hip-toss her to the ground. A feeling of guilt and regret rushes over me, but this is no time for subtleties. I know she does not yet understand, but I cannot afford to reveal my familiarity with her to my mentor.

She looks at me puzzled as if she is about to cry. I flash my eyes toward Gylippus and back at her. I dip my chin slightly in an attempt to not only reassure her but also communicate the purpose of my forcefulness. She lets out a soft breath, and her tense body relaxes a bit, a silent indication that she understands what is about to transpire.

I grab a handful of her hair and jerk her head back. She lets out a distinct but discreet yelp. She grimaced with discomfort when I put my lips to her ear.

"Make this look real, and we'll be gone before they arrive," I whisper. She lets out another soft breath in acknowledgment.

I keep my hand firmly around her throat as she impulsively swings her fist at my face, kicking wildly as I begin pulling up her garment. I position myself, draw my blade, and put it to her throat. Her body becomes tense again, and I feel a shiver roll down her spine as the cold bronze blade touches her neck while I simultaneously enter her. At that moment, her back arches violently. The movement is so sudden that it causes the blade to scratch her ever so slightly. I toss it aside, convincing be damned. I am not going to accidently slice open her neck all in an attempt to fool Gylippus.

Instead, I grab both of her small wrists with one hand and pin them against the dusty floor above her head while placing my other hand over her mouth. I use my knees to grip her thighs and the weight of my body to limit the movement of her hips. With this action, her muffled screams turn into something more akin to a moan. I know she is attempting to keep up the act of resisting, but the movement I can feel in her hips betray the fact that she is enjoying this. I wheel my head around to shoot a glance at Gylippus, hoping that he is not on to us.

I notice the orange rays of the setting sun pouring through the window. They reflect off the cloud of dust Gorga and I are whipping up. As a result, it is difficult to make out the figure of Gylippus still acting sentry by the doorway. Unexpectedly, I see him give me a quick salute before shifting his eyes back out the entrance. My eyes close and open slowly. The dust flickers in the sunlight in front of my face. I feel as if I am in a dream. Perhaps I am imagining things, but the figure of a woman seems to appear within the veil of dust. I shake my head and peer back into the floating particles, but all I see now is the obscured outline of Gylippus darting out the door.

For a moment, I feel a sense of panic. A feeling like I have lost track of time, like I too must go. Just then, Gorga wraps her legs around me and pins me into her. The sensation that follows is euphoric, our intertwined bodies shaking and convulsing. We are covered in sweat and dust. We simultaneously thrust our hips into one another one last time before I hop up and quickly compose myself. I slam my back against the wall where Gylippus had been. I take one brief moment to pull down my cloak and make sure my escape route is clear before I too slip out of the doorway.

As I run across the field, I have not yet spotted Gylippus. I hope Gorga's family is clear and that he is not in the process of slitting her brother's throat. My legs still feel numb, but somehow, I manage to stumble back into the brush.

Without warning, Gylippus yanks me down from his concealed position. Sweat is pouring down my face as I continue to breathe heavily. Gylippus stares into my face, studying my expression. The look on his face is stone serious before blurting out into sudden laughter.

"Hah! That's my boy!" Delight fills his voice as he begins to speak quickly. "Did you notice how that little bitch reacted when you penetrated her? She barely put up a fight, a feeble one at best. Perhaps just enough to convince herself that she was resisting the shame. Ha! But her instincts must have just told her just to lie back and enjoy. By Hades, Nikos! She looks like a delicious slice of leg. I almost envy you, Nikos," he says as he repeatedly throws soft punches into my shoulder and gut.

I say nothing, pushing his shoulder in the direction of our departure. As we creep back toward the barracks, I feel a mix of excitement and terror. I hope I did not frighten or hurt her. Never have I felt her tremble and shudder as she had done beneath me. Gylippus begins to speak as if he is aware of my feelings.

"You realize the significance of what just happened, don't you? She submitted to you. She was powerless beneath you, and she reveled in her obedience to that fact. Being on the other end of you, a strong

Spartan youth, she tilted her head back, lifted her hips, and accepted each thrust in service to you. She received you, acknowledged your superiority rather than make some foolhardy attempt to resist.

"You see, Nikos, war is no different, my young friend. Enemies and allies alike, they will all respond in this way when they witness the scarlet cloaks of Laconia. There in the field, allies will submit to our leadership, and enemies will piss themselves in dread as we advance. Most armies beat drums wildly, hoping the low thumps will stir courage into wavering souls. Yet we welcome battle with an instrument favored by women—the flute. The casual but terrifying taunt foreshadows the bloody exercise of our conquest and their submission.

"A battle ebbs and flows much like what you just experienced. At first, the clash of shields is chaotic, both lines struggling for position before they become locked into a violent dance. The movement is almost rhythmic, and with it, the blood in one's veins pump wildly, causing all feeling of vulnerability or fear to recede. Like the thrust of your hips, every thrust of your spear builds your confidence as you stoke the instinctual fire within. Bloodlust. The push and the penetration, all seems to move in a single motion, like the tides. With one line rolling over the other until it forces an eventual break."

Then, Gylippus takes a deep breath, places a hand on my shoulder, and turns with an expression of despair on his face.

"Your father is dead, Nikos. The island was overrun and captured by the Athenians. Many fought well and died with honor. Your father, Epitadas, and their squires were among them. The rest were surrounded and did the unthinkable. They surrendered, and by Hades, they have put Sparta in quite the predicament."

All I can do is gaze into the valley below as he continues. For a moment, I find myself visualizing his words as if the battle were taking place in the fields below. The rows of wheat and olive trees resembling rank after rank of armored hoplites. Bronze shields and helms shining brilliantly in the sunlight.

Sensing that I am no longer willing or able to pay attention to his words, we both just stand there idle, staring beyond at Sparta below us. The rivers and creeks flow down through the mountains, dissecting the landscape as they creep along down the hills and around the various dwellings that make up our humble city. There on the hill in the middle lies our acropolis.

At this moment, I sense that I am seeing and feeling a vision of Sparta that Gylippus has been waiting to reveal to me. Perhaps he had used the rape of Gorga, not for amusement, but as the substance of a valuable lesson. Why we Spartans are so effective in battle, why we resemble beauty and terror, elegance and chaos. How we churn these qualities into a single force that is able to deter rivals and overpower enemies without an army ever having to occupy the field. In this way, our small city wields tremendous power. In possession of this prowess, necessity demands that we inspire awe and command respect. With this, we can dictate our future; however, if the illusion fails, we will become just another city-state living under the yolk of the more powerful. While I do not discern his words while he is speaking, I can feel the concern in my mentor's voice. I can tell that he fears the survival of that illusion.

After a long silence, my trance is broken. I look back at Gylippus, and he takes this opportunity to continue his instruction.

"You were once a boy, then a man. Now, it is time to see if you will become a Spartan. You are to be sent into the wild soon. Remember, we haven't spent all this time training you for the Olympiad. You were bred to be a warrior, and now, all is out of my hands. Out there, the gods become your new instructors, and it is they who will decide if you are fit to be a Spartan equal.

"Do not fail me, boy. Either come back next winter with skills to survive and an appetite to kill, or do not come back at all. I will not have capitulation in Sparta develop into a trend," he finishes sternly, looking down at his feet while kicking one sandal into the dirt a few times consecutively.

A King's Errand

The still water ripples outward from the boat as I climb into the craft. A simple nod from the speechless captain lets me know that my payment for this journey is sufficient. I check my kit before we depart. It is a damn nuisance not being accompanied by a squire. Of course, I will have to find a suitable one once I arrive at my destination. Nonetheless, I can't help but feel a little excitement as I check over my gear. Each piece has its own story. Every nick, dent, and scratch tell a tale of some trial, triumph, or tragedy. However, all bring back the memory of faces and names, those of friends, lovers, rivals, and enemies. What man would I be today had they been absent from my story? I am no lover of the poets or mimes, but even I recognize that all the good heroes had a strong supporting cast and, of course, a worthy antagonist. While I am no hero, those who accompanied me along the way have certainly crafted my story well.

I look to the shore, hold my hand up, and give the lady one last smile and nod before we push off.

Oh, the women in my life, I think to myself.

All the misery and joy they have brought me. What perfect specimens the gods chose to accompany men through life. The philosophers often debate the source of eros, the preeminence of love, and whether it is stronger among comrades in battle or between husband and wife. We men, so willing we are to die for one another. Ah, but women, women give us not only a reason for life but also a desire to preserve it. Perhaps not our own, but theirs, for they embody the polis and the oikos. They endure the campaigns and politics of men, putting their fate in our hands, only to suffer the consequences of our barbarism. Many think them powerless to the inevitability of strife, but as if divine, it is, in fact, our love for them and what they represent that makes us fight with such vim. We lust for the instant gratification of their bodies, and we strive for the strength associated with their unconditional love. The very survival of our blood depends on the children they bear us. As Homer can attest, men will go to war in pursuit of such treasure.

That is why the loss of a woman's love is worse than their death and, I believe, worse than one's own death. Of course, with death, there is a period of such despair knowing that you will never see them again. Yet there is also a dark and savage peace that comes from knowing that they took their love of you, and your love of them, to the other side, where it will live eternally.

To lose a woman you love and have them still be out there. For my part, the feeling has never been one of jealousy. Only greedy fools are jealous. The most severe wound that can be inflicted upon man is when a lover once saw you as a light in her life and now refuses to accept all that you are willing to offer her. The heart refuses to move on from such a loss, even when its very persistence might have been the very thing that drove her away.

Ahhh, such memories still plague me. They drive a dagger into my heart to this day, every day. Like a fresh scar that throbs every time your eyes catch the flash of the blade. Simple scents, visions, or a slight touch can cause a recollection that produces an ache of which there is no remedy to quell the symptom. Spartans call such feelings possession because there is no place to hide, no refuge from the pain. Unlike a wound of the flesh, there is no pride in enduring a wound of the heart, for no visible scar exists to show. Nothing to say, "See, I suffered this, and it did not kill me." Instead, it shamefully lingers within until it gets you killed or breaks like a fever, only to return again when another memory corrupts you.

Whores help. By the gods, they do. Anyone who says otherwise did not know the women I did the way that I did. Battle also eases the pain of the heart, but only for a moment. On many occasions, I've seen men do their best fighting after being left by a camp wife. Men sacrifice their bodies for their cities, but these whores and camp wives sacrifice their bodies to keep us warriors from possession.

In the midst of battle, men find courage in the presence of comrades by sharing that march through hell. Love for them is often what compels me to plant my shoulder in the bowl of my shield, grind my feet into the mud, and hold some shit-stained piece of earth. I know it is no different for any other man of war. Yet in the wake of bloodshed, I, like most other men, crave nothing more than the touch of a woman. Only their presence, in the form of flesh or memory, is capable of keeping the horrors of battle from penetrating the mind and destroying one's consciousness.

Like many herbs and potions, the difference between a remedy and a poison often lies in dose. They are a race of goddesses, only with the power to heal and destroy. If handled with wisdom and care, they are a divine gift and the only thing capable of saving us from the most persistent and unforgiving adversary—ourselves.

There is now a roaring flame in my heart. Not of love or of anger, but of clarity. A new sense of purpose that has come from a better understanding of the duty associated with my heritage. Here in Sparta, my upbringing has sealed me off from all but tales of past battles and stories about the world beyond our borders. My troop and our training have been all I've known; it has been my life for as long as I remember.

Now, like having awoken from a dream, the wider world seems so tangible. I feel eager and hungry, ready to force myself upon this conflict and prove myself in battle. The source of this awakening, Gorga.

Her father picked a rather uncommon name for a *helot* girl. Gorga, named after the Spartan queen and wife of the legendary King Leonidas, such a symbol of power and strength during her time. As if reincarnated, the *helot* prodigy of the queen has become the foundation of my strength. She is arguably the very reason that I will be a Spartan peer, both in mind and in title. While she pretended to fight me that day with Gylippus, I feel the connection we shared in that moment was necessary for my transition from a young man into a warrior. She instinctually followed my lead and showed me that in all battles, cohesion within chaos produces a beautiful and violent dance that not only has the power to take life but give it. Now, with lessons learned and the *agoge* coming to an end, I am finally at war's doorstep.

During my first winter in the wilderness, I was approached by a group of young men that I recognized. They were older boys from my troop, and they had sought me out to join their ranks in the *kryptea*. To my knowledge, there are several bands of youth assassins in the wilderness, all autonomous. One within our ranks has the task of being sent to a secret temple in a location unknown to me. I suppose it is there where we will receive our orders. Sometimes he returns in a few days; other times it seems to take a week before he is able to locate us, but he always comes back with names, *helots* that have been marked for death, and we are to be the instrument of their passing.

The older boys taught me the significance of surveillance, proper planning, and the instrument of stealth. Every death is to be quick and silent. Those who are to commit the strike sneak in, while others set up ambushes for possible pursuers in order to cover the assassin's retreat.

I am now coming into my second autumn in the wild, and I am plagued by an unquenchable appetite for war. The *helots* were made to be my enemy, and while my thoughts always remained with Gorga, never once did I dare to visit her dwelling in this state of mind. Nor would I want to lead my company anywhere near her for fear of her and her family's safety. Out here, we stalk everything, whether for nourishment or for duty. What we eat, we either hunt or steal. Death and thievery are our closest companions. For now, my presence can only bring her suffering.

The pattering of fast steps through the brush breaks my series of thoughts. Perhaps the hunger is not in my heart but rather my belly. My body aches, and the cramp in my stomach becomes more potent with every step. The past couple of days, I have spied a couple of hares along this game trail, and I have tracked their hole to somewhere in the present vicinity. I positioned myself on some high ground uphill from the site. Just as I anticipated, the hare emerges from its hole, and it is still unaware of my presence. The sun rises over my shoulder, rays emanating across the landscape as it peaks over the mountains. I grip the javelin in my hand and slowly position myself for the throw.

"Nikos!" I hear faintly on the horizon. Down the hill, maybe half a *stade* away, I see a rider on the road. My eyes focus back on the hare. "Nikos!" the rider yells again, oblivious to my whereabouts. The small beast twitches its ears toward the commotion. This is my chance. I let loose the dart, piercing the animal's hind legs. It squirms helplessly as I scramble to claim my breakfast.

"Nikos!" The rider draws nearer now. To call out would be unwise; this rider could be anyone. I must get in close, intercept the rider before he moves on. I rush down the slope, bracing myself as I stumble down the blend of pine needles and rock. Twice I almost manage to filet my thigh with the homemade darts I have fashioned as I dash across the terrain.

"Whoa!" The rider steadies the horse as I burst through the brush and onto the road. It's Shrill. I stand tall to receive his news while subtly brandishing the corpse of my breakfast, ready to skin the animal if this intrusion turns out to be a waste of time.

"Nikos, hop on. We must go at once."

The seriousness of his tone precludes the cause of his unanticipated arrival. Something has happened. I climb aboard the steed, and the Rhodian kicks it into a gallop. As Sparta comes into view, I see people along the Hyakinthian Way. The funeral procession has already begun, and the games will follow soon after. Runners deliver the news of battle prior to any returning army. A solemn but tearless mourning period hangs over the city as they prepare for the arrival of the army and its dead. The next day is supposed to be the celebration of victory and death through glory; however, I fear tomorrow will be different. I can feel a sense of gloom, even from the outskirts of the city. *Helots* tend to the pack animals as the wagons of the dead file into the city.

"Where is the army?" I ask as we trot toward the crowd, noticing no army in tow of the procession of the dead. Spartan armies always carry their dead into the city before the rest of the men so all those behind eat the dust of those better than themselves.

"There isn't one," Shrill says bluntly.

"What?" I query.

Shrill just looks over his shoulder as if to say something, decides better of it, and then turns his head back down the road.

We trot up about a hundred feet from the procession, and I see Theron and Messulius among the crowd along the road. My brother, Theron, has returned with his *pentekostys*, a phalanx unit consisting of fifty men, from their coastal defense post on Cape Malea. Eyes of many of the peers meet my own, followed by a slight nod of their head as if to acknowledge my return from the dead. I am still oblivious for the reason of my sudden retrieval; however, I dare not show disrespect by opening my mouth at such an untimely moment. With each shield that passes by, women place garlands and flowers upon them. Some men of great importance must have died.

The peers sing the paean in absence of the army as each shield moves down the road. The choir girls join in accompaniment from the steps of the acropolis, which is located down the road and up the adjacent hill before feeding into the agora. Shrill and I dismount, and my brother falls in beside us.

"Your friend Gylippus is still in Thrace, and Brasidas is dead. Gylippus sent word to me. He thought it best to have you retrieved," Theron says bluntly.

Perhaps hardened by hunger and death, I feel nothing with the news. Yet a feeling of despair hangs heavy in our city, and morale among the people appears low. When the peers on the island were captured, Brasidas had been the only one capable of rallying Sparta's resolve. He marched Sparta and her allies into Macedon and Thrace at the invitation of Athens's wavering allies, securing many Thracian cities and achieving great victory at Amphipolis. Gylippus had been dispatched with him and is currently somewhere north. However, they have been ordered to return home soon after they negotiate terms with our new allies.

The gloom seems not to have affected my brother, who tersely jabs me in the chest with his shield arm. "Appears you are to join us in this war very soon, little brother." He chuckles.

The feeling around Sparta is tense. With the death of Cleon and Brasidas near Amphipolis, Athens and Sparta negotiated an uneasy peace and a brief respite from the fighting. As everyone has said, this war is different. The horrors of the past ten years have both sides yearning for peace, but I fear many of the atrocities inflicted will not be easily forgotten. A renewal of conflict seems inevitable. It has been a year now since the Peace of Nicias, and it seems all it will take is one citizen within a single city-state to take their revenge upon another, and the whole damn thing will unravel.

While Sparta and Athens try to catch their breath, rumors continue to spread about fickle city-states and their shifting loyalties. It seems fresh grievances have arisen to replace the past grievances recently pushed aside. Because Sparta and Athens struck an accord without consulting their allies, Corinth and Argos still refuse to honor the treaty. Now both have begun sneaking around, establishing informal alliances of their own. As a result, our envoys have been sent to see which rumors are true and to counter this talk of an alternative alliance between city-states.

Thrace and Boeotia balance on the tip of a sword. They remain loyal but dreadfully quiet. The instability of the situation causes many to contemplate the advantages and disadvantages of possible action, while some are not yet committed to one side or another. Each new day brings fresh news, along with the latest rumors. Ironically, the *Gerousia* and the assembly of peers have become so wary of our Peloponnesian neighbors that the peace with Athens was altered to an alliance just to keep the belligerent allies of both parties at bay.

With that development, the captured peers from Sphacteria are finally being returned to Sparta, but the territorial exchanges associated with our accord have yet to be honored. Old friends and former enemies are hesitant to submit to their original protectorates for fear of reprisal. As a result, the original purpose of the treaty with Athens has backfired. Instead of making the rest of Greece dependent upon Athens and Sparta to maintain the peace, the cooperation has made them suspicious of us. Whether intended or not, shifting alliances across Greece are causing tensions to build, and neither Athens nor Sparta is confident enough in the peace to trust one another.

Our daily routines have not changed in drill, and yet the exercises seem almost completely unfamiliar. A mix of nerves and excitement, fear and anger, causes an uneasiness that permeates each exercise and instruction. Like a wrestler expecting a contest against a well-matched rival. Having recently returned from my campaign of murder, the anticipation of war without the relief of violent action is exhausting. Many like me can't sleep while some become possessed with fury during drill, causing others to have to drop what they are doing and restrain the individual before someone is accidently injured or killed.

We Spartans are championed for having the virtues of self-command during battle, but training the mind to endure gossip is another battleground entirely. It seems all of Greece has become breeding ground for talk of treachery.

Early in the last campaign season, a whole levy was dispatched under King Pleistoanax to move on Mantinea. The fort of Cypsela was destroyed, and the Parrhasians of the territory were declared independent. The act was more of a display of force rather than an act of war. Sparta needed to feed their soldiers' appetite for violence while reminding the rest of the Peloponnese that Sparta would not hesitate to meet defiance with action. Now, no city-state feels secure. The mingling of gossip and politics is driving all Greek men of war mad. While politicians and emissaries plot and scheme, words infiltrate each *polis* and infect it like the plague. Alliances are constantly proposed, but the conditions laid down are rarely fulfilled. Even if the emissaries speak truthfully, and the city has the intention to ally, the time it takes for the transition creates an insecurity that makes everyone suspect treachery.

Politicians and generals, warriors and seamen, merchants and farmers, the wealthy and the poor constantly bicker and quarrel like children. Mercenaries hover on the outskirts of each city like buzzards, awaiting the imminent death of a sick fawn. Their excessive drinking, gambling, and constant quest for whores make them a persistent source of trouble. However, with so few Spartan peers to spare, some commanders are reluctant to send them away.

No one can agree on what needs to be done and with whom they need to do it with. With the mounting tension, weaker states scramble to dispatch envoys, hoping to bind themselves into any acceptable arrangement, perpetuating the endless cycle of talk. With so many emissaries coming and going from either side, many have found themselves in the predicament of declaring for both. One day, we hear that friends have now sided with our enemies, and with the next sunrise, some enemy has now become our friend. The confusion, it seems, is beginning to take its toll on the internal politics of every governing body, and Sparta is no exception.

The division between our two ruling factions, the Agiads and the Eurypontids, is escalating. Those loyal to each are constantly in disagreement about how Sparta should proceed. Arguments on both sides hardly seem distinguishable. They often contradict statements they made only moments before. It seems they argue just for the sake of arguing, blindly throwing out reason for the sake of political allegiance.

The return of the disgraced Spartans from Sphacteria has only escalated the tension. Upon their arrival, all have been stripped of their status and rank. However, with the growing need of warriors, the *ephors* judge that initial shame as punishment enough, restoring their rights as peers so that they can swell our thinning ranks. While their status has been restored, they remain outcasts. Even the youth heckle and torment these shamed souls, humiliating men who would otherwise be their superiors. The harrowing is not only deemed acceptable; it is encouraged. Yet I fear an unintended consequence. The sight of the youth shaming these peers makes the entire structure of our society seem out of balance. The situation is only exacerbated by the recent return of Brasidas's forces. While several regiments have stayed behind to garrison various outposts and cities, many are arriving to a hero's welcome.

Even the Messenians are divided. The *helots* that Brasidas conscripted and Gylippus trained distinguished themselves in Thrace by fighting well beside Sparta and our allies. As a result, they have been granted their freedom and now hold their head high. With my mentor's blessing, many have requested to form a *helot* regiment of those trained to fight and remain loyal to Sparta. While most of their countrymen still wish for us a cruel demise, these Messenians are proud veterans, respected for their loyalty to Brasidas.

My mentor stands by their loyalty and can speak of their individual acts of courage. Now, the officers among them look to beef up their ranks. They have even taken notice of my Messulius, now referred to as Stout. Our instructors gave him the nickname for his aggressiveness despite his stocky appearance. I like it; it is a name well-earned with acts of boldness during drills and of loyalty toward me.

One evening, as he strips me of my armor, I tell him that he is a brother to me, as free as any Spartan peer in my eyes, and if he desires, he should join the *helot* regiment. He just laughs, saying, "By

Hades, you can barely wipe your own ass, much less shine your own *aspis*," while using a rag from his belt to polish my armor.

The *karneian* festival begins tomorrow, and all youths of age and their squires shine their *aspis* in anticipation for the word.

"You will be inducted into a *sussitia* tomorrow, Nikos, I am sure of it. Fate surely has led you to this moment. Why else would Gylippus and your brother both return? Your father also died well at Sphacteria, one of the few who did. All the regiments will want the son of a man who died in battle."

"Your father died there as well," I add, interrupting him.

"Yes, anyway, you are also a valuable asset, the prodigy of Gylippus. A man whose reputation speaks only to his ability to train capable men."

"All the same, the peace still stands, and the *ephors* have decided on a strategy. It involves only the coastal defense of Laconia. Even if we are to be inducted, we will most likely end up somewhere like Gythion."

Just then, Gylippus appears at the entrance of the barracks.

"You will not be inducted tomorrow," he says sternly.

"And what disgrace has robbed me of the honor?" I try to contain my anger and disappointment, but the tremor in my voice clearly expresses my frustration.

"Oh, stop it. Do not sit there and pout like an Athenian bitch. Get your ass up. Men greater than you have come to a decision, and you are to perform another duty. We must go now to the shrine of Artemis. There you will be given further instruction."

My heart is pounding, and I am furious. The temple of Apollo, brother of Artemis and the symbol of manhood, this is where the inducted boys will begin the ceremony tomorrow. It will be laden with flowers and garlands. Choirs of Spartan girls will sing praises to the proven youths, while I on the other hand am on my way to the shrine of Artemis, the huntress and a Spartan symbol of youth.

I do not recall any of my elders ever mentioning unworthy youths being sent to the shrine prior to the *karneian*, so the purpose of this outing perplexes me. As we approach, I see Diokles and Estathios, my platoon leader the peers now call Bull, along with their own mentors and squires. My brother is there, along with few other peers I had heard were former *kryptea*.

Then, out from the darkness, a particularly unexpected face emerges, the Agiad king, Pleistoanax. He had been a friend of Gylippus's father, Cleandridas, in the early days of the war. About twenty years ago, both men were disgraced and exiled for accepting unauthorized peace terms from Pericles. Of course, political enemies around the Peloponnese called for their heads, insisting that they had taken bribes. Instead, they were sent away from Sparta as traitors.

A few years ago, when talk of peace with Athens was renewed, Pleistoanax was recalled. However, both the *Gerousia* and *ephors* remain split in their allegiances to him and King Agis II. Now, here I am, standing before him in the shadows. No ceremony, no garlands or singing choirs, just a single torch for light. The glimmering glow reveals only the faces of each man and the scarlet cloaks that hang from their necks. This is no common ritual; this is a meeting of war.

When we all settle in, Pleistoanax nods his head, and the mentors depart. As they exit, the king whispers a few words to each individual before stepping forward and taking the torch from his squire. His attention turns toward me and my companions, acknowledging all of us by name.

"I want to begin by telling you, *paidiskoi*, that you are not here out of disgrace, but don't make the mistake of thinking that I give a damn about your pride because I don't. Each of you has been selected for something critical, and all of your mentors have ensured me that you are prepared for this undertaking.

"As you all know, the treaty with Athens is failing. Even a man of peace understands this. War now is inevitable. This is a trying time for the Spartans, for the future of Sparta, and perhaps the future of all Greece will soon be placed in your hands, our youth. If we are to win this war, we must do so quickly and decisively as Brasidas had wished. We cannot prolong the suffering of Greece by being content with stalemate. Necessity dictates and now requires action. But what actions are necessary, you ask?

"For now, peace bides us time, but many in Sparta have become eager to renew hostilities. As I said before, war is inevitable, and we need to ensure Sparta has the advantage before the peace is lost. You will be the instrument of this advantage.

"Of course, missing the *karneia* means that you will not be inducted into a regiment tomorrow, and for that, I do apologize. Such initiation requires ceremonies and rituals, and I do not have time for such formalities. Many who hold office would not understand or approve of what you are about to do.

"The sacred festival of the *karneia* begins tomorrow, and according to our laws, no Spartan is allowed to leave the city or take any action related to war. This is done out of respect for Apollo, and we must be humble before the gods.

"Of course, I am not oblivious to the confusion you must feel being here. You must think that it is foolish to break our sacred oaths, to taunt the gods at such a time. And while all of you try to conceal these objections, I can see them in your eyes. No matter how treasonous you think my words sound, do not mistake my intentions. This is an undertaking for Sparta. I have already consulted the oracles and asked Apollo for his forgiveness, as well as his blessing, and I can tell you that I have received both.

"The primary terms for peace with Athens required an exchange of prisoners, that we evacuate Amphipolis, and relinquish control of the fort at Panactum. In turn, Athens was supposed to withdraw from Pylos. Of course, after the transfer of prisoners occurred, the Boeotians decided to raze Panactum to the ground upon their evacuation. To complicate matters, our Thracian friends have gained the upper hand in Amphipolis and do not wish to become subjects of Athens after paying for their autonomy with blood.

"Of course, all of this has made Athens reluctant to abandon Pylos. So as you can see, the pillars of this peace are not in place. Greeks have taken their deep breath, and now most are taking action to prepare for the next stage of this war. We too have an obligation to improve Sparta's situation, and I happen to have an asset that may be able to deliver such an advantage.

"An old *proxeni* within the Athenian ranks at Pylos owes me a favor and has offered his help. His name is Pherecydes, and he claims to have information about Athenian agents across the Peloponnese.

This all I can share for now, but take this dispatch with you, and be sure that for each of you, I will make all the proper sacrifices to Apollo. Now, I must retire. Theron, tell them what they must do."

My brother stepped forward as the king and his squire skulk off. Then Theron instructs us to make for our households. The women of each dwelling have already been informed to prepare kits for our departure.

"No armor, this is a mission that will require you to travel light and fast. Again, no Spartan is allowed to take up arms during the festival, so you can't be seen with weapons, nor can you be dressed for war. Leave out of the Aphetaid Road. Just after you pass beyond our borders, at the crest of the hill, look for a lone olive tree next to a large boulder. A perioikoi blacksmith has been instructed to bury light weapons behind the boulder. If he failed in his task, I pray that you will improvise. Consider yourselves lucky, you little bastards. You have been given the honor of making Sparta's first move in the next phase of this war."

When I arrive at my dwelling to retrieve my kit, I see Gorga there waiting for me. As I snatch up the kit, I grab her arm, whisk her behind the house, and pull her down into the grass. I don't know why, but I start to tell her everything. Maybe it is because I am not sure if I'll ever see her again. She places her hands in mine, and I feel a small wooden figure.

"Shhhhh," she says to calm me before placing her hand within mine.

Then, she slowly opens her hand, and I feel a small wooden object being released from her grip.

"It is Athena," she says, surrendering the tiny figure to my hand. "I know Athenians claim her as their patron, but I figured if Apollo takes offense to your actions, then who knows? Maybe she'll make an exception for one Spartan…I know I did." She presses her lips against mine.

I run my fingers through her long hair and down along her cheek.

"I am to be married."

Even though I always knew this day would come, my heart sinks, and I briefly lose my breath. Sensing my pain, she crawls hands and knees over to the tree. As she lightly places her hands on the base of the trunk in front of her, she arches her back and turns back toward me.

"Quickly. Take me one last time before you go."

My heart is pounding as I sprint back toward the temple. I have taken too much time. I needed that moment with Gorga, but I fear that I have held up my companions. We have to be out of Sparta by daybreak, and the soft glow of the sun is already creeping into the ink-black sky.

When I arrive at the temple, all except Stout are breathing deep, so I know that I did not delay our departure.

"Orders from the king, despite the *karneia*. Is this real?" Diokles whispers heavily.

I do not answer but clench the quaint figure in my hand, just a small wooden figurine of a female with a shield and a crudely carved helmet upon her head.

"What is that?" Stout says as he places our equipment at our side. "Been fondling my cousin again, I see," he says with a wide grin, all while nodding his head toward the stains on the front of my scarlet chiton.

I smile back mischievously, trying not to seem embarrassed. Out of the corner of my eye, I see Theron and two other Spartans approaching. Four *skiritai* scouts are also following them closely.

All the men begin to inspect their kits, and I do the same, trying to imitate them in their preparations and act as if the moment is commonplace. We are sixteen total. There are six Spartans, including myself, each with a squire in accompaniment, and finally, the four *skiritai* scouts. I study the group, hoping to gain any insight as to how I am to carry myself in the midst of these occasions.

These *skiritai* are a Spartan middle class similar to the perioikoi; however, they have adapted their duties to become a valuable instrument of war. The perioikoi primarily act as metalworkers, traders, bakers, and engage in many other occupations necessary for the overall function of a community. When called upon, they also fill the ranks in battle as common hoplites. They are considered part-time warriors, but after watching and supplying the Spartans, they have picked up a few things.

While the *skiritai* practice numerous trades, their strategic location within the Laconian territory makes them the first line of defense for the Spartan *polis*. Their community lies along the Tegean road, the only road leading directly into Sparta. As a result, they have sought to emulate their Spartan counterparts and school themselves on various warrior trades. Not only does Sparta not object, the peers actually encourage this. Often, Spartans passing through will stop to offer various instructions to them as they assemble for drill. Simple tips on footwork or how to use a broken spear as an effective weapon are welcomed by a people that now take a certain level of pride in their association with our city.

Due to their eagerness and loyalty, the Spartans have honored them with their own regiments, often commanded by younger Spartan officers. They are our light-shock troops and take a position of honor on the left wing of our battle line. Of course, this usually pits them against the enemies' crack troops, but fortunately, this role has also become an additional source of pride for them.

Highly mobile but lightly armored, their purpose is to occupy the opponents' right by repetitive method of attack and withdraw to draw the enemies' right flank out into the open and extend their lines. The intention of the tactic is to tire the enemy's best warriors while the Spartans rout the enemies' left. The *skiritai* have proven to be very effective in this role. However, if forced into a pitched battle or exposed to enemy missiles, their lack of heavy armor makes them vulnerable to break or slaughter. Nonetheless, Sparta openly acknowledges their importance, and this has made them extremely reliable allies.

Aristocles, one of our companions, was given command of one of their regiments last year. Before that, my brother served him as a platoon commander in the Wild Olive regiment. Both men obviously trust the *skiritai* with their lives and have also hand-selected these men for this assignment. While I have never met any of them, their apparent eagerness for what's to come begins to calm the nervous twitch in my stomach, and I am already thankful for their willing company.

While I look around at each man's face, I study the expressions in an attempt to detect any indication of uneasiness. My blood stirs in a mix of excitement and nervousness. A shudder runs down my spine as a slow breeze rolls over me. It is not cold but rather damp and stiff. Up in the sky, black clouds twist and furl around a full moon, causing dark shadows to creep around the landscape before us.

"All right, gentlemen, let's move," Theron orders. Each man and squire snatch up his effects and follow Theron along the long road out of Sparta, toward Tegea. The movement of our crew is silent and swift. Each man's feet following behind or alongside the other. I smile as I see them move ahead of me. They appear well suited for a task of this type. Obviously, the group was carefully assembled based on each member's unique skills and assets that complement the rest. We are a perfect blend of power and speed, leadership and boldness. The men who devised this plan must have been paying attention to detail, and that gives me courage.

While we Spartans like to think we have a keen eye for strength and weakness, we are not clever when it comes to nicknames. Usually, we stick to something short and easy to yell. The title often represents an obvious trait that speaks to an individual's character or appearance. Accompanying us is a peer everyone calls Beak. His nickname was bestowed upon him in the *agoge* due to a long nose that makes him easy to distinguish from his comrades. He is also known for his terrific speed, keen eyesight, and constant state of awareness. When ridiculed by peers, the most common jest directed at Beak is that his mother had been gang-raped by eagles.

Then there is Archelaus. He is a Spartan of the ancient style, calm, fearless, and mean as hell. The type of man everyone wants by his side in the phalanx. I used to dread his presence in the *agoge*. There were days where we were forced to challenge an older boy. He was one that gave no quarter. If you were assigned to Archelaus, he mercilessly beat you to a pulp, and he always wrestled dirty. He shows a lot of respect for us now, but he is the type of man that requires a lot in return.

"Keep low and quiet, friends. Remember, we are going to be out way past our bedtime," Aristocles whispers with a grin.

The last and most capable man among all of us is, of course, Aristocles. He is already a captain. A born leader and tactician with the humility to follow orders but also enough arrogance to conveniently stray from them if he assumes they will endanger his men.

Theron once told me that Aristocles always puts his men first, and they love him for it. I know my brother has nothing but the utmost respect for the man, and I believe he would follow him anywhere.

As I fall in and follow their steps, I feel humbled and honored to be a part of such a party, but most of all, I feel completely secure.

After retrieving our weapons along the road, we scurry off into the pines to keep our escape from Spartan territory anonymous. I have always considered myself silent and clever, especially after my time in the *kryptea*. However, hiding oneself is a lot easier than hiding a group, but Aristocles's familiarity with maintaining anonymity is obvious. He leads up the front with the *skiritai*, and every patch of terrain we move through seems preordained, allowing us to traverse effortlessly around the outskirts. We race through fields and over streams before finally making our way back to the road.

I turn around and spy Diokles. He looks like he is about to shit himself, and the sight almost makes me burst out into laughter. I am overwhelmed with excitement. I can't stop grinning as our steps transition into a trot, flexible and smooth, as if we were a pack of beasts rather than a collection of men.

I pick up a small stick and bite down upon it, chewing it between my teeth as my heart races and my thoughts wander. *What am I to expect? What will our orders be? Will I get to kill an Athenian? I hope so. Get a hold of yourself.*

I lecture the thoughts in my head, trying to maintain my poise and professionalism. I glance again over my shoulder. Stout is in stride behind me, his face just staring at the feet in front of him, my own. As I observe the darkness from which we came, I can't help but think of what we just left behind.

Back in Sparta, boys are formally making the transformation from youth into peers. Many are graduating from the *agoge* and will be inducted into the various regiments that make up the Spartan army. I have been dreaming of this day my entire life. Since age seven, the thought of my place in that ritual was the only thing that kept me going during the daily drilling, the nightly runs, and the harrowing in the mess. My reward at the end of the *agoge* was to finally become an equal, a peer. Today was supposed to be my prize.

I could have never expected this, but now that I think about it, there is no place I'd rather be than where fate has led me now. Every Spartan back home believes that this is their most gratifying moment. Oh, but what they would give to be me, here, with these men, on a secret task at the request of a king. Fuck the ceremonies and the rituals, the choirs, and the feast. This is it. This is what it was all for—my education is over, and I am going to war.

Clouds continue to move in as we maneuver along the outskirts of Spartan territory. As the moon brightens and fades, the only other light that can be seen are the lamps burning in the scattered dwellings of the *helot* farmhouses. The darkness reminds me of those moonless nights running the trails around Sparta while in the *agoge*. Then, being discovered and ambushed by older boys led to beatings and the ridicule that would follow in the subsequent days. Yet out here, I can't even fathom the consequences of our discovery.

I keep pace with the shadowy figures of my comrades in front of me. Obviously, Aristocles is trying to keep distance from the houses without wandering too far off the road, but then, without warning, we hear a dog let out a deep bellowing bark.

"Shit!" I hear a few voices whisper in unison.

At any other moment, the occurrence may have been comical. Now, however, we all freeze, waiting for something to happen. Then, we see a *helot* emerge from the hut and untie the dog.

"Perfect," I say under my breath as the dog disappears from view, racing into the darkness in our direction.

"I can't see a damn thing," Stout whispers from behind me. We wait and listen as footsteps of the beast approach.

I expect a bark or a yelp, but all is silent.

"Come on," I whisper as Stout and the rest of our party head toward the front of our small column. Sure enough, the figure of a dog appears. The dog is wagging its tail furiously while one of the *skiritai* feeds it little pieces of dried pork. I let out a deep breath, and I shake my head. The young *skiritai* man pulls the rest of the meat off the bone, takes a bite before giving the rest to the dog. Then, he casually places the bone at the dog's feet while tying a short rope to a tree and then the dog's neck. We all just look on curiously.

"What?" he says, shrugging his shoulders. "If you want him dead, do it yourself. He isn't going anywhere."

My brother calmly pats the young man on the back and orders us passed. The *skiritai* just holds his grin and strokes the dog's head a few more times before continuing on with the rest of us.

As dawn approaches, we move into the wilderness to stay a few stades off the road. Now, as we reach the outskirts of Tegea, Aristocles informs us that their path is no longer the same as our own. When we break camp at dusk, we are to head around the mountains into Messenia, making our way toward Pylos. When we get there, we are to locate the Athenian informant and, if possible, make contact with the group of *kryptea* that were dispatched before us.

"*Kryptea*? Before us?" Diokles says with dread, realizing the magnitude of this operation and how difficult it will be to track down Spartans that specialize in not being discovered.

"Shut your fucking mouth! If you would rather go home and explain to everyone why you're arriving late to the festivities, then be my fucking guest!" Aristocles snaps back.

After Aristocles briefs us on our role in the operation, he orders us to get some sleep and tells the *skiritai* to take the first watch.

When I awake, Theron approaches with Beak, and both are carrying a couple of hares.

"Couldn't sleep, but no worries, you didn't miss much, little brother."

Archelous walks up with his arms full of firewood with a wide smirk across his jaw as if he had been laughing to himself.

"I swear to Zeus, that dog last night. I was about to slit the little bugger's throat. Then, that one goes feeding the little wretch. I swear, you draw pork faster than I can draw my blade," he says as he drops the wood and trades grins with the young *skiritai*. Everyone breaks into laughter, but the lightened mood provides only a brief respite from the thoughts that plague my novice crew. This is the weight of inevitable peril, of having to go it alone as soon as the sun retreats behind the mountains. A less-than-welcoming transition into the new reality of war and of our lives, as ordained by the gods.

"You worry too much," my brother says as he hands me a piece of meat. He had caught me staring into the flames, and I had made obvious my thoughts of uncertainty.

"You six have the advantage, you know," he says, talking about Diokles, Bull, and me, along with our three battle squires, Protesias, Ideaus, and Stout.

"The rest of us are splitting up to monitor Athenian movements in the surrounding territories. This Athenian Alcibiades has become quite the agitator. Word has reached us that he moves among our allies in the Peloponnesian League, pouring Athenian honey into their ears. Sparta feels his silver tongue is emboldening our current enemies and working to turn our allies.

"Beak is tasked with staying in Tegea, while Aristocles will try to keep the locals honest in Mantinea. Archelaus will go to Argos, and I will be making my way to Corinth."

"So few at each location?" I whisper out loud.

Although he knows that, despite my protest, I recognize the reasons for this. Still, he decides to remind me anyway, perhaps to fortify my confidence in the plan.

"Remember, this is reconnaissance, brother. We are going to each place only to find out what the Athenians are up to. At this moment, they will be careless with their words because we are not supposed to be there, not away from Sparta at the time of the *karneia*. Citizens, politicians, and warriors alike, none will suspect our presence.

"Unaware of Spartan ears, their loose tongues will likely give us the opportunity to gather much information in a short amount of time. By observing the gossip, we can get a better sense of morale within each city. We also have orders to locate existing assets that have gone silent. Once found, we will reaffirm their loyalty or dispose of them and recruit new ones.

"You see, Nikos, we must discover which way the winds of war are blowing. We must know who speaks what and why. Who can be bribed and who can't. What are the current weaknesses and insecurities within each *polis?* Are their men anxious or afraid? Are their citizens mutinous?

"Spartan emissaries will be dispatched in the days just following the *karneia,* and Pleistoanax wanted to use this ruse as a chance to gather alternative sources of information. Often, ahead of formal negotiations, cities will attempt to display to our diplomats only the image they wish to convey. Pleistoanax is a calculating man, so he wants to know every detail."

"Every fuuucking detail, down to the color of their piss and the smell of their shit," Archelaus utters as everyone breaks into laughter. "I tell you what, those Argive boys are going to be begging for a fight after they find their wives' cunts filled with Spartan seed."

"Calm yourself, my friend. None of our Peloponnesian friends are enemies yet," Aristocles responds.

"Ahhh. You lads are the ones who get to have all the fun. You're walking into a nest of enemies, Athenians and pissed-off *helots* alike," Archelaus says as he nods his head in our direction, the comment only made more unnerving as he gnaws slovenly on his rabbit leg.

"Just do what is required of you, no more, no less. Find the Spartan agents, then the Athenian, and then get your ass out of there. In and out, this is not a six-man assault on Pylos. We can't afford to have you killed or captured, and don't create such a racket that this mission becomes a breach of the peace," Theron states with a glare of seriousness.

"Heh, this is the good killing, boys, not just a rabble of unsuspecting *helot* farmers. Where you are going awaits an experienced Athenian detachment, along with an entire garrison of Athenian trained and equipped *helot* hoplites," Archelaus chimes back in, mumbling as he clamps his teeth onto a bone.

I see Bull smile at his squire, Ideaus, following the comment.

Ideaus is the son of a wealthy Macedonian who wanted his son educated in Sparta. He was supposed to return to his home country after this campaign season, but his father was slain for reasons unknown to us. He decided to stay and serve Bull rather than return home. Bull told me that he asked Ideaus, "For what reason would you stay in Sparta?"

Ideaus replied, "Why go back to an enemy that lurks in the shadows when there are plenty of enemies for me here. Let's be honest." He continued, "Everyone wants a piece of you, Spartans. Only in Sparta do you have rivals that desire your death, not for your material riches, but for your ostensible superiority."

The decision to pair them up in the *agoge* was flawless. Like Stout, Ideaus sees every situation as an opportunity to prove himself. He also has a ready willingness to follow Estathios anywhere. Always eager, never have I seen a look of dread on his face. He is also a hell of a horseman, not that Spartans give a damn.

Again, witnessing such excitement gives me comfort. Perhaps their fearless looks of anxious anticipation are naive, but the confidence they show is contagious. It is the sensation that all good leaders are capable of summoning, the ability to fortify the souls of the men around them without ever having to speak a word. Such zeal and lust for action makes all in their presence eager to confront imminent danger with them.

The sun is getting lower in the sky as we finish our meal, and the sound of Ideaus sharpening spearheads stirs the whole crew into a mode of preparation. I order Stout to make ready our own weapons as I inspect the rest of our kit. Gylippus always reminded me to give myself and those under my command various tasks, even if miniscule, for no other reason but to keep our minds occupied so that nervousness and doubt do not find a way to seep in and scuttle morale. The others are apparently doing the same. The sound of each squire stroking blades generates a sinister chorus of steel, shedding fear from the bones while replacing it with keenness and zeal. Tonight it begins. We will depart from the group and play our role in this expedition, not as youths, but as Spartans.

Baptism by Blood

As we push off into the ink-black sea, I hear the deep yet subtle battering of the water against the wood. It brings back visions of battle. The deafening sounds and smells that accompany the chaos, drums, flutes, the cries of men, shields clashing, spears splintering. The piss and shit, the blood, the dirt, the dust, it all blends together in a harmony that seems to slow time, dulling the senses. Many philosophers debate the ethics and morals of murder, and I can tell you that taking a man's life in battle is much different than dispatching him in silence or single combat. Both are exhilarating, and experience in one surely makes the other easier. The way I see it, cutting an individual down in silence is usually done with a blade and in limited armor. There, both men are exposed—two single beings in a struggle to survive, and the lives present are the only ones at stake.

In battle, the feeling is much different. There, clad in armor, shields overlapped, you march into the dusty, blood-ridden hell as part of something much bigger than the individual. It is as if each army is its own living thing. Men die in one line, and the beast of war falters, but it will rally if courage holds. In such circumstances, the individual is powerless and can only ride the violent wave in the company of his comrades until one beast slays the other.

An army of individuals is an army of cowards, often unable or unwilling to trust the beast. The beast feeds only upon discipline and lust for victory. Unlike single combat, here your thoughts and actions are not your own and should not be your own. For the consequence of battle often decides much more than your own destiny; it can decide the fate of entire cities and civilizations.

I turn to the dark figure steering the boat, perhaps to get his opinion, spark some sort of conversation, or maybe trade a few war stories. However, his expressionless face makes me think he's a shit conversationalist. I catch myself smiling. Could I take him? Even in my old age, killing me is not easy. Although I have no reason to size this man up, he must have already suspected the nature of my thoughts because he is now pushing his long black cloak away from his hip. The blade he reveals is as dark as the cloth that was just concealing it. It is as if he is inviting me to try and assuring me that I am not the first to attempt.

My grin deepens as he nods toward me slowly. I give him a gentle nod in return. No words, just a silent gesture of mutual respect that acts as a reminder that I am no enemy of his. His confidence is intriguing and makes me wonder how many foolish travelers have challenged this seasoned captain. It also makes me wonder what road led him here, to this ship. What a tale it must be. Probably much different from my own. Mine is just a story of the humble trails and travels of a warrior playing his part in a maniacal war.

We take the road north, curving northwest along the Taygetus Mountains, before darting south-southwest across the Messenia plain, passing beneath the base of Mount Ithome. The track takes us about two and a half days to reach hills across the plain that eventually descend to the coast. We continue to move only at night to avoid any confrontation. Spartan peers usually frequent Messenian territory to collect the quota of grain and inspect the *oikos* of each *helot* plot the Spartan is responsible for. However, with the present state of things, they rarely move this far west without notifying the nearest garrison. The nearest garrison is not expecting us, and we are not here to collect grain. With the current treaty and a festival in Sparta, our garrisoned friends will not be in a position to provide assistance. Furthermore, any mobilization from the garrison could be interpreted as an aggressive move toward war. Any action we take must be made with care.

"These hills will be the only cover we have," Bull says as we hump it across the landscape, trying to keep some distance from *helot* dwellings we encounter.

Then it appears. The moonlight bounces off the sea, creating an eerie, almost-beautiful glow surrounding the ominous dark rock in the distance. Sphacteria. The island that saw a hundred and fifty Spartans surrender and where Stout's father along with my own met their end. We all freeze as we stare at it in the distance. Just south of here is Methone, where Bull lost his father. In our silence, you can feel the heaviness of this undertaking start to weigh in each of our hearts.

For the moment, we're done moving, even though Bull has given no order to stop. We just lay down our gear and sit, staring off beyond the coast. Here, at these intersecting game trails, our past and our present now intersect.

"They sent us here on purpose," Bull mutters.

"Makes sense. Why else would they select us?" I respond.

"Do you ever ask yourself what you would have done?" Diokles says as he sits down beside me.

"I do, but I don't know," I reply, looking at the island cloaked in a ghostly darkness. All alone out there, it sits, silent. "I would like to think I would have died out there, either in one last desperate and defiant charge or maybe even trying to swim the channel, but I don't know, Diokles, I just don't know."

"And you, Stout?" Diokles continues.

"I would have done whatever Nikos had ordered me to do," Stout replies in a soft but stern tone.

I should not be surprised by Stout's response, but I can't help but smile to myself. Under the present circumstances, it is comforting to know that at least one among us would share the ferry with me if things don't go as planned. As Bull fingers the soft dirt, he starts to speak again while occasionally looking back up at the island.

"It is impossible to know what we would have done, Diokles. Each of us would like to convince ourselves that we would have done what was right, to die with honor in the company of our mates. However, one hundred and fifty of our peers did not come to the same conclusion, so who are we to judge? Did they not receive the same training and education as we did? Does the same Dorian blood not run through their veins? Look again at that island, brothers," he says, gazing somberly toward the ocean.

"So desolate, isolated, just looking at it overcomes one with dread and doubt. Even the bravest of men can lose hope in such places. Starving, weak, and wounded, on an island surrounded by Athenian triremes. Swimming, maybe a few could have survived before being spotted, but there is little glory in washing ashore after taking an arrow in the back. Little food, dehydrated. In the condition they were in…" He pauses, nodding his head in disgust and despair.

"Standing was to accept slaughter, and right now, Sparta needs every man we've got. My opinion is that our opinions matter not," Stout mutters as he hops to his feet.

We remain still and say nothing. Then, an abrupt rustling in the bushes startles all of us. We are all exhausted. We must have fallen asleep without someone on watch. How could we have been this careless? My hand grips my *xiphos* as I listen to the footsteps getting closer. Something doesn't sound right. I turn my head around as I peer through the darkness, trying to catch a glimpse of the figure. There, I see a large buck walking gently down the hillside toward us.

I can make out the dark silhouette of his antlers in the soft light of the dawn. My grip loosens on my *xiphos* as I let out a sigh of relief.

"Breakfast?" I hear Ideaus whisper.

"Nah, we're downwind. He'll smell us long before we're in range," Stout responds.

I see Protesias unfurl his sling and load a bullet, but before he can get a clear shot, the stag catches our scent and trots off.

"Good hunting in these parts, I'm sure," I declare as I stand up and brush myself off.

"We will have to return here one day, in honor of this first outing as equals. We will sacrifice to Artemis and Apollo, then stuff our bellies with meat until we can't move," Bull pronounces as everyone trades grins. "But now, it is time to make our preparations."

We spend the entire day combing the hillside, scouting most of the farmsteads and orchards that dot the coastal plain beneath us. We note every move of the *helots* to try to understand their daily routine. Who talks to who, and what individuals will be where at certain times of the day.

While many of the huts are scattered across the landscape, most are located near the roads, becoming more concentrated as the mountains edge toward the water farther down the coastline. The center of town is to the south, just where the terrain causes the settlement to condense.

This town, Pylos, is a small and simple community located on the southern tip of the bay, and despite the unique topography, the layout is the same as many other modest communities. The agora is in the center of town, and small humble temples mark various groves or intersections of significance. The location had not been much more than a small trading outpost and fishing village when the Athenians arrived. Now, however, another humble market has been set up near the fort that lies on the northern point of the bay. There are also additional temples that have been erected and another building that appears to be a brothel. Their position adjacent to the fort suggests that these locations are the work of the garrisoned Athenians wanting to make their outpost feel more like home.

The Athenian fortification itself is in a very unusual and yet defensible position. It's wedged between a swampy lagoon and the rocky shoreline. There are only two possible ways to take it by land, advancing from two small slivers of dry land on either the northeastern or southeastern side of the lagoon. They left no room for trickery.

By sea, the position is just as cumbersome. The small rocky beach juts out into the water, and the only sensible landing sites are several stades up or down the coast. It is no wonder why our comrades had such a difficult time trying to take it. From what we were told, brave Brasidas scuttled the ships on the rocks to try to take the fort from the rear, but even he was pushed back due to the disadvantage of the terrain.

Stout and I compile the information we have gathered and head back to camp. As the sun goes down, we go over our notes and discuss the most likely locations of our Athenian agent and the roaming group of *kryptea*. The Athenian must be located either near the fort with the garrison or in the village to the south, where provisions, wine, and clean women can be procured. We all agree that moving toward the fortification is reckless. The Athenian would not expect us to come knocking on his door, and we can't risk compromising our position with *helot* villagers and Athenian hoplites in such close proximity. After brief deliberation, we agree that finding the *kryptea* should be our first priority.

I peer into the tree line along the mountains.

Where might you be? I say to myself.

I do not know if my other comrades were ever inducted into the *kryptea*, and we are not permitted to ask. Bull was, I suspect. His position of leadership requires the skills to lead men in silence, find food and water, and decide when to kill and when to disappear into the darkness. In the *kryptea*, we are required to be experts at scouting, infiltrating, and assassinating. The problem for us, a pack of *kryptea* is anything but predictable, so discovering their location could prove difficult.

My brief stint in that fraternity was during a time of peace. Making a mistake meant putting yourself and others in peril, but our enemies were only *helots*. Here, we are not only surrounded by *helot* villagers but also Athenians and Athenian-trained *helot* hoplites, and any misstep that leads to violence could be considered an act of war in violation of the peace. Our capture would be terrible nuisance for Sparta at this juncture. For our city, the diplomatic consequences would be catastrophic, while individually, the vanquished would receive nothing less than execution or disgrace. If we fail here, better that we die.

After discussing our options for the next day, the sky once again begins to grow dark. To avoid being noticed, we decide to relocate south along the high side of a game trail, hoping to avoid being in one area too long while also keeping upwind of any possible meal that may cross our path.

Stout takes point as the other squires distribute their small javelins among every member of our group. However, as we move, no meal presents itself, and the sun begins its fall behind the dismal island. Now, the day ends with nothing but empty stomachs and a faint red-orange glow in the sky.

"Shhhhh!" Stout turns to us swiftly. We can see him motioning with his hand frantically, his lips mouthing the words "Down, get down."

We all settle in the thicket. The noise is coming from farther up the hill, and as their voices grow louder, we can tell that there is a group of men moving down toward us. They must be moving north along the hillside, back in the direction of the fort. The chattering voices grow closer while I curse whatever devious god has orchestrated this chance encounter. None of us can move without exposing our position, but if we don't do something fast, the light of that torch will do the same. As the flames gradually illuminate the terrain with their every step, I begin counting the number in their party. No larger than our own. They are laughing and passing sacks of wine between them. The third man in the group carries a doe over his shoulders.

"Apparently, they had more luck than we did," I hear Ideaus whisper behind me.

"You forget, it is we who lay in ambush," I whisper back, gripping my javelin to prepare for the confrontation that is now imminent.

Each man in the party is armed, that much I can tell. Like us, they appear to be carrying weapons. Javelins, certainly, maybe a short sword or spear among them. Perhaps they are a recently acquainted group out to quell some boredom, or maybe they are old friends using a hunt to quench their lust for violence during the lull in this war. I will never know for certain, but what I do know is that they will be aware of our presence any moment now as the glow of the fire creeps up the road.

Stout is on point, so he lies about fifteen paces up the trail. He will likely be the first one exposed. I am on the uphill side of the trail, while Bull is higher up the hill to my left, forward about five paces. Directly across me, Diokles and Protesias are about five paces downhill from my position. Ideaus is directly behind me.

The hunting party approaches, and with the flame growing closer, I see Stout's form turn from a black silhouette to dark-red figure of a man, brighter and brighter as the flame begins to dance off his scarlet cloak. Each year, the *ephors* issue those in the *agoge*, with a single scarlet tunic and cloak. Spartan peers wear the cloak into battle and on diplomatic missions while the youth are told to wear it year-round, even while part of the *kryptea*. It is supposed to inspire allies and strike fear into our enemies, but surely, on a mission of infiltration like this, I am starting to question our choice of attire. Surely they see Stout, and I feel Bull senses this too. The tight grip on the hilt of his *xiphos* betrays his anxiety. He then looks to me and puts his hand out.

What? I think to myself briefly, but then I quickly recognize the movement of his fingers. A countdown. Three…two…one…I spring from my post as Bull rushes their torchbearer. No war cry or challenge, just a fast and violent rush toward the man. He freezes at the sudden sight of the charging Spartan rushing toward him in a terrifying silence. As if about to be cut down by a ghost, the man's face is pale with surprise before Bull slams his *xiphos* into his gut.

At that very moment, I sprint past Bull and his foe, not even noticing Diokles by my side until we are simultaneously driving our javelins into the following man's neck and chest. I hear Diokles's javelin snap. Then I notice it. He is wearing armor. Athenian? No time to contemplate as the next man begins to pull his short sword. I too start to pull my blade to show that I accept the man's challenge.

Unexpectedly, I feel Ideaus swiftly brush past, diving into the man's shoulder first before my foe is able to fully unsheathe his blade. My opponent falls to the ground dazed as Diokles moves in behind Ideaus, running his knife abruptly across the enemy's throat. I can see the man with the doe has dropped the beast and is now running along the trail toward us. The firelight of the dropped torches betrays a glint from his blade as he advances. Inspired by this ally, two others in their group fall in behind him.

Diokles and I stand shoulder to shoulder and stare into the hunter's eyes, anticipating a collision.

Sheeeeeeeewwww… Thump. The man's head jerks back awkwardly, the impact from Protesias's sling bullet causing blood to spatter all over his friend behind him. Our blood-covered foe strides over his fallen comrade and rears back, hoping to hit me with a wild swing of his short blade. I quickly step forward and thrust my *xiphos* up through his chest cavity. His eyes bulge, and he gasps for breath, freezing in pain and disbelief. He begins to grab my face in defiance, until Diokles dispatches him with a graceful slit to the dying man's throat. He falls to the ground, my xiphos still wedged in his chest. With a quick tug, I try to dislodge my blade. No use.

I can't see Stout, but I can hear him as he engages two men in the back of their column. The enemy *helots* are fanning out on the edges of the road to try to get a line of sight as Bull lets out a roar to charge to Stout's aid. Ideaus follows behind, hurrying to catch up to them as I frantically try to free my *xiphos.*

The noisy approach of Bull attracts the attention of one of the remaining *helots,* who manage to turn quickly and let loose a javelin. Somehow, the dart finds flesh, piercing Bull's thigh. Seeing this, I leave my *xiphos* and scramble to my feet, running past Bull as he goes down with a cry of pain.

Diokles and Protesias go to Bull's aid as Ideaus spills the innards of the dart thrower in front of me. I rush past him, tackling the next man as he drops his darts and reaches for a knife. The blade falls clumsily into the dirt as I land on top of him with a thud. The young man starts scratching at my face, beating back at me in complete terror. Tears boil from his eyes as his bloodred face grimaces with the anticipation of his death. Emboldened by his show of cowardice, I swipe aside his arms and proceed to pound my fist into the young man's face. Punch after punch, his body goes limp beneath me, my fist no longer slamming into flesh but rather sliding off the side of his face awkwardly as it grows slick with blood.

"Nikos," I hear a voice say calmly.

I look up to see Stout standing over me, his arm extended out to me with the handle of a knife before me.

"Make sure," he says and walks back toward Bull and the rest. I take one last look at the man and then press the blade to his neck and rip it across his throat. Wiping the blood from the blade with my cloak, I survey the carnage that has just taken place. Stout obviously dispatched the two at the rear of the column, which leaves eight men dead at our feet.

"How bad is it?" I say, handing the blade back to Stout as he and other squires assess the seriousness of Bull's wound. Ideaus holds him down as Protesias elevates and stabilizes the leg, breaking the shaft at the top to shorten the length of the dart.

"Ahhhhh, fuck me!" Bull groans as Ideaus rips off part of his jerkin and wraps it around the blade of his knife, putting it in front of Bull's grimacing face.

"Now, Bull, bite down. Stout is going to pull the javelin shaft all the way through. If we try to pull back the way it entered, the tip will pass back through and shred both muscle and flesh. So go on, bite down for me. This is going to hurt a bit," Ideaus says, handing his blade to Bull.

Right as Bull clamps his teeth upon the handle, Stout pulls the shaft carefully, passing it all the way through, slower and more precise than we all expected. Bull begins to scream, but then his head slumps back as he appears to lose consciousness.

"Well, the blood is not gushing, so it did not sever the artery," Stout affirms as he begins to shove dirt into Bull's wound.

"Good to know I'm not going to sit here and bleed out because of you shitcakes," Bull grumbles. All of us break out into laughter at the unexpected comment.

"You should be fine," Stout responds as our chuckles subside.

"I think we may have just killed an Athenian," Diokles says as he nudges the man in the light cuirass with his foot.

"Help me up," Bull utters to the squires.

"But—" Ideaus starts to protest.

"Do it, damn it, I do not have to ask twice," he snaps.

Stout and Ideaus help Bull to his feet.

"Strip the Athenian of his arms and armory. Take anything of value off of the bodies." Almost immediately, everyone understood. Bull intended to make the scene look like a robbery. Assassins and especially Spartans would not burden themselves with baubles.

"We need to leave now quickly," I interject after everything of value is gathered. "We have to move off this trail and continue south. Need to be on the edge of town by morning."

The group moves slowly as we carry Bull. While not life-threatening now, Bull could be in trouble if his injury gets infected, a risk that will increase the longer we remain out here. I look over my shoulder at Stout and Ideaus, who are supporting Bull from underneath either arm. Stout looks up at me and shakes his head back and forth as if to imply that this is not going to work. I walk up beside Diokles.

"We have to get him out of here."

"But to where?"

"We need a roof, but I doubt we will find any reliable quarter here," I assert.

"Back to Sparta then? Abandon our assignment?"

"Of course not. Remember the farmsteads we observed yesterday? There were a number that have stables. Ideaus and Stout are both skilled riders. We need a horse. Then the rest can continue on."

Diokles and I agree that the best course of action is to proceed on as far away from the ambush site as possible until the sun starts to rise. Then we can settle down and make camp. To my surprise, I see Protesias bringing up the rear with the deer he acquired from the doomed hunting party.

"Figured a little meat could do everyone some good," he remarks subtly as we settle into a group of shrubs well off the road.

"Open up," I say, lifting Bull's chin and pouring wine from the sack down his parched throat.

"If you plan on doing something, Nikos, leave Diokles with me. Do not take him with you," Bull whispers as he grabs me by my tunic as if to convey his seriousness.

It is odd to me that Bull would make such a request, but I nod in agreement as my eyes notice the sky over his shoulder; it is growing brighter behind the hills.

"Stout, we have to get moving."

"Wait, what does he expect us to do?" Diokles asks.

I pull him aside and walk a little down the trail to explain myself without having to engage in a group debate.

"Something needs to be done, and we must be decisive. I ask you to trust me and not question my decision. We have lost our leader, and any division will only work to break Bull's spirit. He must not see himself a burden to us if he is to remain our leader.

"We have to get a horse, but neither you nor I are skilled riders. Stout will come with me. Keep your eyes and ears open and stay with Bull. That missing hunting party will not go unnoticed forever. I know hunting trips can usually last a few days, however, we do not know how long they have been gone and who might have been expecting them. I would rather not be careless and leave our wounded friend without adequate protection."

Diokles nods in agreement.

"Stout, let's get moving."

Moving in daylight is not the best idea, but we have little choice. We have to reach an uphill position where we can get good vantage of the dwellings below. The others will stay back and build a fire to cook the deer just before dusk. In this way, fire and the smell of food in the air will not draw attention. An hour or so goes by until Stout and I find an exposed hillside with a break in the trees. The sun is bright, and the sky is clear.

"Well, looks like Apollo has his eye on us today. Not a cloud in the sky," I say to Stout with a grin.

"No shit, Zeus must be pissed he doesn't have anywhere to sit." He chuckles back.

We sit here for several hours scouting the population below, spotting several stables and making risk assessments of each. Some helots are working in the fields; others walk along the road in and out of town. We can even see a boy mounted on a horse doing circular motions around a beast of a man, most likely his father, who is offering instruction. That one won't do. Conveniently, another farmstead lies directly below our location. There is smoke billowing from the small stack, but no movement except for the animal in the stable.

"That's the one," I whisper.

"Agreed. Okay, seen enough?" Stout asks as I nod back satisfied.

It has taken most of the day, but we have decided upon the stable and confirmed an animal was inside. The location is close, and there is also an accessible route to and from the location. We decide to return to the group briefly, fill our bellies quickly, and then move down the hill just as the sun falls behind the sea.

I stuff the meat in my mouth hurriedly while I watch the sun moving quickly toward the waves. We must reach the bottom before sundown, and Bull needs a physician sooner rather than later. A horse riding with a small *helot* and a wounded man will take a couple of days. I know Ideaus is skilled enough to keep the wound clean and ride Bull out of Messenia; however, they must begin to move out of hostile territory while it is still dark.

Stout and I leave the trail and start down the hillside at a silent sprint. The light is fading fast as we race down the hillside. The small pines create a low-lying canopy that stretches out over our heads, blocking any view of our approach from below. We zig and zag through the trees, swift and quiet, over rocks and under the low branches. Rays of the falling sun beam through gaps in the trees. Through one of these gaps, I catch a glimpse of the sun, the sea, and the island in the distance, and my blood begins to boil with anticipation.

We move with such quickness and furtiveness that my heart is beating pure adrenaline now. Sweat pours from our faces as we glide through the terrain like ghosts draped in scarlet. Not even the wildlife we encounter is aware of our sudden approach until we are directly upon them. We dash past a doe and her fawn, while even the hare that is present has not the time to flee. The startled beasts only jolt and freeze as we fly past. This is how I always must move; this is how to manipulate fear.

My confidence is building. I can feel it with every step, a rush that I have never had in my entire life. As we near the base of the hill, I ponder the possible scenarios in my head. Will we be in and out without confrontation? Will someone get in our way?

When we reach the bottom, Stout and I crouch behind the tall wheat on the edge of the wood. The sun is bright orange as it finally touches the sea. The grain glows in its reflection, dancing as if it were flames. I can make out the roof of our target stable and the hut adjacent to it. We chose this stable because we saw no men at the location when we scouted it earlier, but now there appears to be three women. One is obviously the mother; the other two we assume are the daughters. One is very young, and the other is just about the age to marry.

The light begins to retreat as the sun disappears. The orange landscape gently turns to scarlet until finally fading into shadow. We move quickly and fast, timing the wind intervals while we approach. The steady breeze muffles our steps as it whips off the sea and against the slope of the mountain. We settle beneath a tree in the field that is only about twenty strides away from the stable. Both of us try to catch our breath as the sweat streams down our faces. Stout looks around and then peers back at me. I shoot a little grin at him, and he responds in kind.

The moment almost seems surreal. During my training, Gylippus has always told me combat and war are different. Not more difficult, just different. He always warned me not to become intoxicated by the moment but to focus and use the heightened awareness to my advantage. That I should not let overconfidence undo me but wield it within the realm of memory and training. Until now, I did not fully understand what he meant.

Without a word, we're off again. I crouch low as we run, so low I feel as if my knees are about to ram into my chest. The grain whispers, and waves crash as the ocean breeze helps conceal our approach. We reach the small stable and draw our weapons, pausing only for a moment before silently storming inside. My foot catches on something as we rush into the stable. A horse is definitely present; however, it also has company.

I reach down to free my ankle and notice a loose jerkin wrapped around my foot. I follow the trail of loose clothing and see armor. I move forward cautiously as I unsheathe my knife. There, in the darkness, the scene of a *helot* girl and a hoplite humping in the hay. Our arrival is so still and sudden they have not yet noticed our presence. I motion to Stout to move around to the right flank while I slowly approach the couple from behind. Their lips remain locked, and the steady rolling of the man's hips means that we still have not been discovered.

Stout nods to me quickly, and we make our move in one cohesive and decisive move. I grab the man by his hair and jerk his head back, quickly slicing his throat, while Stout pulls the naked *helot* girl from beneath him. Blood spurts from her lover's throat, covering the poor girl's bronze skin. Stout covers her mouth with one hand and holds a blade to her throat with the other. Her terrified eyes lock with mine as I stare directly back into hers. Her legs begin to give, and her green eyes begin to swell as tears start rolling down her cheeks. Horror and fear begin to overcome her, and I can see Stout is struggling to hold her upright. I nod to him to let her go, and she falls to the floor as I gently kneel down beside her.

"Shhhhh, lady, we are not going to kill you." I barely finish my statement when she slaps me with tremendous force.

I grip her throat and push her to her back. She tries to scream, but my grip cuts the air from her pipes.

"Stop struggling," I say calmly. "Crying out will only lead to your death and possibly that of your mother and sister. I am no criminal, and we are not here to rape you. Stay quiet and your family will come out of this unharmed."

I pull my blade from its sheath with one hand and gently place it upon her throat as I loosen my grip with the other. I can see the heart beating under her breast. Her brown stomach glistens with sweat as it rises and falls with each heavy breath. Her eyes grow wide as she sees Stout standing by the door in his scarlet cloak before staring back at me with defiance.

I explain to her that our friend is wounded, and we need her horse. The hatred in her eyes shifts, and I can tell she is looking through my own for any sign of trustworthiness. Stout is preparing the steed as I lift the blade from her throat. I look over to the body of her lover and, almost by accident, let out a sigh of regret. My heart hurts for her, and my face must betray this because she then raises her chin and quells the tears behind those striking eyes. As they hold my gaze, I can't help but see the image of Gorga in the girl's face. Then, I shake my head to break the glance and look away to chase the image from my mind before it has a chance to sink into my heart.

"The horse responds to Gryphon, Spartan," she whispers to me triumphantly.

"We will take good care of him. Where is the closest trail back into the hills?"

"The trail up to the pass is back towards the north," she replies. "Not even a *stade* from here, it should be clear of travelers at this hour."

"Thank you," I reply. "I told you I would not kill you, but you have to understand, I cannot just let you go."

Terror again starts to creep back upon her face as I place my hands back upon her throat.

"Shhh, just trust me. I am going to starve you of breath, but it will only be for a moment, and you will fall asleep. I promise, you will wake, I promise," I whisper in a comforting voice as I can.

How ridiculous. What comfort can I offer her? I just killed her lover, and I am trying to explain to her why I must choke her out? But to my surprise, she slowly tips her chin to communicate her understanding. The delicate way she leans her head back exposes her smooth, gentle neck as I begin to squeeze the air from her throat. She then places her soft hands gently around my wrist but offers me no resistance.

What a brave and beautiful young woman she is, here in her most vulnerable moment. I cannot help but be moved by such a display of valor. After she passes out, I check her breathing, clean the blood off her, put her clothes back on, and place her in the hay beside her dead lover.

"What the fuck are you—" Stout starts to exclaim but stops midsentence when I snap my head around and give him a stern glare.

He knows better than to question me. I often encourage him to speak his mind to me on matters, but this one is not up for debate. I can tell that he realizes his mistake because seconds after the exchange, he begins to help me with the process. I will not leave her bloody and shamed, not after proving to be so virtuous. We also dress the soldier back into his armor and lay him in a more honorable position. I do so not for his sake but for hers. I drag his body on top of a shield that had been propped up in the corner of the stable, assuming it had to belong to him. Then I cut a curious pendant from his neck and gently tie it around hers.

As we mount the steed, I survey the place. While futile, I seek any other way to leave this place in such a way as to express my gratitude.

"Ah, nonsense," I scold myself, and with a hard kick from Stout's heel, the horse bolts straight into a gallop out of the stable and back into the field.

The moonlight casts a ghostly blue tint across the landscape as the clouds remain absent. The light is more than enough for the horse to navigate the track ahead, and it is not long until we discover the trail that the girl mentioned before.

I smile to myself, knowing that the only words she ever spoke to me were true. Perhaps it was out of fear or maybe just pride. My mind wanders back to the instructions of Gylippus and the mock rape of Gorga, his words about the submissiveness of people when they encounter a Spartan. I had known that Gorga was playing along, but perhaps what I had just experienced was the true manifestation of that lesson.

We did not yell at her or beat her into submission. Stout and I exercised the most elusive of virtues: self-control. Her submission came in the recognition of our restraint. She herself was no threat to us. She knew that. When I removed my hand from her lips, she understood her life was in her own hands.

Gylippus always said that confidence and self-control are the finest weapons that Sparta carries. In the midst of battle, when others are consumed with terror, shitting themselves and loading up to flee, our confidence, respect for the gods, and contempt for death will shame men into following us. When all seem lost in the chaos, show a sense of awareness and purpose, and the shields will start lining up beside you. It is not just some image we Spartans use to venerate ourselves. Truly, the force of our presence is a powerful asset.

We gallop up the hill, and I can see a fire still burning. Diokles and the others must have kept it lit to assist us in our return. Stout slows the horse down to a slow trot before turning his head slightly back toward me.

"I was thinking."

"What is it?" I ask.

"Well, Diokles might be right. The armored man on the trail and the man in the stable, they did not look like Messenians. They looked Athenian."

"They weren't Athenians. At least the one in the stable wasn't," I retort.

"What? How do you know?"

"Well, first, the one on the hill had on a cuirass and a short sword, but did you see the blade? Terrible condition. The Athenians are sloppy, I know, but any Athenian his age would be ashamed to have equipment in such disorder. Especially if it was an heirloom, such symbols of honor are not so easily disregarded. The same with the man in the stable. That shield hadn't been polished in years and had too many dents for a man of that age. An Athenian shield it probably was, but a very old one. Also, did you not notice how they moved?"

"Who?"

"The hoplite and the girl. They moved as if they had known each other forever. Such brutes we men can be. Men of war who are on campaign do not wander off in the night and hold a woman so gently. Besides, *helot* whores are probably lining up at the gates of that Athenian fortification in the hopes that some strapping Athenian lad will fall in love with her hips and haul her home to an extravagant life in Athens.

"No, she knew that man for some time. These were *helot* militia. Trained by Athenians and issued discarded Athenian equipment. Furthermore, both men were out after dark with *helots*. Gylippus always said Athenians were social butterflies and only wander away from the barracks to drink and whore in packs."

"Still, if they are who you say they are, Athenian-trained *helots,* then they must be of some type of importance."

"Go on," I say, encouraging Stout's line of thought.

"Well, these men boldly walk among the populace armed in Athenian armor. If they are not Athenians, then they are Messenians, Messenians who are openly displaying their defiance of Sparta. If you are correct, we should be killing as many of them as possible."

"The *kryptea* we are tasked to find. What do you suppose they were sent here for?" I respond as Stout nods his head in recollection.

I cannot help but be amused to hear Stout speak in such ways and by the irony of the entire conversation. Stout, a *helot* by birth, now proposing which among his kin would be beneficial to elimi- nate. Of course, I dare not voice this, for I know that he has fought his entire life to earn his place among us. And other than his imme- diate family, I doubt that he would even identify himself with these people. I imagine that he sees himself as a part of our army, a part of Sparta, and only to her does he feel he owes any loyalty.

When we arrive back at camp with the horse, Bull's and Diokles's faces are serious and somber. Bull is speaking to Diokles as if giving instruction. Diokles's expression is sturdy now, although it looks as if he had been crying. It is obvious to Stout and me that they have been having a very intimate conversation. Diokles has always admired and envied Bull. All through the *agoge*, instructors often used Diokles as the example of what not to do, then would ask Bull to step forward to display the opposite. This fostered animosity throughout our early years that Diokles has not yet let go of. Perhaps this is the weakness that Bull is now confronting, and although I do not know of what they speak, I am thankful that we left the two of them together.

Bull is wise for his youth. He speaks his words with frankness and listens with understanding and does so with overwhelming confidence. His approach would have been designed to break Diokles down, forcing him to internally confront his doubts and his feelings. Gylippus once told me that comrades are there for us to point out our imperfections, but we must be willing to confront our faults, fears, and insecurities alone. He said that learning how to do so gives you a steady soul, and this is important because if one has weakness in the soul, he too will have weakness in his knees.

Insecurities cloud our judgment, causing a man to see only chaos, when focus is what's needed to maintain discipline and order. Emotions can take control for good or for ill. Untamed emotions are a liability, the consequences of which are more often at the expense of those by your side. If Diokles needs to address such internal enemies, Bull is indeed the most capable adviser among us.

Stout and I leap from the horse as Ideaus finishes re-dressing Bull's wound. No one asks about our excursion, and no one needs to. Our bodies are caked in a combination of dust and blood. As Protesias brings us a sack of cut wine, I take a swig, pull out my dick, and proceed to urinate on the fire.

"Ahh, what the hell are you doing?" Diokles looks up with disdain.

"The sun has been down for quite a while now. There is no benefit in putting our position on display. Besides, we all need to move. Bull, you need to be well on your way home before sunrise, so we need to be leaving this campsite behind. Ahhhh, and there is nothing like that urine-on-fire smell to get everybody motivated," I say as I shake out the last drops.

Stout looks at me with a grin as he notices everyone looking as if I had gone mad, causing the whole group to break out into chuckles.

Even Diokles shakes his head with a smile as he brushes away the drops of piss that he imagines splattered upon him.

"As much as I hate to admit it, the sick bastard's right. Ideaus, let us not loiter. We must be getting on our way," Bull declares as he attempts to help himself up. I stuff myself back under my jerkin and scramble over to help him to his feet before hoisting him up onto the horse. Protesias hands Ideaus some dried venison and his own sack of cut wine. We tell them farewell, and with a strong kick, they gallop off down the dark trail. Now we are down to four.

Bull had been our troop leader, but like I remember in the *kryptea*, there is sometimes no formal method to transfer leadership among equals. However, Gylippus spoke to me once about such circumstances and that the natural world, by the gods' design, has its own way of establishing hierarchy. He told me that men follow reason and action but are often hesitant to respond to one without the other.

When Bull fell, I assessed the situation, gave commands, and up to this point, those commands have been acknowledged and followed. That night, I move our company farther south away from the Athenian fort, even past the fishing village on the south end of the bay. After settling in around sunrise, we now have an elevated position that puts us just above the rooftops. We are also well off any trail, and our concealed position has a surprisingly decent view of the sea-level terrain below. Word of the missing hunting party and the stable raid must have spread. The *helots* in the area seem agitated and alert, like an anthill that has just been disturbed. *Helot* sentries are posted along the roadside, and there are a few patrols moving along the edge of the fields, their eyes constantly combing the hillsides. I also notice many of the young men are carrying daggers or slings on their belts.

As we monitor the locals, it seems they too are looking for any sign of us. Occasionally it seems as if they are staring right back at us. With the day coming to a close, we observe more militia patrols assembling in the distance, so I order our group to move farther into the hillside before constructing our hides about twenty feet apart. We cover our makeshift blinds with pine straw and any other plants within our vicinity and curl ourselves up to make it through the night.

During my watch, a few patrols pass within fifty strides of our position. The men are chatting and laughing as they trudge through the hills. I almost laugh at the sight of their carelessness; a deaf man could hear these imbeciles coming from twenty stades away. Stout is beside me, shifting to get comfortable, obviously disturbed by the racket passing by.

"By Hades!" I whisper, laughing. "We could be sleeping on the side of the road, and I don't think these sons of whores would even know we were there."

Stout keeps his eyes closed, but I can see him smiling in silent acknowledgment. Gylippus says that poorly trained men often act in this way. At their post in daylight, they can be sturdy and aware for a moment before they become hot, cold, or bored. After that, they become worthless, letting their mind wander to a far-off place until it is time for them to be relieved. On patrol, they are even worse. They clearly know we are around; however, the darkness makes them uneasy. Untrained men always look to humor and chatter to conceal their fears in the darkness, and this patrol is a walking racket. Shit, I would not be surprised if they secretly hoped that we heard them so that we could choose to avoid confrontation.

If only we had Bull and Ideaus. The hunting party had surprised us before, but if we were at full strength, we could easily overtake these dawdlers. If all their patrols are this noisy, at least we won't have to worry about being stepped on in the night.

The next morning, we discuss our situation. With the *helots* aware of our presence, how can we infiltrate the village and find the Athenian without being spotted? Diokles points out that the Athenian ships are mooring occasionally to trade and stock up on simple provisions. This seems to be our Athenian's best chance to mingle with outsiders without the watchful eye of other Athenian officers in the garrison.

We decide to wait till sundown to move into the town. Once there, we will wait until morning to locate our informant, when Athenians and traders are occupied unloading and inspecting cargo.

"Nikos, come look at this."

I swing my head around to see Stout waving me over.

"Something is going on," he continues as we both observe multiple *helots* on horseback galloping to and from the village and farmsteads to the north.

"Looks like messenger boys," Diokles includes.

"Indeed, something is amiss, and we need to figure out what it is," I assert.

"Ha! Finally, it's about time we get down there and shake things up," Diokles responds, slapping me on the shoulder with what seems to be excitement.

As I ponder his words, I can't help but think that this enthusiasm is uncharacteristic of Diokles.

Shake things up, I think to myself. I hope we don't stir up a hornet's nest down there. We have a job to do, but the *helots* are alert, and there is a tension that hangs heavy over the terrain. I glance at the lone island, hoping this place is not cursed. A place where Spartans now go only to be captured or die. I try to shrug off these thoughts, forcing a smile back to Diokles before telling everyone to prepare to move.

Night falls, and the air is thick with anticipation. I can still feel it here in our camp, and it seems the same down below. As we stare down into the town, it appears that the entire village appears to be eating at once. Not a person can be seen outside their homes, only the glow of the lamps and fires inside. The sun has fallen behind the island and into the sea. Then, as the sky grows black, the village comes alive.

Almost at once, people emerge from their abodes. Traveling by torchlight, all the locals seem to be heading toward the agora. Diokles looks at me as if unsure of our next move, and a sense of urgency overwhelms me.

"We have to move, now!" I pronounce to the group, that strange smile again creeping across Diokles's face.

I almost laugh as I smile back.

An eager Diokles? I think to myself. I have no idea what Bull has said to him, but so long as he is not reckless, this change of personality could be a welcome addition to our shorthanded party.

As soon as we reach the bottom of the hill, Diokles spots two *helots* moving north on the road toward the agora. We follow them for a short time but are forced to move off into an adjacent field to avoid a few dwellings in our path. We use this opportunity to get out in front of them. Diokles and Protesias peel off the road on their left flank, Stout and I to their right. When we are several strides ahead of them, we stop, lower our heads below the stalks of grain, and wait for their approach.

The wheat is waving wildly around us as the breeze whips off the sea. We continue to keep our heads low as they pass, trying to pick up a few words as they walk by. I look at Stout, and he just shrugs to show me he didn't pick up any of it. They are about five paces past us when Diokles moves out from the other side of the road, moving up behind them. He glances back at me as if he was expecting me to follow. I tell Stout to stay hidden and watch for stragglers before following Diokles out into the road.

We need to find out what is going on in town, so I assume Diokles intends on taking them alive. Diokles and I move in so close behind them that I feel that at any moment, one of them might turn on us. Carefully, we time our steps with theirs until we are within striking distance. At once, we grab the men at the mouth and put blades to their throats. Both men struggle, and it looks as if Diokles might lose control. In an instant, he rips open the man's throat, letting the limp body drop clumsily to the ground. The *helot* in my clutches goes still as Diokles drags the body out of the road and into the field. I follow him into the grain, stopping conveniently next to the *helot's* dead companion. I can feel his heart beating frantically, his body expanding and contracting with every heavy breath as Diokles steps forward.

"Surely, *helot*, you know why we are here," Diokles says with a calm, stern voice. Both his words and his tone are to my surprise.

Shit, I think to myself. Even I don't know exactly why we are here, but I play along.

"Tell me about the man who called this little gathering," Diokles continues.

I release my grip on the man's mouth to allow him to speak. Just then, he attempts a shout. I immediately slam the blade into his throat and jerk it across his jugular.

"Well, shit, looks like they were both an enormous waste of our time," I avow, taking my scarlet cloak and using it to wipe the blood from my blade.

"Defiant little bastards, weren't they?" he responds as we both calm our nerves with an awkward laugh.

After regrouping with Stout and Protesias, we continue to move into the village. Passing from cover to cover, from one hut to the next, we weave our way through the settlement. The voices of women and children are all that remain in each dwelling. We turn the corner behind one of the small houses and see the *agora*. Men of all ages are assembling in the square. With torches in hand and weapons on their belts, they chat among themselves while they await whatever announcement or proposal is about to be made.

"What do you think?" Diokles asks.

"I don't… Wait." I pause as I spot a shadow move behind the adjacent hut. "We are being followed."

"You sure?" Diokles says as he and the others begin to look around.

"No!" I whisper stridently. "Eyes on me. I do not want them to know we are aware of their presence. Whoever it is, they are not bringing alarm to us. Stay here and keep an eye on the crowd."

I move across the front of our hut to stay out the line of sight of the unidentified shadow. I try to move quickly so that the light projecting from the dwelling's doorway does not expose me. Once I reach the other side, I pause briefly before scurrying across some open ground to another hut in an attempt to flank the unsuspecting intruder.

I can see that Diokles and the others are still peering at the gathering *helot* crowd as if oblivious to the presence of whoever is behind them. I dash quietly to the north end of the next hut where I originally spotted the stalker. If my vision is correct, he should be on his belly on the southern end of the building. I draw my blade and make my way around to the corner that should be his blind side. I turn the corner with swiftness, but nothing.

The impression in the dirt confirms that a body has just been here. I freeze as a feeling of near panic starts to shiver through my veins. I examine the print in the dirt again. It is smaller than I expected. I stay still, my body frozen as I ponder my situation.

Is it just a youth curious of our lurking through his village at night, or is it worse? Could an ambush be imminent? Are my comrades and I doomed? Then I feel something strike my shoulder. I whip around, gripping the handle of my blade as I expect to be overtaken by a horde of *helots*. Instead, there is only a small pebble at my feet.

"Spartan…here, over here," I hear coming from the darkness.

I slowly make my way toward the field, knowing not what lies within the waving grain. Then, I squint my eyes in an attempt to focus on what appears to be the undersize figures of two *helot* boys.

"Go retrieve your friends, Spartan. We wait for you here," one boy says as the other looks around cautiously.

Questions race through my head. What sort of trickery is this? How did the boy know? No time. I ignore my suspicions for the moment, knowing that these boys were the first real contact and potential source we have found since we got here. Theron had told us "in and out," and yet we have already killed many. I gather the others, and I lead them back to where I had met the boys; however, when I get there, I see nothing.

"What in Hades is this?" Diokles proclaims.

Just then, I spot the boy running toward us through the grain. I look to either flank. The two other boys are keeping watch over our extraction from the edges of the field. Clever little bastards. We move across the terrain about two stades and into a small gathering of dwellings near the ocean. As we follow, the boys unexpectedly run inside one of the dwellings while the rest of us stop in our tracks.

I look at the others, trying to gain something from their expressions that will help me decide what to do next. Where did I think they would lead us? A friendly house does not seem to be an unreasonable location, but still, I hesitate.

Just then, one of the boys runs back out and waves us in.

"What are you doing? Inside quickly. Quickly!" he exclaims in a shouting whisper.

We walk inside past two women and a girl preparing food. The boys lead us into the next room, where three Spartans and four *helots* sit around a humble table in the center of the room.

"Ha! My boys, you found them," an older *helot* exclaims as he grabs one of the boys and rubs his hand wildly across his little head, making the hair stand up as the boy just grins wide with delight.

"Come sit down, please," the man says, motioning to the boys, who scramble about to retrieve any stool or box that could act as a chair.

Before we sit down, the other Spartans rise to greet us. Two of them I recognize, Eukleides, more commonly known as Edge, notorious for being sharp in both wit and tongue, along with his friend Stelios or Stone. Stone's instructor used to say he was unmovable, a powerful shield mate. However, the peers often joked that his mother must have fetched him from the mountain chasm where he was supposed to be discarded, the impact with the rocks the reason he is a bit slow. His mates in the *agoge*, however, have a contrary opinion of him. They claim he always takes orders willingly, can be relied upon to stand firm under any circumstance, and though he rarely speaks, he leads by example. Fitting that he was born Spartan, for we are more often judged by our actions as opposed to the substance of our words.

Finally, there is Kritos. I only know him vaguely because of his reputation as a commander. He will not accept promotion because a rise in rank would not allow him to continue being an instructor in the *agoge*. He apparently is in a unique position that allows him to train, select, and transition youth to the battlefield. This is a post he takes very seriously and that most other peers abhor. He obviously is on this assignment due to his reputation as a man who can produce results by bringing out the best in young recruits. I can only assume his prolonged absence caused enough concern in Sparta to lead to our dispatch.

Kritos begins by introducing us to the *helot* men in the room. Not including the young boys, all the men are military age, between thirty and fifty. As we take bread and cut wine, Kritos unexpectedly turns his attention to me.

"What in Hades are you thinking?"

"Well, sir, I assume the reason for our presence here has something to do with you," I respond meekly.

"Likely, but what kind of reckless stupidity overcame your senses when you decided to enter the village on such a night?"

"Gathering intelligence, sir," Diokles blurts out.

"Tell me then, what good is intel when you are captured or bleeding out?"

"Point taken, sir, however, we came to the conclusion that this gathering was of some importance and that it would be in the best interest of Sparta to discover why the *helots* are gathering in this way," I assert.

"Ahhh, you ignorant little shits. It's all just *helot* gossip, important *helot* gossip, yes, but nothing that Sparta does not already know. I am sure you have heard the usual. The Argives are doing this and the Athenians saying that. We Spartans all know where this will lead, but the rest of Greece still feels the need to tittle-tattle over trivial details. All we can do is hope that we are at war again with our Athenian friends before our Peloponnesian allies abandon us.

"Here I go again rambling. I do not mean to lecture you, and I thank the gods you all made it here in one piece. It is true, we have been expecting you."

I pause to ponder just how long he has known about our presence here.

"It did not take long for word to spread about a missing hunting party, followed by rumors about Spartans murdering a *helot* and stealing a horse from a local farmstead. The Messenians cried out that it was the work of Spartan agents, but the Athenians remained unconvinced. These boys overheard Athenian officers at the port saying that it was just as likely the work of bandits who ambushed the hunting party and needed a horse to make their getaway. I have to say, I am surprised that all of that was the work of just two of you, Spartans, I mean." I see Stout's body shift next to me as if he is irritated by the comment. Yet Kritos continues, the stir of my squire going unnoticed by the veteran.

"I am curious, why steal the horse?"

"Actually, sir, our party was six in total. The other Spartan among us was wounded in the run-in with the hunting party. Due to his condition, we commandeered the horse so that his squire could return him safely to Sparta without compromising our mission."

"Typical, Sparta decides in its wisdom to send a bunch of unproven goatherders to blow our cover," Edge interjects with hostility and frustration.

"Well, what fuckup of yours caused Sparta to feel the need to send a bunch of goatherders to check up on you?" Diokles snaps back immediately as both rise to their feet to face each other. Edge's posture denotes superiority, while Diokles's, one of defiance.

At that moment, I feel everyone in the small room growing uneasy with the abrupt escalation of tension. Even I am taken back. Never have I seen such aggressiveness in Diokles since the events of the last couple of days. Then, as things look as if they are about to calm, Diokles smashes his head forward directly into Edge's face, sending him flailing backward from the unexpected blow.

Edge recovers and looks as if he will charge, but Stone grabs his jerkin and restrains him, chuckling slightly as he holds back his enraged friend. I even notice a small grin appear on Kritos's face, his only response to the fiery episode.

Most who know Edge are aware that he is a smart-ass, but Diokles? Diokles is known for his reputation as being soft and that he is a Spartan only due to the former reputation of his father. I imagine that this sudden display of aggression is a sort of comic relief for them.

For me, however, I now realize there is a warrior hidden within Diokles, and perhaps it was Bull that found it that night when we were stealing the horse. While Stout and I were occupied with the assault on the stable, whatever Bull said to Diokles, it was his intention of unveiling this man. Bull found that part of him that even Diokles was not sure he had. Like drawing poison from a wound, Bull used words to extract his shame, uncertainty, and fear.

Although I do not know his exact words, I have seen this done in a mess in Sparta. The technique often involves defining the individual's reality, offering a choice, and then posing a direct challenge associated with the consequences of failure or cowardice. Defeat your fear, and kill the version of you that others currently perceive, or live under the shadow of your lineage and set yourself up for dishonor. Now, my own fear is that this excursion will either refine him into a mature warrior, or it will possess him. If he becomes obsessed with killing that old part of himself, the loss of self-awareness, discipline, and control will lead to an untimely death. Ah, why do I ponder such things? It is out of my hands now, and this is an internal battle that only Diokles can face.

"How did they find us?" I ask, nodding toward the *helot* boys, and I take another swig of wine, trying to change the subject within the room as well as within my own thoughts.

"After word spread about the missing *helots* in the hills and the incident at the stable, we thought that the rumors of Spartans in the area might be accurate. The helots have had their guard up over the past couple of days, and it has made *helots* loyal to Sparta nervous about their hospitality to us. Our gracious hosts that feed and shelter us tonight are among those who remain loyal," Kritos says while raising his cup and looking around the room. "That one even swam the channel to Sphacteria to help your fathers," Kritos exclaims, pointing to one of the older boys.

I tilt my head toward the boy graciously as a gesture of thanks and respect, and he responds to me in kind. Kritos then continues.

"I too have questions. You spoke earlier about the nature of your assignment… If I may, why did they tell you to come?"

"An Athenian named Pherecydes. We were told to locate him," Diokles responds.

"Ha! Well, good luck with that. That sea-loving bastard was a whoring drunk. Got recalled to Athens about two days ago, left on a single trireme last we heard," Edge interjects.

"What? You know of him? Why was he recalled?" I react.

"Apparently, he was fraternizing with the wife of one of the Messenian men the Athenians had made a militia commander. Perhaps the Athenians were concerned that his antics would have a negative effect on their recruitment efforts. Anyway, what business did you have with him? Surely, killing him could not have been to our benefit," Kritos states in an almost-careless tone.

"We were told he had information that would benefit Sparta's efforts to regain Pylos, but I suppose it is of no importance now," I conclude.

I feel Kritos's eyes upon me, analyzing my words with playful suspicion. He chooses not to query, however. He likely thinks that our original task was futile but decides not to voice this outright, knowing better than to challenge the absent authority by which we were dispatched.

"The circumstances have changed then, and being that my men and I are shorthanded, you will now be taking commands from me. Is that understood?" Kritos says with a calm sternness.

"Yes, sir," we all reply, almost in unison.

"Very well then, let me update you on our current situation. We departed from Sparta a few weeks ago with a list of *helots* that need to be dispatched. Ever since the Athenians fortified Pylos, it has been a boil in Sparta's ass. If that boil is not lanced, it will fester. We are here to purge the source of this infection.

"We had seven *helot* marks, three of which we have already taken care of. With the Athenian garrison so close and constant militia patrols, there has been some delay trying to locate and execute the others. After three assassinations, we figured we would lie low during the *karneia* and give the locals the impression that any potential Spartans in the area had departed. For a short time, things appeared to be settling down, but that is when you all showed up. But now that you are here, four objectives remain, and I need all of you to help us get rid of them.

"The *helots* are suspicious again, and despite your reckless advancement into the village, these boys preserved you by discovering you first. All of them are sons of the men you see before you." I nod to the *helot* men again, and they nod back as Kritos continues. "Sly little foxes they are. They can approach any location, observe anyone, and listen to everything without raising suspicion. They are the resources we must utilize. Skulking men draw too much attention, and right now, we Spartans cannot take unnecessary risks, wouldn't you agree?" Kritos looks at us as if making sure we are paying attention.

"Yes, sir, absolutely," I respond.

"Good, we leave tonight, after the *helot* crowds have dispersed. We do not want to put our *helot* hosts in more danger than they already are," Kritos says, addressing the entire room.

Everyone nods in agreement without speaking as we continue to fill our mouths with food.

"Boys," he continues, waving over the *helot* children. "Gather what you can about the men we spoke of. We will meet at the house on the far side of the field tomorrow evening."

I cannot help but notice how familiar Kritos is with our hosts. It is clear these men mean something to him. Perhaps he has known them since his youth, or maybe he served with one of them on campaign. Also, if what Kritos says is true about them making the swim to Sphacteria, I am truly grateful. They brought us in willingly, and for the first time in days, we are eating something other than dried pork and stale bread. The place reminds me of home and makes me think of Gorga. I pull out the little figurine of Athena and stare at it, feeling a sinking feeling in my heart, a fear that I may never see her again.

"What's that?" Kritos says, eyeing the wooden figure in my hand.

"Just something I took off a man we killed. A figure of Athena."

"Ah yes, the patron of Athens. Little good she will do us tonight but wouldn't hurt to honor her with a prayer. We will likely need all the help we can get, and maybe she'll take pity on us, ha ha. Now, put her away and let's get ready to move."

By the time the sun rises again, we are back in the hills. There are seven of us now, five Spartans and two squires. Throughout the day, we observe the townspeople to the south and Athenian movement outside the fort to the north. Kritos points out one of the marked men, and I almost have to keep myself from laughing aloud due to his bold, smug demeanor. It is almost too obvious that he is one of the men we are supposed to kill. He is strutting around in Athenian armor with a small entourage as if he is the Messenian Pericles. Some Athenian brat gave him rank, and now he is walking around, barking personal commands.

Outside the fort, the Athenians are arranging the militia ranks to begin the day's drill. The *helot* hoplites are so sloppy it is almost painful to watch. If not for the *karneia* and the peace with Athens, Sparta would march right in here and slaughter the lot of them. Now, however, the Athenians are here, and the defiant are rallying to their standard, eager for the chance to emerge from Sparta's imposing shadow.

I suppose it's man's nature to boast behind the image of themselves as soldiers, especially on the eve of war and after a life of servitude. Seeing this enemy forming ranks in the field is even rousing a fire in my belly. They joke, laugh, and march around haphazardly as if they were preparing for a parade rather than a fight. The sight makes me want to charge down the hillside and slap these haughty assholes across the face with a shield.

Their time will come. Sparta cannot afford to have an Athenian garrison here for much longer. The Athenian presence among the Messenians is too destabilizing. Necessity demands their death; I just hope that I will be here to help deliver it.

All day we sit and critique them. Finally, when the drills are done, most of the men begin to disperse. Some look to be retiring to the barracks while others head for their homes. Then, I hear Kritos whistling like a bird to grab my attention. I turn to see him pointing out our Messenian Pericles heading down the path close to the hillside.

We are well hidden in the brush as the man passes our position, only about twenty strides ahead of us. Kritos holds his hand up to tell us to hold our ground and motions for us to follow the marked man to his home. I notice sporadic pockets of men traveling home on other paths. Perhaps they are all comrades, companions, or just neighbors. I guess it is of no consequence, for this man's previous entourage is nowhere in sight, and he is alone.

We continue up to the side of the man's dwelling just below the window of a vacant room. A woman's voice can be heard, along with the grumbling voice of our doomed man as I hear him stirring in the window directly above us. Kritos nods to me to take a look inside. I etch my back slowly up the side of the abode, my cheek pressed against the dusty wall. The thin cloth covering the window blows lightly in the breeze as I catch a foul stench drifting in the air. As I peer inside, I see the sweaty bare back of the man as he sits on the wooden plank of his privy.

Ugh, what a shame to be this man. His last breath will be inhaling the fumes of his own shit. I bend my knees as I crouch beneath the window. After adjusting my belt and my *xiphos*, I pull my dagger and propel the upper half of my body through the opening. I quickly grab the man under the chin and pull it back, letting my weight fall back out the window, clamping his jaw shut and stretching the man's back toward me violently. I drive my dagger into his throat. As I slide back out the window, we hear the shriek of a woman.

Kritos looks at me sternly, his head cocking slightly and his eyes growing big as if he is not pleased by the sudden alarm.

"Deal with it," he whispers loudly.

"Shit," I say to myself as I sprint around to the front of the house.

When I step into the opening, the woman runs directly into me. She was likely running to retrieve help; instead, she literally ran into me just inside the doorway. My momentum carried me forward, causing her to hit my chest and fall straight to her back. I immediately jump on her, scramble to cover her mouth, and slam the butt of my knife into her head. Dazed but not unconscious, she bites my hand and tries to scream once again.

"Silence!" I scream back, but the defiant bitch won't stop. "I really don't want to kill you, woman." But she doesn't submit.

Without warning, I see the shadow of a figure appear on the ground in front of me. However, before I can turn around to challenge, the blade of a *xiphos* thrusts past my head and right through the woman's throat.

"I told you to take care of it. Shit!" he barks angrily, rubbing his sword's arm over his mouth. "Bloody business though, I take no pleasure in killing wenches either," he says more calmly.

The air is heavy and humid as we make our way out of the house and through the fields. Stars fill the sky, making us seem so small and insignificant, giving me a weird sensation, like we are being observed somehow. I barely pay attention as Kritos gathers rendezvous with the *helot* boys to gather information on the remaining marks.

The breeze waves the grain all around us, causing familiar but unsettling noises across the landscape. I try to gather myself, telling my anxious heart to remain calm. The woman is dead, and she is now silent. No need to have nervous blood running through my veins. I look around at everyone else. We are spread out about five to ten feet from one another, but I can tell that the others also appear uneasy.

"You all right, what is it?" I hear Stone whisper to Edge.

"I don't know, brother, I feel something. I feel—"

"Shut up, both of you," Kritos snaps back. "Nothing is amiss, so stop your grumbling. By Zeus! Get a hold of yourself, Edge. The goatherders are acting with more zeal than you," he states, referring to us to remind the older peer that he should be leading by example.

Kritos is definitely not happy with my recent performance; however, I think I know what he is trying to do with his speech. Whether or not he feels as we do, it makes no difference. As our superior, he cannot afford to show fear; otherwise, it could contaminate the morale of the entire group. Being possessed by such emotions could cause all of us to lose our composure and become careless.

Still, my palms continue to sweat as I continually try to adjust my grip on my *xiphos* as I scan the shadows along the horizon.

After speaking with the boys, Kritos has learned the locations of the last two marked men, but despite his efforts to quell our fear, something has overcome us all. Kritos turns our party east, back into the hills. Yet Edge is growing irritated.

"Now what the fuck is it?" Kritos turns around, whispering loudly.

"Kritos, listen to me. Something is wrong."

"Oh really, and what is that?"

"I cannot place it, but I think our *helot* friends have been compromised."

Kritos jerks toward Edge and grabs him by the throat.

"You believe them to be treacherous? You know nothing of them or their loyalty!" he exclaims defensively.

"I do not know, Kritos, but I think we should head to their dwellings now. Only then will I be able to settle this fear or confirm our suspicions."

"You mean *your* suspicions, Eukleides, not mine. Now you have the whole group second-guessing me," he says, letting go of Edge's throat only to push off it violently with a single stiff index finger.

"Upon our return, have me flogged if you wish. But I beg you, heed my warning, Kritos," Edge pleads.

"And you, goatherder?" Kritos says, turning around at me.

"Yes, master?" I say with sarcasm, looking around, pretending to be confused as if there were someone else he might be referring to.

No matter what I think about our situation, I feel I have to throw this "goatherd" nonsense back in his face. We are peers now, or at least we were supposed to be. Still, Kritos swings the back of his hand forcefully across my face.

"I have no time for your foolishness."

"We can either sit here, cowering in the wheat discussing my foolishness, or we can get out there and start killing something," I snap back, spitting the blood from my teeth and onto Kritos's sandals. "The only way we are going to satisfy *phobos* is by feeding him flesh."

Kritos just grunts and starts off in a crouching sprint back into the grain in the direction of our *helot* friends. The wind from the sea blows through the grain as we move with it in unison. The soft, salty air muffles all noise as we move silently across the darkening landscape. Confidence is growing again. Idle, we felt exposed, but moving, we transform back into a pack of wolves in search of prey. I have no clue where we are or where we are going, but I know the hills are to my left and the ocean is on my right. South, Kritos appears to know the area well, but just as my nerves seem to recede, we hear them.

Voices are on the wind, followed by faint shouts and cries. After that, no one so much as pauses again to question what we had heard. Our pace quickens. Kritos rises out of the grain in full sprint, and we follow in suit. No longer in a crouch, we are running in full stride toward the house of Kritos's *helot* friends. The racket has grown louder now as the dwellings come into view. I draw my *xiphos* in preparation of whatever lies ahead.

When we arrive, the outside of the house is littered with blood and dirt covered with bodies, some I recognize, others I don't. By the look of it, it appears our friends put up a hell of a fight and died with honor. Kritos scrambles from house to house and from room to room to check for any survivors, disregarding any attempt to conceal our presence. In each, the scene is the same. As we dart in, ready to fight, no one inside draws breath.

I pop out of one doorway only to see Kritos scramble onto a wounded man who is attempting to crawl over the road in a feeble attempt to find shelter in the fields.

"Who did this?" Kritos yells as he stands over the *helot* clad in Athenian armor. The man just smiles defiantly back at him.

Kritos slams the butt of his *xiphos* into the man's mouth, smashing his teeth into pieces. Then he proceeds to cut the straps off the man's armor, using a combination of blade and foot to remove it from its master. We all watch as he begins to open the man's belly with an agonizingly slow slice of his *xiphos*, leaving the man screaming in pain as he reaches to contain his spilling entrails. The whole scene is out of a horrible dream. A grisly scene, Kritos spilling a man's guts, while we stand there surrounded by bodies of the dead. Not even the women or children have been spared.

"Kritos! Come look at this!" Stone shouts from inside one of the huts.

As we all scurry inside, we see the facedown body of one of our friends, his arms and abdomen covered in slashes. Beyond him, we recognize another man in armor. He is one of our marks.

"Looks as if we have only one left to kill," Edge responds solemnly.

We all look to Kritos as we breathe heavily, waiting for the next command. He grabs a wine sack from the table, takes a clumsy gulp, and passes it among us. We walk out into the open, and Kritos stares up into the sky. His eyes water slightly. His face, angry and sick, as if he is either about to scream or to throw up. Then, out of the darkness, we hear a cry. One of the *helot* boys survived. Kritos runs toward the bawling child, squeezes him tightly, and then pulls back, placing his hands on the boy's shoulders.

"Wipe those tears from your eyes, boy, quickly now," he says as the boy tries to stiffen his posture, whimpering slightly as he rubs his fists into his eyes. "Now hold your head high. Your family fought bravely. They now carry their honor with them to the afterlife." Kritos smiles and gives the child a stern nod. The boy looks back into Kritos's eyes and, holding back tears, returns the gesture with several heavy nods of his own.

"Now tell me, did you see how many of the killers escaped?"

The boy's demeanor shifts from an inconsolable child to a rooster dutifully hollering at the dawn. The story floods out of the child's mouth and paints a surprisingly clear picture of the events that took place. A group of about fifteen men came through and started killing, and only about half of them escaped. The boy states that, as the men retreated, he heard them speak the name of the last marked man.

"Follow me, boy, and stay close," Kritos says to the child before trotting off to the south, not even acknowledging us.

As we follow, we do not even bother staying off the road. Kritos obviously knows exactly where the man lives and is looking to make an example of him. As the faint glow of the sky appears to the east to betray the coming dawn, my gut tells me the day is going to begin in blood.

I look around as we near the farmstead.

"Is this the one?" I ask Edge. "The terrain looks slightly different from up the hill."

Edge just shrugs his shoulders.

Kritos looks to be sure about our whereabouts, running up to the outside wall of the house before waving us forward. With the boy still by Kritos's side, we all line up on the wall behind as he takes a careful peek inside. I watch as he hastily ushers the boy forward, gripping the back of his neck as he presses him against the wall, guiding his head carefully around the corner of the door.

"Are those the men?" I hear Kritos whisper to the boy.

"Stout, Protesias," Kritos whispers. "Take position in that field, lie low in about thirty strides out and about ten apart. Stay out of sight, and make sure nobody comes this way unopposed."

Both nod back in affirmation and run off into the field just as commanded. Kritos then instructs us on what we are to do when we get inside. Diokles and I are told to follow Kritos inside while Edge and Stone are going to guard the entrance to make sure no one comes in or out.

The sun is peering over the hills now; we do not have long until Pylos comes to life. We burst through the entrance. In the corner of my eye, I see a small corridor. At the end, there is a wounded man being tended to on a bed. In front of us, two soldiers at the table jump in surprise at our arrival. The first goes for a spear; the other draws his sword. I dash past Kritos and swing my *xiphos* down upon the wrist of the man who had just acquired the spear. His hand flails about, shredded flesh the only thing keeping it attached to his arm. I bring the butt of my blade back hard straight into the man's face, feeling his jaw snap as he falls to the floor. As Diokles engages the man with the short sword, I slam my *xiphos* into the spearman's chest. By the time I look back to Diokles, the swordsman is lying dead at his feet.

Kritos slowly walks down the short hallway toward the wounded man. In an instant, a young man wheels around the corner, thrusting a spear forward at Kritos's face. Kritos makes a quick sidestep, only barely avoiding a spear point through the eye. Instead, it grazes his cheek, and in one fluid motion, he grabs the boy's spear shaft with his left hand and brings his own blade down across the youth's body. The slash opens him from the base of the neck, down across the abdomen. The women tending to the wounded man stand up and scream in horror in response to the carnage that is taking place before them. Diokles and I grab the two wailing women as the man on the bed pleads with Kritos for his life.

"Silence them!" Kritos snaps as Diokles and I struggle to secure the women as they flail about. Kritos looks at us with anger and frustration.

"I said silence them!" Just as he steps toward Diokles, I whisper a prayer of forgiveness in my captive's ear before reluctantly slicing my blade across her throat. Kritos is less particular, pushing Diokles aside so he can swing his *xiphos* forcefully across her neck. Diokles looks to me in horror, but Kritos already taught me this lesson, so I did not intend to defy him now.

As I let the women fall clumsily to the floor, the *helot* child we brought begins to cry in the entrance of the corridor. Edge and Stone still peer dutifully out the doorway.

"We are going to have company very soon!" Stone yells.

Kritos then pulls the wounded man to the floor and grabs him by his hair, forcing him to his knees. I turn toward the window as Kritos puts the edge of his sword up to the man's eye. The man lets out a horrible scream, which is quickly muffled by the sound of Kritos brutally striking him with the butt of his sword multiple times in the face.

"There goes one eye," Kritos growls savagely.

Gazing out the window, I can see a group of *helots* congregating down the road. Obviously, they have noticed the commotion and are now talking and pointing this way. I fear that Stout and Protesias are going to be outnumbered if this leads to a confrontation.

"Kritos! We do not have time for this!" I shout over to him, trying to break this trance of rage. He just peers back with the eyes of a lion, holding off his assault briefly as the man crawls on all fours while trying to mumble something through his bloodied mouth and shattered teeth.

"Help me get him up," Kritos says to Diokles. Both men lift the battered man to his knees and drag him over to the teary-eyed *helot* boy. Then, Kritos leans down and begins to whisper in the man's ear.

"You missed one," he says as he places the dagger into the hands of the boy.

The boy is trembling, frozen with shock and fear in the chaos of the moment.

"Quickly, Kritos, we've been exposed!" Edge yells as he and Stone sprint out of the door of the dwelling and out into the field.

"Do it, son," Kritos says calmly as the boy shakes his head in protest. Kritos pulls the hair back from the beaten man's face, exposing his neck. The single eye of the man stares into those of the little boy as he continues to try to mumble words through his shattered jaw.

"Do it for your mother and father, for your brothers," Kritos encourages him.

Just then, the man spits a mixture of phlegm, teeth, and blood at the boy's feet. The boy looks up. His eyes move from Kritos's, to Diokles's, and then meet my own. We all nod to him in approval. The boy raises the dagger in his right hand and, with a clumsy stabbing motion, strikes the man in the neck, barely breaking the skin. The boy recoils in astonishment, but before he has time to lose his nerve, Diokles takes control of the matter by grabbing the boy's hand while it still grips the dagger. Without hesitation, he guides the boy's hand so that the blade digs across the jugular, and with a gurgling sound, the man falls forward at the little *helot's* feet.

Seeing that the deed had been done, I run out the door to assist the others. I immediately notice two *helots* lie dead on the ground. Six more are running forward as I arrive, halting their advance briefly with my sudden presence. Understanding now that they no longer have a sizable advantage in numbers, they've stopped about thirty strides in front of us. One of the men then turns his back and yells down the road, perhaps to rally others to the assault. Protesias targets him with his last javelin, and the throw pierces the man's left shoulder. His companions recoil with astonishment, eyeing us nervously.

In the distance, however, more *helots* make their way in our direction. Diokles and Kritos have now fallen in behind us. Kritos has the boy in his left arm and his *xiphos* in the other. Diokles has a spear and shield that he acquired from inside the house. Now we are five warriors, two squires, and a boy. We form up and move slowly backward with our weapons drawn to deter any bold *helot* from a senseless attack. More of them are gathering now. I count twenty that stand before us, approaching slowly as we withdraw with equal caution.

"Slingers! Watch your heads, boys!" Kritos yells as the bullets begin to whiz past our heads.

After a barrage of bullets, a few brave militiamen arrive and decide to charge, likely in an attempt to embolden the crowd that is growing. One of them dashes toward me. I bend my knees to prepare to parry. His shield is raised as he barrels toward me.

"Step right! Now!" Diokles yells.

No time to question. I dive to my right and hear a loud crash as Diokles meets him shield on shield. The jolt causes Diokles to bounce back slightly, despite delivering the majority of the force. The *helot* hoplite tumbles backward, but I recover quickly, slicing my *xiphos* down behind his knee. I feel my blade cut through the tendons, preventing him from rising. Before I am able to take another breath, Diokles finishes him off with a spear thrust to the throat.

I turn to see Edge and Stone make quick work of three armorless *helots* while Diokles and I move to cover Kritos and the boy. These poorly trained farmers are no match for highly trained warriors. A couple of loud dings and bongs ring out as Diokles deflects bullets off the bronze face of his shield. Again, following the volley, another group of *helots* decide to make a foolhardy charge. Protesias has now pulled out his own sling and drops the lead *helot* with a well-placed bullet to his chest. Seeing their comrade fall so abruptly, the rest stop briefly in horror.

"Back! Back!" Kritos calls out in an attempt to take advantage of their hesitation.

We retreat, hopping a short fence of olive wood before dashing through the field toward the hills. Diokles covers our retreat with the heavy shield, but it is growing cumbersome. Our enemies gain ground and charge forward, perhaps motivated by the prospect of our potential escape. I stand beside Diokles to make sure he does not fall behind by himself as Kritos continues to scream at us. Out of the corner of my eye, I see Edge and Stone quickly fall in beside us in an attempt to deter the advancing *helots*. However, we soon realize the folly of our boldness.

We seem to come to the same conclusion, and our feet begin to kick up dust as we all shuffle backward.

"Go, now!" Edge shouts. We simultaneously turn and run, passing another set of farmsteads. Outside, a few confused *helots* just watch us sprint through the grain. Those approaching call to them for aid, and I see the men quickly retreat back into their homes, likely to retrieve whatever weapons they have. I hear their women begin hurling insults and realize that the entire town is turning on us. More helots are about to join the fray.

"We have to make it to the hills now before we are overwhelmed!" Kritos demands.

While pursuing *helots* try to draw others to the chase, the small lapse in their advance gives us just enough time to make a break for the woods. A sling bullet skips on the ground at my feet as we sprint toward the hills. We take the path north and then double back, moving off the trail and heading south in an attempt to shake the pursuit. While we continue to move south, parallel to the coast, we stop to wait until nightfall before heading north, back toward a small game trail that will take us through the hills and inland to the Messenian plain.

The maneuver appeared to work because through the night, we were able to pass unnoticed by the many *helot* farmsteads scattered across the plain. With the rising sun, we come to the end of the plain and reach the relative safety of the Tegean Mountains. Perhaps we were blessed with swiftness from the gods or just fueled by adrenaline; either way, we made fantastic time. If the sun had risen before we crossed the plain, we might have been stuck out in the open and exposed. Once in the foothills, we stop for some brief respite, and all stare back into the plain. The ground we covered is vast, and we spot what must be Athenian horsemen from the fort. They appear to be going from farmstead to farmstead to search any potential hiding place or ask about suspicious activity.

"Good thing we are not still down there," Edge says, echoing what we all are thinking.

"Just pass me the water and the damn wine," Kritos grumbles, passing the water to the boy before putting the bottom of the wine sack vertical.

I watch as Kritos and the boy likely empty the sacks of water and wine. I can't help but be surprised by the thirsty boy's stamina. He ran most of the way with us, with Kritos only picking him up occasionally to give him unrequested relief from our quick pace. He kept right on the heels of Kritos, like a young pup following his new master. I do admire him. Not since this moment did I ever see him look back.

We never even considered leaving him behind, and no one questioned Kritos's decision to bring him with us. Still, I can't help but wonder what will become of him. I can't even imagine the thoughts that must be running though his head. As he holds the empty water sack, he just stares blankly back across the terrain. His thoughts are starting to plague him. I can tell he is fighting back tears, but no words come from his lips. Perhaps he is afraid, afraid that if he cries for help, we will abandon him. We are all that he has now, and I now believe he would walk till his feet were raw and bloodied before he risked disappointing us.

We continue into the foothills a short while before making camp at dawn. We will rest and sleep for much of the day before we continue north in the hills. Of course, it is folly to pass over the mountains, so we must go around them before heading back south to Sparta.

The mood is light now that we are in no immediate danger, and so comfortable are we that our decision to build a fire is somewhat reckless. However, we feel it is a reasonable reward for our diminutive victory and successful escape. While we all reminisce about the part we played in the skirmish, the boy succumbs to a deep sleep.

"Probably best if we all get some rest. Bed down, boys, I will take first watch," Kritos mumbles, looking at the boy's peaceful nap with envy.

Heeding Kritos's advice, Stone appears to pass out almost immediately. However, the rest of us decide to stay up and keep him company. Whether it is because we can't sleep or because we want to show our respect for the man, we decide not to leave our leader to sit silently alone in the darkness.

"That boy… I have no words," Diokles utters.

"Tough little bastard, isn't he?" Edge says with a smile.

"You have no idea," I respond.

"No idea? I watched the kid walk on splintered and bloodied feet all day without complaint," Stout replies as he takes a swig.

"That's not what he means," Kritos interjects.

"Why, what the hell did we miss? What happened in there?" Stone enters the conversation, slightly opening his eyes and revealing that he has been awake all along.

Everyone looks around at each other, and then finally, I decide to give a short recount of how the boy avenged the death of his family.

"Ha ha, ole Diokles, helping the boy flay the bastard. I have to say, I truly am impressed by that little fella, and by you, Diokles," Edge says with a slap to Diokles's shoulder. "You are not the youth I remember you to be, truly."

Diokles just nods in acknowledgment and stares back into the fire. I watch his eyes. The flames appear to dance within them with each crack and flicker. Wrapped in his scarlet cloak with reddish-orange flames in his eyes, he looks like a warrior that just crawled out of Hades. Clearly, Diokles is a different person after this excursion. Like the *helot* boy, he has left something behind him. His innocence. I never asked, but I know Diokles was never *kryptea*. This must have been the first time he has taken life. The last time I saw his eyes staring into the flames like this, he was receiving guidance from Bull. It must have been then that he discovered the fire within himself.

Now, his eyes revisit Hephaestus at the site where the new Diokles was forged.

"At a loss of words regarding the part you played with the boy, Diokles? Understand that under the care of any other Greeks, this boy would not have been able to mentally and physically endure the events of the last day. Our actions, your actions, they may seem cruel and maybe even barbarous to our neighbors. 'He is too young to witness war or deal death. Are you mad? You will wound his fragile mind,' they would say. But make no mistake because of what we did for him, the trauma will be short-lived.

"Seeing your family murdered before you is something we Spartans are fortunate to have little knowledge of. And yet we are the only ones with the proper tools and the mental discipline required to cope with such an event.

"From youth we are trained to focus only on what is necessary, trained to not let our soul search those forbidden places within the mind and the heart. We are aware that these have the power to drive all men to madness. Our strength lies not in our tactics on the battlefield but rather our ability to confront the emotion, eradicate it, or dismiss it entirely. We learn not to let ourselves dwell in those places that can only bring us harm.

"Had we not forced the boy to kill the man that murdered his family, it would have allowed these demons to spawn within his soul. His whole life would be consumed by a quest for answers and an unquenchable thirst for revenge. We all know revenge does little if the quest for it causes us to ignore our destiny, if it is allowed to define our path instead of following the gods, the ancestors, and the dictates of necessity.

"Swift and immediate closure, by his hand, is the only way to cauterize such a wound to the heart before it has a chance to fester. Without it, what then? The boy's mind would be poisoned, his judgment forever clouded. He would become reckless and vengeful to all who come to know him. He'd be cruel and corrupt, like a rabid fox endlessly wandering the earth day and night, and for what? He would not even know."

Everyone's eyes are trained on the sleeping *helot* boy as Stone directs his attention to Diokles.

"Diokles, you did an honorable thing for that boy. You could have killed that man yourself after the boy had failed, but you did not. Without having to be told, you sensed what Kritos was trying to accomplish. With your hand guiding his, he will trust you, and perhaps Sparta, for the rest of his days. As Kritos said, you saved him from a cursed existence."

"Aye," Edge chimes in. "Not to mention the misery and horror that boy would be facing if he were still back there, surrounded by the corpses of his kin. None among those *helot* bastards would have taken this stray, a boy considered to be the son of traitors. He only sleeps soundly now because of us and because of you, Diokles."

The journey home is pleasantly uneventful. We reach the Tegean road without need of any sneaking or skulking about. In friendly territory, we take the road and come across the occasional group of travelers and street vendors packing up to depart following the festival. Of course, mercenaries are still gathered at the crossroads. At any other time, all but the mercenaries would be a rare sight on this road. However, during the few Dorian festivals, outsiders are sometimes invited to witness the Spartans in celebration of the gods. We stop only once or twice to quench our thirst and engage in some small talk.

Here and there, we are able to pick up small details of the *karneian* festival we missed during our recent exploit. Some avoid us, but most are curious why Spartans, caked in dust and blood, travel the road in the opposite direction. One mercenary cavalryman in particular trots right over to confront us, slowing his beast to match our pace as we continue along the road.

"Spartans on the road, I thought the festival was down that way?" he says sarcastically. "Is this not an offense to the laws of your land?"

Kritos just smiles and responds, "We too must eat, Athenian. Spartans grow hungry during a festival, and what better way to honor

Ares than with a good hunt. Oh, and since when does an Athenian question a Spartan about his own laws?"

"He is an Athenian, Kritos?" I whisper.

"Of course, they question anything having to do with law. Besides, look at that smug look on his face."

"I was not born yesterday, lads. I can hear you," the horseman continues. "And I have seen many more summers than you. Covered in blood? A hunt perhaps, yet I see no game. You have no javelins nor bows and arrows. So spare me this production. I am no fan of actors, poets, and mimes. I was trained in your *agoge*. I always knew you Spartans to be good and honorable men, but that was back when you Spartans believed in a prosperous Greece."

"You mean a free Greece, Athenian?" Diokles chimes in with a smile.

"Do you claim to be free, Spartan?"

"I do. Oh, and what freedom do you claim to have, sellsword? I fight for a city, not a paymaster."

"One can gain much wisdom by fighting on both sides of a war, my friend. For your sake, I hope you reach my years and learn what I have come to know. I have survived this long by seeing things for what they truly are, not by what I was simply taught to perceive. You Spartans speak of freedom while enslaving other Greeks. Athens claims democracy and alliance are the only true path to freedom. Yet they too force capitulation on such terms that their allies find themselves in only a slightly better position than your *helots*. You force men into the field because the grain feeds the might of your army. Athens forces submission because money is the only sustenance for a great navy. Coin, not slaves, buys the timber, builds the ships, and drives men's hands to the oars."

"And the whores are what keep their hands there," I utter.

"Ha! True enough, Spartan, we are all slaves to women. Ah, but enough politics and philosophy. I fuck, fight, sleep, and drink on my own terms. If that is as free as I'll ever be, I give thanks to the gods. Have a pleasant war, Spartans, for you know that your city is the prized jewel. The city without walls, yet to witness the fires of rape and war. Well, we shall see, won't we?

"There is not a man in Greece who hasn't pleasured himself to the thought of pissing on your corpses and raping your wives!" he yells over his shoulder as he trots back to the huddle of mercenaries.

He looks back over his shoulder to show us his smug grin. Then, in a most unexpected move, he wheels his horse around and straightens in the saddle to project a more noble and sincere posture.

"But all the same, my heart knows that I would get more pleasure fighting and dying alongside you! The name is Theopompus. Just ask any hired man if you ever need my services, and word will reach me."

He waves back around, giving us an Athenian salute. We all just laugh and shake our heads. I wonder, would I ever want to overlap my shield and stand with a man of that type, or would I rather see him on the other end of my spear?

As we come over the hill and see Sparta, the fresh scents of jasmine and lavender fill my nostrils. The road is still laden in the remnants of the *karneia*. My eyes take in the few of all the gardens surrounding the quaint Spartan quarters that riddle the countryside. Never have I appreciated the beauty of this place so. The olive orchards, rivers, streams, and mountains, they all seem to dive into the landscape and come together at the center, at our city.

The youth, in their bright scarlet cloaks, are immersed in their exercises. A few wives and daughters tend to the *oikos*, taking pause from their chores to give us faint smiles as we pass, trusting that we had probably just been obeying one strange order or another. Contrarily, most Spartan males that see us stop what they are doing and take notice, looking bewildered and even angry as we approach.

"We must look like hell," Edge utters, causing us all to look down and inspect our appearance.

A feeling of nervous pride swells in my chest as I see Kritos just continuing to look forward, chin high, with eyes trained on a rider approaching ahead. I have no idea how our city will receive us. We are not a common spectacle, especially just following the *karneia*. However, there is a sort of swagger in Kritos's steps that gives me assurance. Seven armed and bloodied men, not in war gear, and a small boy with battered feet. It is clear that Kritos carries home no fear or shame; we obeyed the orders of our elders and carried out a task in the interest of Sparta.

"There are a few peers that request your presence. This is a request, friend, that would be wise not to ignore," the rider says as he approaches.

"And it would be wise, friend, never to speak to me in such tone again," Kritos responds arrogantly, obviously recognizing this man is not a peer.

"My apologies, sir, I do not wish to do so, only trying to convey the importance of the message I was instructed to give you," the squire replies as the horse stirs a bit.

"Very well, lead on."

In a gesture of respect, the squire dismounts and walks alongside us with his horse the remainder of the way. We walk across the agora and over to the assembly house. There, the squire tells us to wait outside while he enters to announce our presence. That is when I see Gylippus in the corner of my eye. He trots on horseback down the hill toward us. He slows up halfway down the hill, and he and I lock eyes. He salutes me, and I see a large grin on his face before he wheels the horse back around, kicking it softly as he heads back the way he came.

I can't be sure, but it feels as if he wanted to make sure he was the first to welcome me home.

"Okay, it is time," the squire says, stepping out to usher us in.

After entering, we line up and stand at attention before the assembly. The assembly of peers is not present. Instead, it is only the *ephors* and King Agis.

Oh shit, I think to myself as Agis eyes each of us and begins to speak.

"Any other collection of men, I would deem irreverent and insubordinate, but I suspect you all to be neither. What you must understand is that the gods favor Sparta, but only because we obey their laws. This foolish errand of yours has the potential to cause many problems for us. We can't have the rest of Greece believing that Sparta is willing to disobey our obligations to the gods for trickery and expedience. Our strength is in our discipline and our consistency. Tell me, what do you think you accomplished in Messenia?"

Kritos begins to speak, but he is silenced. Agis instead decides to question us individually. We explain to him the status of Pylos and the elements of armed *helots* that exist there. It seems he and the *ephors* were aware of the *kryptea's* original assignment to dispatch *helots.* Of course, this means he is more concerned with the errand that we were selected for.

Diokles and I say nothing of the Athenian for fear of the speculations that already surround King Pleistoanax and his reputation.

"Nothing? As I said, foolish. Kritos, we already know the information you have given us. We also know who was dispatched with you. These youths were not, and yet you all did have another objective of which we also know. The men who put you on this task have already been punished. Yet I find myself in a difficult position. I feel I cannot punish you because you did as you were trained. You obeyed your superiors without question, and it is for that reason only that I will not have each of you flogged. However, I hope for yourselves that you have taken something from this experience," he says, addressing only Diokles and myself.

"Permission to speak, sir," Kritos says.

"Go on."

"We completed our task in Messenia."

"With some difficulty," Agis interrupts.

"There is no excuse for that, sir, but each of these men acted with bravery and did what was necessary under the circumstances."

"Get to the point, Kritos. I do not have time for this."

"I wish to say only that without the reinforcement of these youths, we would have been unable to eliminate the objectives. All were prime examples of Spartan discipline and resourcefulness. However, one stood out above all, without whom we would have all been lost."

"And who might that be?" Agis asks sarcastically, getting tired of this commendation.

"This boy," Kritos says as he steps aside to reveal the little *helot* boy to the council, all of whom erupt into loud whispers.

"Silence!" one of the *ephors* declares, shifting to a calmer tone before asking, "And who is this?"

"This boy led us to each objective. His father and uncle both had been granted their freedom by Sparta after we enlisted their help at Sphacteria. However, Sparta failed to honor that promise when Pylos was not taken. As a result, he and his kin were forgotten. Still, they remained loyal to Sparta."

"Why is he here?" Agis snarls, seeming upset with this development.

"While he was providing us with information, his family, my squire among them, were ambushed and murdered by those loyal to Athens. Our last objective died by this boy's hand. That is why, with the permission of all of you, I would like to sponsor this boy for admission into the *agoge*," Kritos concludes firmly as he places his hands upon both shoulders of the boy.

"Of course, we will have to inspect the boy ourselves," an *ephor* exclaims.

"Very well, that will be all," Agis says as we turn for the door. "Oh, and by the way, Adronikos, you and Diokles will be serving under Kritos now, as Wolves."

The words fill my soul with honor. I fight off a smile as I give him a dutiful nod as we turn for the door. The Wolves of Nike are a *mora* comprising of approximately 576 men. The *lochoi* is regimental size, representing particular Spartan communities with 144 men. Kritos was now our *enōmotarches* in charge of an *enōmotia*, or platoon, which is comprised of 36 men.

My father had been part of the Wolves. He always spoke about how the Wolves were the Spartans who were always in the most danger. They held the middle of the line, on the left flank of the royal guard and on the right of the *skiritai*. While formidable allies, they are not Spartans, and they wear lighter armor, making them more prone to break and run. The Wolves act as their example, displaying virtue on the field so that the *skiritai* have the courage to die with honor beside you or risk the dishonor of abandoning you.

My father once said, "The Wolves are not there to maneuver or win battles with tact. Our job is to prevent the break, to keep the line intact. The Herakliens and the Crown Laurels get all the glory for routing the enemy on the right flank, but it is the Wolves who the gods favor, for they die in the most sacred of places, the middle of the field. We act as the mill of murder, holding our prey in place as the rest of the army envelopes the flank. Only humble Laconian men with courage and self-control are welcome among the Wolves, for in battle, they reside in the realm of only death, confusion, and chaos."

Gylippus obviously knew, for he and Diokles's mentor, Aristonike, now charge into the room to greet us in congratulations at our acceptance into a mess. Due to our peculiar situation, the *ephors* decided to put all of us into the same mess. This was obviously done to limit explanation and discourse regarding our absence during festival. However, I also suspect that this was the case made by someone of greater rank in our absence.

The mess is important because you have to be recruited into one in order to be deemed a peer, a Spartan equal. Once an equal, you are eligible for military service. The group with which we will dine is comprised of equals from all communities within Sparta. In this way, Spartans know and relate to all Spartan peers, regardless of politics or rank. This way, each man can learn from one another's experiences, gathering details of an engagement from a variety of perspectives. Furthermore, an army functions with more cohesion when all men have an interest in preserving friends that stretch the entire length of the line. A Spartan is only a member of multiple messes when he is given the honor of being selected to the ranks of the king's knights, three hundred men that serve as the king's bodyguard on campaign. Gylippus has just received this honor, while I take my place in a unit that used to be under his command as a *lochagus*. I do not know if my selection had been the design of Gylippus all along, but to be following in his footsteps and under Kritos's command, I am honored and, most of all, thankful.

Gylippus asks me of our adventures, so we tell him everything, trying not to be overdramatic or enthusiastic. Of course, the last grim days were not a pleasant story to tell, and I feel tears run down my cheek as I describe the scene where I had to slit the woman's throat. Gylippus and Aristonike inform us about the plots of land in Messenia that have been allocated to our charge. My brother received his years ago. I am now being given those that had belonged to my father.

"Helots have already begun preparing to build your new home here on the outskirts of Sparta, and I know you want to oversee its construction, so let us go and check their progress," Gylippus says, patting his hands on both my shoulders.

As we depart, all notice Kritos still pacing outside the assembly, waiting intently as the boy is interrogated inside.

"Come, Kritos!" Gylippus yells. "The fate of the boy is no longer in your hands, no sense in stirring up dust. We wouldn't want to blur Apollo's vision from these events now, would we?"

"Ah, you're right, Gylippus. My worry is of no consequence to them or the gods. His father was a brother to me, and I shall treat this boy as if he were blood."

"We know you will," Gylippus states encouragingly as we depart.

Loves Lost

A wise man among my enemy wrote a work to honor his mentor. It is a record of a debate between men regarding eros and whether the love between men is superior to that of a man and a woman. Although we Spartans are not known for our depth in thought, I would have very much enjoyed taking part in that argument, for neither is truly superior. Instead, they each have their place and their purpose. My mind has already pondered the divine duty and allure of women and their love. All of them sirens, sent by the gods to live among us, both to save us and to torment us. To drive us mad and bring us back from madness. It is this reality that drives all men to seek the company of comrades to escape their women. Whether it is the unnatural calm, the meaningless banter, or their unhinged mind when their legs flow red, love between a man and a woman is a constant unwinnable battle that offers great rewards and devastating defeats. Men share their trials of death, and it is also why we seek out our companions to share meat, wine, and whores. For marriage and companionship is a war where the shields and spears of our comrades count for nothing. However, like recounting the horrors and glories of battle, so too do men share the triumphs and tribulations of their quarters.

Love between a man and a woman is like religion. It takes discipline and faith. Due to the violent ebb and flow that comes from our relationship with our women and our gods, it may sometimes seem futile. Contrarily, the relationship with the comrades that we bind ourselves to is constant, consistent, and unbreakable. Even if some unforeseeable circumstance forces a man to kill a dear friend, the distasteful task is done with as much respect as the situation allows. Still, the fracturing of that bond will torment the soul of the survivor, making him long for the day to be reunited with his friend in the afterlife.

The source of unrest between man and woman lies in perception. I think that is the essence of the philosophers' debate. I have seen women fight, fuck, and drink as well as any man, but this dick between our legs forces us to see the world through a particular lens. It is not that we lack the wisdom or the curiosity. Instead, the gods chose to balance our world through selectively imparting divine wisdom into each half of humanity. Men find knowledge, understanding, and purpose through death. Women find these through life. Even the gods share this torment with us, for both are a natural and necessary part of this world.

Many may call me a heretic, but I'd like to pose this question to the philosopher. If the beasts within us are present even in the gods, how did they come to be divine? By what design or purpose did they arise with such flaws? Could there not be an all-powerful god, one that reigns above even our own, guiding our world down a specific path to some unknowable end?

I will never get to pose this question; however, I heard the Athenians put this thinker to death, forcing him to drink hemlock and take his own life for some trivial offense. Fucking Athenians. So willing are they to act on envy, putting their best military and philosophical minds to death in the name of one fickle law or another. They say our ways are inferior, but what is superior about forcing a wise old man to end his own life, alone in the dark, through some trickery of words? Of course, we Spartans also condemn or kill those among us who break our laws, but our laws are old, and we carry out those sentences while looking the accused in the eye.

Ah, this old mind, wandering again through a maze of memory of war, love, and philosophy.

Everyone is eager; the army has been waiting for orders since we've heard about the Olympic Games in Elis. With the summer nearing, the games are about to begin without Sparta receiving an invitation. The Eleans, the host of the games, declared Sparta's occupation of Lepreum in violation of the Olympic truce; therefore, we are banned from the festivities. All in Sparta are outraged. Lepreum was taken before the Eleans formally conveyed the truce to Sparta, as is custom. Rumor has it the rest of Greece is traveling to the games under armed guard, fearing that Sparta will march on the games in protest. They should fear us because most in the barracks desire such a reprisal.

The seasons continue to pass as my regiment endures their daily training and exercises. In the barracks, rumors fly about the diplomatic and political adultery that is playing out throughout Greece. The Athenian, Alcibiades, had deceived the Spartan envoys that had been sent to Athens to explain our relationship with Boeotia. As a result, the assembly in Athens turned the Spartans away in insult, voting to join with the Argives, Mantineans, and Eleans in alliance. My brother, Theron, after returning from Corinth, said that they would still stand behind Sparta; however, much time has passed since his return, and more recent emissaries speak of their wavering loyalty. A statement the formal envoys later confirm. At mess, all the conversations are consumed by these city-states making their preparations to ride out renewed war.

It's been over a year now since the rest of Greece decided to spurn Sparta by excluding us from the games in Elis. Since then, there has been a lot of posturing on both sides. Tension remains high, both sides have taken actions to provoke their adversaries, but neither side has taken the bait and committed to pitched battle. The Argives invaded the region of Epidaurus, just north of the Peloponnese. For the past year, they have ravaged the countryside and tried to encourage their allies to join them and reignite this war by provoking the locals to battle. While here in Sparta, we have continued our endless drilling. As new members of the regiment, we make up the opposition force during training, taking endless beatings from seasoned Spartan warriors. The only respite has been a few occasional expeditions to Epidaurus as the Athenians, and we look to mirror one another's moves. However, the gods do not approve of battle as the sacrifices are consistently unfavorable for both sides.

With the season of war approaching, everyone is again convinced that battle is inevitable. Word spread that the Argives plan to once again make moves on Epidaurus and possibly other allies of Sparta, so King Agis marches our army to Argos to inquire about these rumors in person. The Argives meet us out in the field, in full battle order. We all feel the battle we have been waiting for is moments away when King Agis rides out to meet the Argive leader. Instead, they agree not to fight, and we are begrudgingly ordered to march back to Sparta.

Lucky for us, the Athenians arrive to join the Argives shortly after we leave. There, a charismatic leader among the Athenians, Alcibiades, spurs them back into action. All in Sparta see this as a pivotal moment. If there is not an adequate show of Spartan strength and leadership, many worry that Corinth will abandon the Peloponnesian League, causing the entire alliance to dissolve, leaving Spartan territory open to invasion and without allies to come to her aid. The war would be over, lost. The fate of Sparta now hangs in the balance, and everyone is eager for the elusive battle that will decide the course of this war.

I excuse myself and proceed with Stout to my quarters to check on the status of what will one day be my home when I move out of the barracks at thirty. Gylippus accompanies me to the location of my new home. It is located on the edge of my father's humble estate, just up the road, northwest of my brother's. At first, I think the layout of the place would be of no concern to me. Now that I have arrived and seen what the *helots* have already accomplished, I am most pleased. They have laid a beautiful stone walkway leading into the quaint dwelling that they have cleared on either side for the addition of a garden or courtyard. I am so impressed by the layout that I assume this has been the work of my mother. This is what I have worked my whole life for, to be a Spartan equal. Gylippus too seems as happy as I have ever seen him.

"I appreciate you making preparations and starting all of this in my absence, Gylippus. I have never felt this complete in my life."

"Ha! Many more than me have been behind this, Nikos, and as for complete, what sort of Spartan is complete without sons? What you need is a wife."

The *perioikoi* builder and his *helot* assistants have left for the night, and Stout and I walk among the walls that have just recently been erected. Perfectly proportionate rooms surround the dining and kitchen area. My mother has always preferred this layout, and I can see her handprints all over the manner of construction. I am most pleased and decide to walk down the road to my father's house to express my gratitude. When I arrive, I immediately start giving her praise, which she of course dismisses with a smile.

"All I did was assign your father's *helots* to the work. I also told Gylippus to tell them that the structure must be sound and sturdy. We don't want the thing to fall in on you during the first downpour. Sit down, have some wine," she says softly as Gorga rounds the corner with the shallow bowl of wine and a slab of cheese.

I pass her a devious smile, but my heart sinks as she ignores me. My mother pretends to take no notice as she begins to speak about the land that I have obtained. She informs me that while I am on campaign or assigned to a garrison, she will watch over the *oikos* and all its obligations until I find a wife. A topic she is eager to discuss. She tells stories about meaningless events while I was away, dropping names of females from certain families as if I did not notice what her intentions were.

"Please, Mother. Do not worry for me. I will find a suitable woman eventually," I say, trying to bring an end to the conversation. However, she replies almost insultingly.

"I do not worry for you, boy. My worry is for Sparta. You're of no use to her without a woman who will bear you sons. Do not get an arrogant feeling of accomplishment from your recent fortunes. It is not welcome here. You may be a peer by title, but you will be no equal in the eyes of your fellow Spartans until you produce sons."

Stout casually eyes me from across table as he leans back in his chair, shifting a piece of hard cheese in his mouth as if he is waiting for me to respond. I know my mother has been recently agitated by the fact that my brother's wife has given birth to his second daughter, and she worries about the survival of my father's line.

"Point noted, Mother. While I appreciate all you have done, you should mind your tone. I have not dishonored my father's name yet. Plenty of time to choose a wife."

Stout swings his head back toward my mother, his eyes perking up and a grin creeping across his face. I can tell he is enjoying this little back-and-forth, but just then, Bull's squire appears in the doorway.

"Ideaus!" I swallow my bread with a gulp of cut wine, noticing that his face is flushed as he leans over to catch his breath.

"War," he says softly, gasping for breath. "The Argives have taken Orchomenos and are moving on Tegea. We are going to war!"

"I'm sure you noticed that your quarters are already furnished? Perfectly adequate if you choose to—"

"Thank you, Mother," I interject softly before heading out the door in haste.

The sun has not yet risen as we all scramble to the barracks. Our officers storm in, telling us that this is no exercise. We are all to head to our homes and make the necessary preparations to march. The army will assemble any day now.

Diokles punches me in the shoulder, hardly able to contain his excitement and anticipation. Usually known for our stoicism, laughter and smiles spread throughout the barracks. Some of the officers join in the banter, while others quickly scold and attempt to quell the giddiness. Kritos is no exception.

"Save the smiles and laughter for after the battle, when you confirm that your friends still live and our enemies lie dead. Do keep your spirits up. I want you to welcome battle. Remember your footwork, cover your comrade's spear side. No gaps, we will need to keep it tight. The phalanx cannot break. It must not break! Now, go home. Pack your kit. Make love to your wives, *helots,* or goats. Remember their company, men, because those that surround you now will be your only company after we depart. Whether on the march or in the phalanx, our formation is going to be tighter than your lover's asshole."

Those without wives are to remain in the barracks, but this night, I refuse to be alone. After being dismissed, I send a message by Stout to Kallias and her *helot* attendants to prepare for my coming. I wanted to see her, feel her warmth, and lose myself in her presence.

I have been courting her for almost a year now since Gorga was married, recently giving birth to a child. Kallias has promised to fight off all other suitors, to be my Penelope no matter how long I am on campaign. I spotted her during the last *Hyacinthia*. Of noble Spartan birth, she is a girl with hair of gold and brown, but it was her legs I spotted first. Long and fit, her skin is the color of worn bronze, dark yet elegant and strong. In the months since the festival, I have sneaked out of the barracks many nights so that I could spend them with her under the stars. Her naked body wrapped in my bruised body, with hair that feels like the finest silk as I run my fingers through it. Such moments fortify the soul and do more to mend the body than the rarest ointments applied by the finest healers.

I trust Kallias will be a more than adequate wife, and with the army once again preparing to mobilize, I plan to kidnap her tonight and make it so. If this is to be the moment where Athens and Sparta meet in battle, then I want to make sure I have a wife who can properly mourn my passing and make the proper sacrifices to the gods to facilitate my passage to the afterlife. Who knows, perhaps I will also plant a son in her belly before I go.

While beautiful and more than worthy of my affection, the thought of Gorga still plagues me like a splinter in my heart that I am unable to dig out. Ah, but who am I to long for her in this way? I cannot keep her for myself. I am of Spartan blood, and she is a *helot*. She took a husband and gave him a son, as all woman of her age dutifully seek to do. At times of exhaustion, when I feel neither asleep nor awake, I sometimes find myself imagining killing the little whelp and running off with Gorga into the wilderness.

"She wishes to see you," Stout says sternly. "Among the olive trees by the creek below your father's house."

Strange. Kallias has no right or reason to request such a location. I am to come to her and take her from her home as is custom. My face must have betrayed my anger as Stout quickly clarifies.

"I speak of Gorga. It is she who wishes to meet with you."

Without pause, I burst out the barrack doors and off into the brush. All thoughts of my marriage seem to have left my mind as I sneak beyond the field toward the creek and the olive trees that line the shore. Even though it is a moonless night, I know this track well. Gorga and I used to skulk away to this spot as children, so I have spent many days and nights along this course. Even if the gods were to strike me blind at this moment, I could still make my way to our meeting place. The gentle rush of water drowns out all talk of war and the anxiety that comes with it. For just a moment, I lay waiting for her, already picturing my head in her lap and her stroking my scalp. Then, I hear the light patter of footsteps.

"Gorga?" I turn to see her face. Her eyes were swollen with tears and her hands clutched together.

"My husband, he is taking us away."

"What? Where? When? Gorga, tell me!"

"He says if I tell you, then he will kill me."

"That shit-eating piece of *helot* swine, I will flay the skin from his bones," I blurt out in anger and disgust.

"Adronikos, please. There is nothing I can do, and even if there was, duty demands that I follow my husband," she says with a solemn sternness, as if lecturing me on what I should already know to be true.

"Where are you going, Gorga? When will I see you again?" I plead as she stares deep in my eyes.

"I must go. Please do not follow. Your fate is in the hands of the gods now. Let us hope your ancestors have made friends with a few, and if they didn't, do you still have the goddess? She has always been kind to me. May she guide you," she says lightly, pressing her lips to mine. I then look to my pouch to retrieve the wooden goddess; however, by the time I pull her free, Gorga is gone.

"Athena?" I say, looking up toward her as if requesting an explanation; however, Gorga is not there.

In the darkness, I cannot see her, but I can hear her small body creeping back up the hillside toward her new home. She asked me not to follow her, so I will not. I have taken too much time already. I need to get to Kallias. She and her *helot* attendants are expecting me.

I make great haste, running through the fields, crossing roads, jumping low walls, and weaving through small trees and brush until I finally make it to Kallias's dwelling, just adjacent to her father's house. Shit, I am supposed to be wearing my scarlet cloak. As I scorn myself for not dressing appropriately, I notice something else out of the ordinary for such an occasion. I hear talking in the room where I am supposed to take her. Also, a candle is lit. That is strange. All is supposed to be silent and dark so that she can be taken by me in secret as is customary.

I burst into the room, startling the *helot* maidens who look up at me in confusion.

"Where is Kallias?" I demand.

"Master?" one of them responds in a confused and terrified voice.

Just then, I realize what has happened. Someone else has already come for her. The stupid whores, did they not know I was coming?

Perhaps out of habit, I grip the hilt of my blade, a reaction that often accompanies my anger. The two young women let out a terrified cry and begin to back themselves into a corner against the wall, dreading my wrath. A feeling of shame rolls over me as I realize my terrifying appearance.

"I am not here to harm you, women. Just tell me who it was and where he took her." I raise my hands and try to control the hostile nature of my tone.

"I am sorry, Master Andronikos. It was Pidytes. They have been gone for quite some time, but I saw them head south after exiting the doorway, possibly down the road towards the agora."

I nod to each of the women as I try to muster the boiling anger within me. I dart out the door and head down the road, looking in either direction, trying to determine their path.

My mind shifts wildly, trying to determine the best course of action. Do I find them and kill the other man? Does she need my help? Is she trying to fight him off as we speak, or did she go with him willingly? Is she receiving him now as she has received me so many times in the past? Ah, it is no use. She went with a man that was not I. If she was unable to resist him, then I am already too late. I cannot lose myself and quarrel with another peer over a woman if she did not choose me. To interrupt them during this sacred ceremony of marriage and begin a quarrel with another peer, even Pidytes, would be to succumb to *katalepsis*. With the potential of battle so near, to display such weakness of heart and mind would demoralize any man forced to stand beside in battle. I cannot afford to be reckless.

I stare out into the black night, breathing heavily as my heart beats out of my chest. Part of me wishes to cry as I did as a young boy, while the other part of me just wants to kill something. I turn my head behind me and walk back toward the dim candlelight of Kallias's house. I move back into the doorway, and the young women gently bow their heads and give me a soft, almost-sympathetic smile, even though there is a look of dread on both of their faces. They know I did not find what I was looking for, and now I have unexpectedly returned.

"Either of you married?" I ask, even though I already know the answer to that question.

I know neither have taken a husband, but I ask anyway as a small courtesy, considering what I plan to do. While I do not know the names of these women, I am familiar to them, for they have been tending to Kallias for as long as I have known her.

"You can have me, Master Adronikos, if it pleases you," one girl says as she bows her head again.

"You are dismissed, lady," I say softly to the other young woman.

Both women comply, perhaps hoping not to provoke some sort of violent outburst, or maybe this girl does feel some slight sympathy for my predicament. In any case, the *helot* girl does not resist as I remove her clothes, run my hands along the curves of her bare body, and proceed to enter her.

Although I feel as if my heart was ripped from my chest when I found Kallias already stolen away from this chamber, there is a strange comfort being here with this girl that I had never thought to give notice before this night. I treat her gently, for her willing submission to me after such a night speaks to the sacrifice this brave girl is making for me. Kallias always told me that she suspected that one of her servants was fond of me. While it does not make this right, all I can do is hope that this is not painful for the girl as I feel her soft breath on my shoulder and her erect nipples against my chest.

As she grips my back and moves her hips in unison with my own, I know I could never take my anger out on this servant girl. I can't help but feel like she is a small gift from the gods, and as such, I find myself not wanting her to ever recall this night with terror. Perhaps it is too late.

I lean down and kiss her softly, trying to soften my mood and my posture. She recoils momentarily, apparently surprised by this display of affection. Then, she relents, pressing her lips against my own, allowing her soft tongue to gently meet mine. Even if she feels compelled by fear to meet my demands, she is doing an impressive job pretending otherwise. Likely, I am just being foolish, and it is my wishful thinking to hope that this girl isn't completely terrified. Then, soft moans bellow from within her throat, easing my troubled mind.

Entangled in this sudden passion, I do not notice a figure enter the door, but apparently, my partner has. She starts squirming under me as if to put up some sort of sudden resistance, just as I begin to climax. Following the servant girl's eyes, I look to find a battered Kallias in the doorway. Her hair was cut short in the ceremonial fashion. The dust on her body might speak to some sort of struggle to defy her suitor, but the seed dripping from between her legs reveals what I had feared. Kallias's eyes lock with my own as I finish inside the servant girl, staring back at her shamelessly as I thrust into the girl a few more times.

As I rise from the bed, put my jerkin back on, and walk past Kallias, she just stares at me. No tears, no words, no expression, just her strong face.

"Lady," I say to her with a nod as I excuse myself.

"Evening, comrade," I hear as I exit.

I turn to see the smug smile of Pidytes leaning against the wall outside the dwelling dressed in his scarlet cloak. I pause dumbstruck, only to hear the voice of Kallias behind me.

"Collect my things. The mules will arrive shortly. We go to the house of Pidytes tonight." I hear Kallias command the *helot* servant girls.

No other words or actions could have pierced my heart more in that moment. I am sure I could have handled Pidytes's arrogance and Kallias's cold stare when she found me in her chamber, but to hear her declare herself to him caused a pain unlike anything I have ever felt.

In truth, I want to speak to her. I want to break his fucking jaw and then ask her why she wasn't able to resist him. However, she is not obligated to me. We had made love often and spoken to each other with great affection, but until I had stolen her, she had no obligations to me. I was late, and she had chosen another. I turn around toward the house, Pidytes chuckling at my expense. I hardly hear him, for at that moment, I see the *helot* girl carrying belongings to the roadside, and she passes me the most beautiful and genuine smile. For a second, the brief personal exchange lifts the burden from my heart and causes me to unexpectedly chuckle to myself as I recall deliberately finishing inside her as Kallias watched.

Obviously perplexed by my lightheartedness in such a moment, I can see Pidytes in the corner of my eye tilting his head as if to try to ponder whether or not I have gone mad.

"You and *helot* bitches," he says finally.

"Indeed. *Helot* bitches indeed!" I chime back before breaking into a long and satisfying laughter as I turn back toward the barracks.

Of course, the mere smile from a *helot* did not elevate the pain caused by the loss of Kallias, but my peace at that moment is genuine, and it is due to the sudden realization that I am incapable of envying that man. There, in what Pidytes thinks is his first and finest triumph over me, he watches as I strut away scratching my crotch in laughter.

Gods of War

While I sit here and carve my name in the bench of this ole ship, I recall those moments where the gods have provided a subtle hint of their presence. At the time, I did not know what caused my laughter that night. Perhaps it was the relief that I had not hurt the helot girl and that she actually might remember our moment with fondness instead of fear. Maybe it was the memory of my defiance in the face of Kallias's blank stare and the confusion of Pidytes as I departed in apparent jovial satisfaction. Now, I know it was not one or the other, for I never wished any harm or ill will upon those two. Nor did I want my defiance and satisfaction from the moment to trouble them, for I always knew the true convictions of their heart and my own. The gods willed it.

I believe my laughter was due to that realization that the gods were present, and that I now understood that my feelings were insignificant. I could have cursed them for sending Gorga away and having me lose my potential bride to another. However, there is a nervousness and unsettling comfort associated actually feeling the tangible presence of fate. I felt their eyes on me there, on the eve before marching off to battle.

I have always known that the gods operate in ways only familiar to their own kind, and I guess I found humor in their timing. That they would choose to reveal themselves to me while I coupled with a random helot servant girl speaks to their canny. To this day, I think one of their greatest gifts to me in life might have been the spontaneous affection she gave me on that night. It allowed me to forget the wrong I thought had been done to me, diminishing the pain in my heart just enough to allow me to focus on the trials ahead. I know now that I was only a pawn, but without the gods' subtle and sporadic grace, I would not have been able to maintain my soundness of mind.

Perhaps they do know what they are doing. Like men attending a contest, the gods choose their horses among the mortals and weave our destinies into the greater game being played among themselves. I had felt beasts within stirring emotions from my past, present, and some yet to come. I was angry, afraid, uncertain, and lost. Possessed by the unnerving feelings that lead men to untimely and dishonorable deaths. The departing humor from Kallias's house came instinctively as if it had not even been my own. A simple reaction sent by the gods to expel those beasts and remind me that I may die at any time, but that moment will be of their choosing. That my petty inconveniences were well below the games the gods played with fate and destiny.

The helot girl had all the right to hate me, to want me dead. Yet her smile as I departed—mischievous, sly, erotic, sensual, divine. To not have seen it would be to disregard it as trivial or insignificant. However, I believe her smirk might have saved my life. In doing so, the gods provided her with the power to realign my fate so that I might be another useful tool for them to alter the course of history.

Although right on Sparta's doorstep, the two-day march to Mantinea seemed like an eternity. The feeling of anticipation is unlike anything I have felt before. I can feel my heart thumping against my breastplate. Every beat feels like it is pumping fire through my veins. Within my ranks, I can barely see the outside world as we march, only the blue of the sky above and the sea of scarlet surrounding me on all sides.

Of course, I have marched with the army before. During my deployments to Epidaurus, we marched out of Sparta in the same fashion. However, this is different. For years, the armies of Sparta and the Athenian allies have postured and jostled for position, sacking one town or laying siege to a city. For whatever reason, men began to never expect or anticipate pitched battle. Instead, they began to assume another withdrawal, despite recent violent encounters in Thrace or at Pylos only years earlier. Everything about this march is different.

After refusing battle at Argos, foul words spread throughout Sparta about King Agis. Some accused him of being a coward, fearing defeat to such an extent that he would avoid battle if given any alternative course of action. Others accused him of having more treasonous motives. After being chastised by the *ephors* and *Gerousia*, they stripped him of his command in an effort to diminish the influence of his rank.

However, with Argos moving on Tegea, King Agis is determined to restore his name, vowing battle and victory. Now, with almost all of Sparta's military might at his disposal, he must gain victory or forever be known as the king that lost Sparta.

The next day is spent cutting down olive trees and burning down farmsteads in Mantinean territory. The Mantineans had offered the Argives allegiance upon their arrival, so King Agis hopes to provoke them into action by ravaging the Mantinean countryside despite the fact that the spring harvest has already been collected. Now, the task becomes merely the destruction of property, and it is tedious business. Each man puts his armor off to the side and proceeds to dismantle walls, break fences, and destroy everything from grain stores to wagons. Anything that burns is set alight, and any tree of value is chopped down. Any animal capable of carrying a man or pulling a cart has already been taken by the Argives; however, all other livestock we come across are butchered.

By the end of the day, we all stumble into camp as *helot* attendants pass around black soup. No one complains; they just gulp down the bloody brew furiously as it spills over their cheeks and runs down the length of their necks. The men are bloodthirsty. Only pockets of us are able to sleep. Instead, warriors gather around different fires with their comrades, and officers move among the groups to share a laugh at one or recall their recollection of one story and another. I smile to myself as I realize I will be one of the lucky ones, as the constant chatter and the crackle of fires cause my eyelids to grow heavy. I may get to sleep.

"Up! All up! Move! Move! Move!" I hear officers screaming as I pull my back off the dirt.

Stout runs up with my armor, shields, and spears.

"Morning, sunshine," he says with an eager grin.

"Today is the day, lads. Remember, the Argives broke the truce and are here to take Tegea, and the Athenians are committed to their betrayal of peace. As we know, the misplaced arrogance of our longtime foes has also attracted the Mantineans. Without the presence of our Corinthian allies, it is up to Sparta to stop this incursion in its tracks.

"Men, look to your *enōmotarches*. *Enōmotarches*, look to your *pentēkontēr*. Repeat orders and keep formations tight. We march to greet our enemies today, so let us be gracious hosts and honor our guest into our domain!"

Stout finishes strapping my armor, and we fall into our place within the regiment, and then a roar from beyond erupts beyond a hill, a joyous sound that lifts my spirit, as if a goddess is reaching out her hand and offering me a dance.

"The Tegeans!" a voice calls out.

Peasants from the surrounding countryside and villagers from Tegea have gathered along the road to see us break camp and depart. Children run along the column as it moves up the road, some marching alongside the warriors, imagining they are embarking with us on some new adventure. As much of the column begins to march, they leave a cloud of thin dust in their wake. While it looks like nothing from here, I know each man can barely make out what is in front of him. Fading into the unknown beyond, they follow nothing but the scarlet cloak in front of him. I see one of the Spartan peers reach out and rub a child's head in a playful manner before pushing him aside so he does not get caught up in the cloud and trampled. The spectacle is inspiring, a river of scarlet, bronze, and leather, leaving our baggage behind as we move up the hillside to finally face our enemies after a tedious peace.

Stout and I fall into order and disappear into the dust. The thundering sound of footsteps mixes with the clamor of armor and shields. *Could this finally be it? Are we actually marching into battle?* My heart wants to think so. While I have learned to steady my breath to control the pace of its beat, it is full of fire, thumping hard against my armored chest. Ahead of me, light is shining brighter as the dust begins to clear. We must be stopping. The men in front of me start filing in each direction, falling into place as we have practiced many times before. Being an officer, I am not able to stand by Gylippus's side. Instead, Diokles covers my spear arm, Edge covers his, and I cover the exposed side of Kritos, one of the *enōmotarches* on the far left of our line. We are the fourth row in a phalanx that consists of around 8.

The whole Spartan presence is 7 *lochoi*, each divided into 4 *pentekostyes* of 128, and 16 *enōmotiai* of 32 men, a total of 3,584 Spartan warriors in an army of about 9,000. We hold the center of the army, our more experienced troops in the right three contingents, then the Spartan Hippias in between the other three contingents. The Spartans take their place of honor on the right flank of the line, while the *skiritai* and the auxiliary units who fought for Brasidas hold the left. My regiment is in the last Spartan contingent on the left of the main body of the Spartan army. To our left are the Tegeans occupying the center, then Brasidas's *helots* and Thracians with the *skiritai* holding the left flank of the battle line.

When the army is assembled, we march over the hill to find the Argives and their allies assembled on a small hill across the plain.

Ravaging the Mantinean countryside, their army is lined up for battle in a strong position. As we move forward, the Argives stand idle. Despite all the orders being shouted across the line, I hear no flutes from our lines or drums from theirs. Nor do I do see any slingers or javelin skirmishers being mobilized on either side.

"Shit," I say out loud to myself. I see Kritos's helmet turn toward me, likely giving me a sharp look that I choose to ignore.

If each commander is unwilling to make the first move, we will face one another, commanders will talk, and the armies will once again withdraw from the field. If we do fight, we will have to fight uphill. All I can do now is follow the man in front of me and look up at the Argive army standing motionless in front of us. As expected, we are given the order to halt. Any further and we would march right into their line. So close are the two lines now that a trained man could easily reach the opposite man with a well-thrown javelin. *What in Hades is this?* I roll my eyes beneath my helmet when I hear the new order making its way down the line. We are to withdraw.

"Mmmrrrgh," I hear Kritos growl in frustration.

I know he wants to scream out, "Dammit, Agis!" but in his position of leadership, he must check himself and carry out the order. The Argives look nervous while we stand voracious. Everyone wants a fight, so the men are reluctant to move. Officers are forced to repeat the order before the men slowly begin their orderly withdrawal from the field.

As we depart, the hillside erupts. The Argives and their allies begin shouting and beating their shields. With impending death no longer upon them, they release their fear and summon the courage to taunt us as we remove ourselves from the battlefield.

No one says a word. We just march, expressing our frustration in our steps. Up and down the line, men keep their heads high and move as we were trained to move. Filing into marching formation, everyone is eyeing one another, spreading the unspoken discontent. The commanders must have picked up on it too because one of the cavalry officers begins to ride up and down the line to reassure men and make them privy to our next move.

"Men! We move to flood the countryside and divert the river into Mantinea. We must force them off the high ground."

"Go back to your post, horseman, or I will have you flogged. We follow orders and need not your explanation!" the stern response coming from the strong voice of one of our *enōmotarches*.

It is likely that the man on horseback outranks our officer, but the gesture from our commanders is so out of place that the *enōmotarch* must have felt compelled to remind him that we were still Spartans.

Almost immediately, men pick up on the insult conveyed by our superior and begin taking out their frustration by continuing to verbally abuse the horseman. Unable to yell his message over the mounting jeers, the horseman relents. He then wields his steed around, galloping away to the sound of men laughing and celebrating the small victory of his retreat.

Not being able to see anything but scarlet and bronze ahead of me, my thoughts begin to ponder the actions of our king. Despite our frustration, a withdrawal was the proper course of action. One's own greed for victory or glory should never outweigh the realities in front of us. Other than small garrisons throughout Greece, we are the entire Spartan army. To force battle despite the Argive advantage would risk the loss of this army and, thus, the survival of Sparta. With the Mantinean countryside ravaged, diverting the Saradanpotamos River would do further damage to the countryside. The Mantineans will surely press for battle in an attempt to salvage their property. Furthermore, the Athenians have not committed their entire army. Our reinforcements from Corinth and Boeotia are only days away, so the Athenians will want to force the Argives into an engagement while the Spartans are alone and the risk to Athens is minimal.

Diverting the river does not take long. The scar in the earth remind us that this has been done many times before in the occasional skirmishes between the Tegeans and Mantineans. Following each, earth barriers had been constructed to fortify the river's edge and allow it to flow along its natural course. Our men hardly do any of the work. By the time the entire column has reached the river's edge, many of the Tegeans following the army are already aware of our intention. Their familiarity with the earthwork and the behavior of the river allows them to make quick work of rerouting the river. Almost as soon as we arrive, we are ordered back to the camp on the edge of the plain. As we depart, we can see the river beginning to flood the smaller rivers, sinkholes, and dried creek beds.

"Let's see those sons of whores loiter on the hill now!" Kritos roars.

I know Kritos is projecting and trying to raise our morale. What he is likely thinking is that Agis better hope that this tactic works; otherwise, he might miss his opportunity to redeem himself. Now, the army is taking a detour back through the Pelagos Wood and to the plain to perform the miscellaneous task of setting up and fortifying camp.

Although I can't see anything from my place in the column, being in the woods just appears more pleasant. I can't really put my finger on why, because I am still eating the dust cloud being kicked up from the army. Maybe the earth just tastes a little sweeter here. For a second, I can even make out the faint song of a bird and the smell of the pines, but it's more than likely my imagination. No one would be able to hear such things or smell anything but the stink and sweat of thousands of men on the march.

"File out! Form the line! Form the line!" I hear the order being passed down the line.

I look over to Kritos as he passes the order, a simple tilt of my head communicating my confusion. He just gives me a sharp nod back to remind me that my confusion is not relevant, nor is it needed.

As we file into my place in the fourth row of our phalanx, the field comes into view, revealing our Argive hosts already in battle order in the plain. It worked. The Argives abandoned the hill. The fire in my heart ignites, and almost immediately, the flutes begin to play the battle hymn. No intention of talk or retreat now. The flutes are playing; we mean to charge.

The army seamlessly files into battle order out of the woods as if we had been preparing for their presence all along. However, because the Tegean contingent of the army was leading the column, as we file out of the woods, they find themselves on our right flank with the

Spartans occupying the center. My phalanx is still the last one on the left of the Spartan body, and Brasidas's *helots* and the Thracians are on our left, while the *skiritai* are still on the left flank.

We advance out of the wood, and the pace of the flutes quickens, guiding us into a slow trot. I adjust my grip on my shield and spear. My palms are sweating. No time for the anticipation of battle. It is upon us, and the sudden rush is intoxicating. The feeling must be spreading through the entire army because the flutes quicken their pace again before the sound of the charge fades as we break into a controlled run. No turning back now. Even if the order is given to halt our advance, no man would hear it, and even if they did, they are so drunk with bloodlust that they'd likely ignore it.

I look down the line, shields still overlapping. In the corner of my eye, I see Kritos turn to look down our line. The suddenness of the gesture and the lack of orders must mean that we must seem to be maintaining our order despite the growing speed of our advance. How terrifying we must look.

Over the crests of the men in front of me, I can see the Argives now advancing toward us. No time to think. I can hear men yelling now and see slingers between the lines whipping projectiles at us, each other, as well as toward our foes. I can hear orders being issued, but I don't understand a word. Everything is muffled. It seems as if all I can hear is my own breath and the beating of my heart. The lines are spreading out ahead of me. I see it as much as I feel it. Our slingers are retreating into the cover of the line. We rush one way, and they are sprinting in between us in the other direction. Flawless, I think to myself as the formation begins to close again. Then it happens.

The force of both lines colliding jolts our entire formation, but apparently, the Argives receive more of the blow. Our men are quick to recover, and I can see them pushing one another forward as the front line pushes against the foe with their shields while the second line thrusts their spears into the faces of the enemy.

A cloud of dust has caught up to us now. It follows our charge and is now rising from the earth beneath us and where the lines are engaged. I feel the push of the men behind me and put my shoulder into my own shield to push into the man in front of me. With my head down, my own feet are hidden from view. We have practiced and drilled this so many times before that my moments are instinctive, even though this experience is very different. While sight and sound are obscured, the sense of smell is acute. Combined with the dust, the smell of blood, piss, and shit is so profound one feels like they can taste it.

Death, but not my own. My confidence is overwhelming. The repetition of training and force of discipline makes this moment mine. Instead of it being repulsive, my body is reacting much differently. My extremities are numb, and the smell is making me crave the taste even more. I feel the line give just a little. One of ours has fallen. Sure enough, a *helot* servant burrows forward past me and, through our line, retrieves the Spartan and pulls him back through. As I push, *helots* move forward and back again, sometimes taking additional spears to the front or pulling a man back. Most appear wounded, not dead, but through the dust and muffled noises, I cannot be sure. Then I feel the shift and look to Kritos. Sure enough, rotation of the ranks.

The whole line heaves into the man in front of him, pushing the Argives back. This unlocks the armies, while the front line of the Spartans give one thrust of their shield before turning sideways between the shields, allowing the army to move past and the second line taking over in front. The men coming from the front are covered in blood and shouting encouragements to us as they move toward the back.

One of the men in my column goes down, so after the rotation, I am now the second man. The Argive line smashes into us again, and the Spartan's spear in front of me snaps immediately. I feel the phalanx pushing into my back as I cover the man in front of me. All I can see are a mass of shields and faces as I thrust my spear forward over my comrade's shoulder as he takes cover beneath his shield and pushes forward against the enemy. His comrade on his right also recognizes his predicament and does his best to position his shield to better cover his friend's exposed side.

I can see the Spartan in front of me drawing his *xiphos* as he looks back at me. We lock eyes. No words are needed. I push into his back hard to get the enemy off him, and then simultaneously, I thrust my spear point forward as he opens his shield and performs a blind thrust with his *xiphos*. The Argive moves his shield up to counter my spear only to have my comrade's short sword tear into his groin.

"Nikos! Nikos!" I hear through the muffles.

I barely turn my head, and there is Stout with an extra spear. I turn my head back toward the fight and continue to cover the front ranker with thrusts of my spear, feeling the point smash into the mouth of a helmet, shatter my enemy's teeth, and punch through the back of the neck before I twist and withdraw it again.

"Give it to him! Give it to him!" I yell before thrusting my shield forward again.

Incredibly, the Spartan ahead of me must have heard the exchange. I see him begin to sheath his *xiphos*. His left shoulder still buried in his shield, pushing against the enemy. Stout is already on him by the time he is able to turn and reach his right arm back to complete the exchange before Stout returns to my side.

"Nikos! Listen! The left flank is broken! The left flank is broken!" Just as he repeats the words, I look at him briefly in disbelief.

"Your regiment must hold! A gap is forming, but the commanders cannot send anyone to your aid. They are ordering the Spartan right forward, but if we break, their flank will be exposed! We have to hold!"

Perhaps Agis did not know what to do, but our officers did. Then, Diokles pushes Stout aside and taps my spear arm with his shield. We are to rotate to our left.

"Nikos! On me!" I hear Kritos yelling now. "Hold your ground! Do not move forward, or they will envelope us. Hold here!"

As we reposition and turn toward our left, we move to the front line. The Spartan who was in front of me gives me an affectionate nod and tap on the shoulder as he rotates out. I can see the phalanx on our left also falling apart, and Argive auxiliaries are quickly filling the gap. The whole damn army is being rolled up. A few brave men among Brasidas's regiment are still holding their ground. Spears long broken, they are out in the open, hacking at men with their short swords as we move to advance toward them. A few of their remaining officers point their swords toward us, shouting encouragements and telling their men to fight like lions, that the Spartans are coming to their aid.

To our right, the Argives and Athenians have broken their phalanx to charge forward toward our faltering line, attempting to encourage the flight of our flank and finish us off.

"Move to them now!" Kritos barks.

Like the Argives, we break our phalanx to fill the gap ourselves in a desperate attempt to prevent being enveloped and overrun. Our line charges forward through the dust, catching the disorganized foe off guard as we smash through their scattered ranks. Without the momentum, we risk our own formation breaking down. However, if we move too far, we create another gap that could leave us surrounded and cut off from the rest of the Spartan contingent. I knock a foe to the ground and smash his face in with my shield before frantically scanning the dust cloud to determine the most prudent course of action.

Out of the corner of my eye, a spear point flashes through the dust and quickly withdraws. He misses. All I can see is the bowl of a shield and the top of a helm peering over it. The man thrusts his spear toward me again, but I parry, jolting my own spear forward. The point pierces the exposed side of my enemy, but as he recoils, the spear point gets lodged in his armor, and I hear the shaft of my spear snap. I can barely see him writhing on the ground. He is not yet dead. He sees me coming for him, kicking at the ground in an attempt to get away. I smash the butt end of my spear into his face as I pass over him and unsheathe my *xiphos*, quickly looking around for the next foe that is sure to come upon me.

Just then, I feel another Spartan appear next to me and cover my spear side with his shield. I give him a nod in relief, but at that very moment, a warrior launches himself into the shield. Cleverly, my Spartan companion lets his shield give as he moves aside to the left, allowing the foe to roll off his shield and fumble to the ground between us. I turn to dispatch him, but he already has a short sword in his back. Stout. He is without armor but has picked up a shield and *xiphos* and has fallen in beside me on my left.

There are three of us shoulder to shoulder, nothing but a small island of order in a field of chaos. I choke on dust as I try to catch my breath as I reach for a discarded spear on the ground. My spear arm feels like worn leather, clumsy and flimsy from fatigue. Any attempt for respite is met with another charging foe. My chest swells and caves as my heart struggles to pump blood through my constricted veins. The fire within preserves me, providing the needed strength at the pivotal moments. In one fluid motion, I raise my shield, plant my feet, step into the foe, push him off, and drive my spear just below the helmet of my foe. I feel the shaft shatter as the point snaps through the spine. Then my body goes flaccid again, only as another foe appears.

We see no order, no officers, and no battle line. We are just lost in the dust, fighting as individuals like the heroes of Homer. Maybe it's the chaos around me, or perhaps it's the fatigue, but everything seems like a dream. I watch men come, and I see them cut down, falling beneath the cloud of dust as if Hades himself is pulling them directly into the underworld. I no longer feel like a man but rather a spirit of death, an agent of Hades. My armor tightens and loosens steadily with each deep inhale and exhale of my chest. The strong beat of my heart beneath the leather feels like there is a beast within me fighting to escape.

As the three of us move through the fray with shields overlapping, surviving allies rally to us. This is hardly a formation, but we still appear to move in unison. Engaged in a death-dealing dance, floating across the field of dust, oblivious to the rest of the world around us. There must be ten of us now, and then finally, we reach a small break in the dust cloud and find ourselves alone. Through the haze of grit, we can make out the blue-and-black cloaks of our enemies as they turn their backs and drop their shields. They look to be retreating.

"Hold here!" I yell to my small band of allies.

"Nikos!"

Something comes over me, and I break from the small formation. I have to find out what is happening. All of a sudden, the ground rumbles under my feet. I raise my shield and swivel my head frantically to locate the source of the quaking earth. A large shape is moving toward me in haste, a horseman. Almost as soon as I recognize what he is and where he is charging from, a javelin is let fly. I am fortunate to turn from the dart just as it glances off the base of my helmet, slicing past my neck instead of piercing my throat.

A strong throw, I think to myself, the rumbling ground growing softer and then stronger again. Oblivious to his location, I can only feel him rapidly growing closer. I quickly roll to my left before being trampled by the beast and blindly thrust my spear up toward the rider, causing him to lose balance and pull back on his reins violently. Just as I hoped, the horse rears back and throws him.

I scramble to my feet, furiously moving through the dust to try to find the fallen man. He, now helmetless, also manages to find the feet beneath him. We lock eyes. He's a handsome man, obviously brave. He looks back at me confident, determined, and unafraid.

This man could be dangerous, I think to myself as I bend my knees, bring my shield to port, and improve my grip on the spear. He unsheathes his short sword, awaiting my arrival. Then, I feel them again, hooves beating earth from behind me. As I turn, I only see a glimpse of the beast's chest before it barrels into me at a gallop. My head spins and my ears ring fiercely. I peer up through the dust and see the man mounting the horse. I struggle to bring myself back to my feet. His horse is steady now, not lining up for an attack. Though I can only make out his silhouette, the horseman appears to nod at me before spurring the steed around and charging back into the cloud of dirt in the direction that he appeared.

I just stand there gasping for breath, wondering why the enemy that had just overrun our flank had now begun to retreat. I circle back around, hoping to see my friends. Sure enough, they are where I left them, their numbers greater now as the dust slowly recedes in our immediate vicinity.

"Look there!" one of our men shouts, revealing the source of our salvation. The most splendid sight I have ever seen, a wall of scarlet marching out of the dirt moves across the field in front of us. Shields overlapping shields, the main of the Spartan force has swung about, crossing the field to flank the enemy formations that had already overcome our left. They too must have overrun the enemy's left flank, but instead of pursuing the vanquished, they doubled back to relieve us.

Like the wave Gylippus had once described, they are rolling over the enemy and forcing a break. All we can do is watch as the phalanx glides steadily before us, devouring any stragglers or those foolish enough to rally and face them. I see one Spartan on the front line halt briefly and drive the butt of his spear toward the ground, likely dispatching a wounded enemy hidden beneath the dirt. Just then, I hear a loud and familiar voice that breaks my trance.

"Reform! Reform on me!" I hear Edge shout.

I see him raising his spear above his head and shouting, and now the rest of our scattered phalanx is beginning to fall in beside him.

"On me! On me! Forward now! March!"

Scattered Spartans continue to rally to our standard while we move through the field to meet the larger formation. Occasionally, those beside me stumble, rising again before driving the butt of their spear into other figures still hidden beneath our feet. Then I feel a hand grab my leg. I glance down quickly to make sure the man is no Spartan and then slam the butt of my spear into his face, putting the poor fool out of his misery.

This is what is left of the battle now. The enemy is en route, but until the dust completely settles and we can confirm the enemy's departure from the field, all we can do is gather prisoners, put an end to the dying, and try to avoid taking a dagger in the groin.

Finally, we find ourselves at the edge of the field and are able to look upon our enemy. We shift our formation to face our opposition. Bloodied and battered, they can do nothing but stare at us from the embankment. Both armies gaze at one another in silence for a moment before the flutes and drums sound again, and the order comes down the line to withdraw. Turning our back to our foes, we depart, singing a solemn hymn of victory.

The occurrence at the end of the battle was peculiar given the inexplicable and merciless violence Greek citizens have unleashed on one another during this war. With each siege and capture of a city, rape and death are all that follow. Here, however, among warriors, I think all acknowledge the sanctity of what's just transpired. With the enemy broken and exhausted, we could easily have overtaken them and slaughtered every last one on that hill. Instead, we just stood there in formation. We do not batter our shields, scream insults, or loot the corpses of their fallen brethren. We only acknowledge their surrender of the battlefield before making our way back to our camp.

Now men's knees grow weak. As we reach camp, many begin to stumble; others puke, hungover from the overindulgence of death. Gylippus had warned me of this, claiming that a lust for blood was one of only two emotions capable of overcoming us in battle. The alternative being *phobos*, fear. Men often die when experiencing the recklessness that develops from bloodlust. Only through strength of discipline and habit of training have Spartans learned to work with this emotion instead of trying to wield it.

"Nikos!" I hear Edge shout, shattering my thoughts just as they had begun to ponder the gravity of what had just occurred.

He is alongside the formation now and waving me toward him.

"Sir," I respond.

"You wounded?" he says, acknowledging the gash at the base of my neck, a slash across my right bicep, and the deep cut above my left knee.

"No, sir," I respond.

Although what Edge can't see are the ribs beneath my cuirass. They are surely broken thanks to that Athenian warhorse.

"Good. Our Tegean and *skiritai* allies believe that they deserve spoils from the battlefield, and perhaps they do, but the Spartans will take no part in it. Stay here. Men of each regiment are being tasked to guard the bodies of those cut down by our spears."

I know my role and take my post without protest. Still covered in blood, with the stink of sweat and shit everywhere, I would have liked to be back at camp swigging wine or collapsing into the dirt. However, Gylippus had taught me both the sacred and political reasons for preserving the dignity of enemy dead. He would say, "We do not rob those who had the honor and courage to stand before our line. We are not barbarians. We have no need for their armors, shields, or baubles, and we certainly don't need personal trophies to prove our valor. We want all of Greece to know as they collect their dead, still adorned in battle regalia and lying there in glorious splendor, that their kin died well at the hands of great men."

"Spartan," I hear faintly, as if a man's scream decided to leave his lips as a whisper.

While standing still, eyes still beneath the cover of my helmet, I scan the bodies to locate the source of the cry. Just as the man begins to echo his call to me, I see him. He sits leaning on the body of one of his fallen comrades with his crested Corinthian helmet still upon his head. We Spartans all wear helmets of this style, a Corinthian with a crest running down the length. Our officers display a horizontal crest that runs across the helmet to distinguish him from others.

In the Athenian ranks, only the officers wear the crested Corinthian. His is horsehair dyed in a brilliant dark blue, with white specks and columns that mimic whitecaps in the sea. What affinity the Athenians have for the sea.

I quickly make my way over to him and address him with the respect that an officer deserves.

"Sir?" I say as I go down to one knee beside him.

He holds his blood and dust-crusted hand out to me reluctantly, not because he fears my response, but because his armor and other hand are the only thing keeping his innards from spilling from his open stomach.

"Finish me, son." His voice sounds like a soul tired of the lingering life that his strong body is binding him to.

Quickly seeking to end his prolonged suffering, I draw the *xiphos* from its scabbard and place it on his neck. His bloody cough turns into a soft laugh before he calmly scolds me for my clumsy and unintentional disrespect.

"No, no, my boy…if this greedy old man can be so bold as to make one last request, I'd prefer to die like a soldier."

I nod to him, my helmet hopefully hiding the shame I feel. I quickly right myself and harden my hidden expression as I stare into his eyes, barely visible through the black holes of his magnificent helmet, only made more spectacular by the blood that covers it and the man whose head it rests upon. I grip his wrist firmly and his strong hand responds in kind.

I rise to my feet, lay my shield down at my side so that I can grip my spear with both hands.

"I'll greet you in Hades, son," he says, taking one last deep breath as he lies his head back on the body of his kinsman.

"It would be my honor, sir."

I drive my spear into his chest with as much force as I can muster so that I am sure to pierce his well-made armor. The force of the blow snaps the shaft of my spear in half, making a loud crack that draws the gaze of everyone nearby.

"A fitting end, sir," I say softly to the dead officer, feeling the eyes of those around me as they all try to catch a glimpse of the man that passed to the next world with such proclamation.

Beneath my helmet, a tear of relief rolls down my face. No suffering, my strike was true. I feel no heartbeat on his neck and no breath from his lips. Nearby, I find the officer's shield and an unbroken spear nearby. Gently I slide the shield under the officer's body and position the spear beneath his forearm so that his comrades can carry him with honor from the field. With scavengers, both man and beast, moving among the dead, I stand beside the officer's body. Athenian horsemen in the distance are moving toward the center of the field, and I notice a handful of our commanders ride out to meet them. As is custom, the Argives and Athenians are conceding and asking our commanders for permission to remove their dead.

After the short exchange, an animal and rider I recognize peels off from the main group, trotting in my direction.

"Spartan," he says in a somber tone as his confident animal high-steps to an eventual stop.

"Sir," I respond plainly.

"*Pheeeeeeeew*. Here!" He whistles loudly to other Athenians beginning to collect the dead.

With his comrades making their way across the field, the horseman peers down at the man lying on his shield beside me.

"I see he is already prepared to leave the field with honor," he says, his eyes never leaving the figure at my feet. I say nothing.

The horseman slides from his horse, takes off his helmet, and places his hand on the chest of the man, just below the spear point still lodged in his breast.

"So it is, Laches," he says, gently nodding his head in some sort of acknowledgment.

"So where were you today, Spartan, which regiment?"

"Wolves of Nike, sir. Right in the middle," I respond stoically.

"You Spartans are all wolves," he states sternly as he looks at the Spartan army beyond me. "And this place, Laconia, your lair," he continues as his heavy gaze surveys the bloodied field. "Perhaps the wise men have always spoken truth. Cornered beasts are always dangerous."

I dip my chin slightly in acknowledgment.

Laches. I stand motionless as I repeat the name uttered by the Athenian in my head. The notorious Laches was second-in-command of the Athenian army and one of the primary authors of the short-lived Peace of Nicias. He was once formally prosecuted by his own citizenry as their renowned "democracy" sought to place blame on one Athenian blunder or another. We Spartans, however, always recognized him as a good man and a competent commander.

When his companions arrive, the horseman moves to my side to allow them to lift the man and shield from the field. Unexpectedly, he places a hand on my shoulder, right next to the bleeding wound on my neck. He peers into the dark eye slits of my crested Corinthian, giving me a sharp nod before grabbing the reins of his steed to lead it behind those who bear his fallen leader.

While the Athenians depart, I see the dead from either side being carried off so that kin and comrades can identify them. It is as if I just begin to notice the scent of stale piss, shit, and death when I see Diokles on the edge of the field where we are gathering our fallen. He is holding his helmet at his waist, and his dirty, blood-covered face is serious and strong as he helps direct men arranging the corpses. When he finally detects my encroaching presence, he comes forth to greet me with a quick smile and hug.

"Ha ha, you made it!"

"As did you," I reply thankfully as we walk along the line of dead, each man lying on a shield with a spear or *xiphos* in hand. "We are fortunate, so few."

"Our friend Kritos was not so fortunate." Diokles's voice turns again toward a more somber tone.

"A good death?"

"From the looks of it," he replies as we come to the place where Kritos lies.

"That deep sword wound on his upper thigh likely immobilized him, and then the bastards finished him with two spear thrusts to the chest," I say out loud as I kneel down to examine him and pay my respects.

As I get back to my feet, I look right and left down the line of the dead. Instead of grief, a moment of pride sweeps over me. The pride stems not from my own survival but rather the sight of my betters lying here on the field. They look stronger and more magnificent now than they ever did in life.

"A most glorious sight, is it not?" I hear Edge's voice from behind as if he was reciting my thoughts. He walks over and puts his arm around Diokles as he looks down at Kritos. "He really must have given them hell, eh?"

"Indeed, sir," Diokles responds. "We found several bodies of Argive and Athenian men beside his own."

"I would say I envy him had I already borne a son. To die victorious in such a battle..."

"His ancestors will certainly be greeting him on the other side, sir," Diokles says reverently.

"Ha ha, yes, and the legs of every whore in the underworld are going to be spreading for him tonight," Edge yelps out, summoning laughter from all within earshot. "Come, let us go find some wine and sit."

We move through the camp, seeing men expressing all forms of emotion. Some feast and laugh as if battle never happened, while others just sit in silence. Men looking for company gravitate toward the fires where one boastful soldier recounts his moments of glory, reenacting the battle as if he was part of a theater display. Everyone eventually looks to humor to dilute the smell of death that still lingers heavy on the field; however, many seeking this refuge find little to lift their spirit. Death was too near, the muscles still ache, and the hearts of men are still overcome with the weight of battle.

Soon, we come upon Stone and some of his comrades.

"Friends, my victorious friends. Please, join us," Stone says as he tosses Edge a wine sack. Protesias and Stout help Diokles and me with our helmets and shields. After a large swig, Edge walks over. I can't help but notice his strong arm still caked with dried mud and blood as he offers the sack to me.

"You and your companions fought well today. I did not expect such steadfast valor from any of you. A year ago, I would have bet a horse that you and your friends would have fled from the situation you found yourselves in today. Look, over there. You see those men summoning officers to King Agis. They will be punished for disobeying orders. We could have easily lost that battle today. Our left flank had collapsed, and in that most vulnerable moment, those men were left with a choice. Had they chosen to follow the king's orders, you, me, and our entire formation would have been surrounded and cut down like stalks of wheat. We had no knowledge of their choice. All we could do was stand alone and hold our ground, and all of you did just that. Had you not, I could be lying over there next to Kritos. You understand what I am saying?"

"Of course, we stood our ground, sir. There was no other choice," I acknowledge.

"Exactly. That is why we do what we do, Nikos. Why we train, live, and pray as we do. That is why we are not only taught to merely live by Lycurgus's laws but to understand them, to believe in them. Our survival depends upon it. The discipline we gain from our rearing allows us to keep our composure while the world collapses around us. That is why the gods favor us. You say we had no choice even while you watched others flee the field, both allies and enemies alike. Some, perhaps most, of the men in our unit had brief thoughts of preserving themselves when they saw our flank collapse. You know why they didn't?"

"Yes, sir," I say confidently.

"But of course, you do! Go on then, tell us, Nikos," he states almost sarcastically as he sits back with his comrades by the fire, making me address all those who had been eavesdropping on the lesson that Edge never intended to be private.

"Fear, sir, fear of being the only one. That to abandon his comrades meant an undying shame would follow him and his family forever. He would be an outcast. As a formation breaks, we anticipate our own death. While this sudden terror may overcome us briefly, all one must do is look to either side. Even if a man decided to turn and flee, he would be unable to avoid the sight of other Spartans conquering their own fear. Of his comrades, with feet planted and shoulder within shield, covering him as he fled by facing chaos and horror head-on. The shame following just that thought of flight must have made their souls cry out at a chance for redemption."

"You speak as if from experience," one of the men chimes in.

"No, sir, all I could do was look for my commander, my friends, and hope that my training and the gods would keep me alive...but I felt it, sir."

"Felt what?"

"The fire, sir. The divine fire Gylippus has told me about. The one only a shamed soul can spark, and as it seeks its redemption, the gods stoke that spark with rage from within. An unquenchable thirst for valor, to show your comrades that you are not the coward that you were forced to confront in your own head. And as with any fire, it can spread. The blaze emboldens those around you and rallies men in the midst of confronting their own demons. What started as a flicker of fearlessness turned into a raging row of scarlet that engulfed the field, leaving only death in its wake. That fire emboldened me. In fact, it likely saved my life."

For a brief moment, some of the men stare at me in silence while others just poke at the fire. I feel as if every man is now recalling the moment during the battle where they either were the source of that flame or one of those emboldened by it.

Sensing the heaviness around the blaze, Edge realizes that it was he who began the lesson, and with morale building around the camp, it was also time for him to conclude it.

"Very good, Nikos, it appears your *helot*-loving mentor has actually taught you a thing or two. Now finish that sack of wine right now so you're not so damn serious for the rest of the night."

Everyone begins to laugh, and others cheer as I turn the sack of wine vertical. The liquid feels warm and delicious as I guzzle it; some overflow out of my mouth and begin to stream down my neck. Another roar of laughter and good cheer rings out as *helot* attendants show up with food and more wine. Diokles looks at me, tips his sack of wine toward me, and laughs as men from all over camp start yelling out, "Victory!" For the first time, I feel the scale and significance of what has just happened. Many officers are walking among the fires, congratulating their men.

"Victory!" I hear a man roar from behind me.

I turn to see an officer, still in full armor. His back is arched, and he is bellowing repeatedly while holding his shield and spear above his head. The horizontal crest at the top of his helmet waves with the gyration of his powerful arms. The armor is decorated with streams of dried blood that had flown like rivers through curves in the metalwork, and despite this, the bronze still gleams in the dying sunlight. He is truly a sight to behold, and he appears to recognize this as he struts around from fire to fire. All the various emotions from within the camp funnel into this man, and the men erupt. The volume of the outburst rises to a great roar that is so loud that I can feel my bronze armor trembling against my body. Surely, the departing Argives and Athenians can hear this war cry, and this reality is likely feeding this overwhelming feeling of triumph.

The moment seems to last forever until drifting into chants by one unit or another. Everywhere, groups by one fire or another break out into laughter as everyone tells their accounts of the day. There has clearly been a drastic shift in morale throughout the camp, and what was once a large collection of fatigued men has turned into something more akin to a celebration.

"Nikos! Edge! Get your asses over here!"

Bull is waving to us and motioning us over. He has a wine sack in hand, laughing with Diokles and Stone while Stout tends to a wound on his hip.

"Either sharp edges are attracted to you, or you are just accident prone," I say jokingly as we lock arms, and he winces in pain.

"Perhaps a little bit of both. You would think the Athenians have a bounty on my head. You think that foreign girl I humped last *Hyacinthia* is one of Cleon's mistresses?" Edge exclaims as we all break into laughter.

As we continue to eat, drink, and recount our personal deeds of the day, I notice the still-armored officer walking our way, pausing occasionally to shake a hand or make a joke.

"How's the hip?" he says, approaching Bull and our mess with peculiar familiarity.

"Nothing serious, sir."

"Heard you boys had a hell of a day. Your regiment put up quite the fight, I've been told. It's good to see you all alive and in such good spirit," he says as I finally recognize the hoarse voice.

"In good spirit indeed, all thanks to your theatrics...brother," I respond.

"Glad you enjoyed that, Nikos," my brother, Theron, exclaims as we embrace. "I almost shit myself when I heard that the Wolves were the ones responsible for holding together the Spartan left. Ahhh, but let me sit. My voice is almost gone, and my bloody feet are killing me. Pass me that sack of wine!"

Theron finally removes his helmet and begins to swing the sack to its conclusion, just as I had been instructed to do earlier.

"Now," he states, wiping the excess wine from his face. "Tell me about the hell you all marched through today. My superiors tell me that officers were ignoring orders."

All of us begin to speak, but Theron raises his hand slightly to signal to us to remain silent and let him finish.

"Ah, but let me say one last thing before each of you tell me of your deeds. Very likely, the quick thinking of those officers preserved us all. For a moment, the enemy had us. Scouts now report that they may have doubled their ranks on their right flank in the hopes that they could quickly rout our left and fold up the rest of our line."

"Sir, many say that those officers you commend might be charged with insubordination," Diokles interjects as Theron uses the pause to grab another sack of wine.

"Do not concern yourself with the politics, my young friend. We defeated our enemy on the field, a pivotal moment in this war, I have no doubt. Yes, they might be disciplined, and I am sure each of them will accept the consequences with honor and grace. They understand that their decision, while correct, was a dangerous gamble. Lack of cohesion can cause panic and confusion, which can dismantle the phalanx and lose the battle. It would have happened to any fighting force other than our own, and even we will not always be immune. Orders must be followed. Today was one of those rare occasions where individuals decided to hold their positions, cover their neighbors, and ride out the storm rather than try to maneuver the entire force to victory. I don't know about you, but I know the first thing I am going to do when I get home. I will announce myself, then retire to my bed and politely ask my wife to treat me to some oral sex."

"Knowing your wife, she will spread her legs and say, 'You first,'" Stone states dryly.

"That might be the funniest thing that has ever left your mouth, Stone!" my brother exclaims as everyone enjoys a good-natured laugh at his expense.

The march home passes much more quickly than the march to battle. We maintain our discipline, marching in an orderly fashion; however, mood in the army is light, and my mind is at ease. Visions of the fray scatter my thoughts, but instead of anticipating my own death as you do marching into battle, I smile to myself in admiration as I recall my own performance. It seems many are doing the same and speaking such thoughts out loud. The chatter can be heard up and down the line, embellished tales of who was doing what and where. I could easily dismiss the stories by immersing myself in my own memories. Yet as I sift through the bullshit, I actually start to get a better understanding about the course of the battle.

After flooding the plain at Mantinea, we were marching toward our intended spot to set camp when we came out of the wood line and stumbled upon the Argive and Athenian forces. Each army put their best forces on the right flank, and from there, it was a race between who could fold the other's left first to force a break. The Argives actually stacked their right with additional forces, easily overcoming our left flank. Agis reportedly ordered the units commanded by Aristocles and Hipponoidas to maneuver away from the center to reinforce our left. Whether they did not hear the order or they ignored it, they stayed in their position while the weight of the enemy right fell upon my regiment. We held our ground and were only saved by the enemy's own greed as they pursued our allies and started to raid our camp. Against other armies, this can actually be an effective tactic that causes chaos, tempting some to leave their post to go back and defend their belongings and supplies. But against Spartans? Had they stayed organized, turned in force, and surrounded us, we might have lost the battle.

As the Argives pursued our fleeing left, the Spartan formations broke the Athenians and Arcadians on their left and then maneuvered back across the field. With the Argive units scattered and caught out of formation, the Spartans cut down all left in the field and prevented any hope of retreat for their greedy comrades who looted our camp.

Now, we march home victorious. Men and women of the countryside line the road, smiling, cheering, and laughing along with us. We march like warrior gods as the sky darkens and a smooth thunder rumbles in the distance. The flutes start to play, and the men erupt in song with the accompaniment of nature's drums. The air is thick and heavy as the wind picks up. The people along the road, the dark sky, the rolling thunder and music, it all lifts the soul and makes all feel that we are truly favored by the gods.

The moment is fleeting. The night before entering Sparta, the heavy rain we heard in the distance begins rolling in, and one can feel the fatigue of both mind and body weighing on the men. As we make camp, the temperature drops and so does morale. The fig eating and wine drinking has ceased along with all the laughter. In the deluge, men find little solace or refuge without a fire to congregate around.

To make matters worse, the baggage train slowly moves down the road past the camp. They continue now so that we can catch up tomorrow, that way we all enter the city together, just behind our honored fallen.

The sight is overwhelming. As the carts with our fallen roll by, memories of comrades also pass over our heavy hearts. The runners dispatched days ago carried the news to Sparta, carrying news about our victory, about the honored and dishonored, and about those who will not be coming home. Wives, sons, and daughters are likely taking this opportunity to mourn. With the rain and thunder, none will be able to hear their cries tonight. Tomorrow, they will greet their fallen kin with the dry-eyed honor we Spartans have come to expect. While tonight, each of us dwell on the moments we watched others fall. Could I have thrust my spear faster? Could I have somehow shielded that missile that I saw split another Spartan's head?

I comb my wet hair. Such thoughts plague me. Then, I see Stout, a welcome distraction, making his way toward me, carefully stepping around men in the midst of the downpour.

"Can't sleep either, eh?"

I don't even respond because clearly the answer is obvious.

"How is the soreness? Take off that chiton," he demands as he pulls a concoction of mint and olive oil out of his pouch. "Don't let your mind be so troubled. Each of your countrymen died victoriously with honor and glory. I pulled some from the fray and tended to many that did not survive. They all had wounds of the face, neck, chest, and stomach. They fell advancing forward, not in flight. They will carry those scars to Hades so all will know of their deeds. Quite a brilliant thing, really, would you not agree?" he says as he digs his elbow into the knot above my right shoulder blade.

"Brilliant indeed."

Despite my dismal tone, the combination of his words and his work on my tense muscles is soothing.

"Now, try to get some sleep, master."

"Don't you ever call me that, you piece of *helot* shit, understand?" I snap back. "You are a dear and loyal friend and an equal. Master over you, I am not and will never be. You have your role, and it is just as pivotal as my own. Besides, you do much more than what is required of you."

"Heh, you hardly ask me to do anything," he jabs back with a smile.

"I meant not only for me, but for Sparta, for this army. You willingly put yourself in harm's way when the need arises. I do not need someone to help me wipe my arsehole."

"I meant no offense, sir, but I will say this, it is my life's honor to be bound to you…and do tell your family to put me under the service of another warrior if something happens to you. For if you are crippled in the next battle, I don't think I'd be very good at wiping your ass."

"Nah, I'd rather have your nephew do it," I say, chuckling, referring to Gorga's young son.

"Have your laugh, Spartan, and later tonight, I will be polishing your helmet with my piss."

We share a good laugh, and he puts my armor aside to polish after the rain subsides. I lay back against the tree, wrap myself in my scarlet cloak, and try to get some sleep. As I watch Stout tend to my gear and my eyes grow heavy, I can't help but think how lucky I am to have him as my companion. Without him, I would still be lying awake troubled. Not tonight. Instead, now I am drifting with the visions of heroes in my head. Men, glad in their gleaming armor despite the desolate darkness. Their heads held high while they file one by one toward the awaiting ferry that is going to bear them to the other side.

I slowly awaken, the moon still shining brightly on the damp ground, casting a pure light that causes everything to take on a faint blue silhouette. Everyone appears to be asleep, lying still in the shimmering grass. However, there is a rustling in the bushes that sounds too deliberate for wild game. I move to investigate and look to the perimeter to see if I can locate the men who are supposed to be on watch—nothing. Maybe the noise is just the sentry taking a shit, but then I spot movement. As I come into a clearing, there it is, the rectangular shape of a wicker shield leaning against the far tree.

"Persians? What are they doing here?" I whisper to myself.

I turn the corner of the meadow and see a Greek hoplite in the center of a group of five warriors. All are in full armor, with shields, helmets, breastplates, and their weapons of choice. Two of the men are Persian, another Greek hoplite, and two others who look like barbarians. One is perhaps Thracian, while the other looks Eastern, but unlike anything I have ever seen. I pause and listen to hear what they might be discussing, but there is no sound. They aren't speaking at all. In fact, they are all facing the hoplite in the middle and standing there motionless, the blue light of the moon making it look as if they were made of marble.

I decide to walk into plain view and allow them to see me, and still, no response from the figures. When I move into the circle, the center hoplite's eyes fix upon my own, the bright beads I can see through the small slits in his helmet, and it feels like he is looking straight into my soul. Without warning, he faints toward me. Startled, I move to parry, but instead of coming at me with his spear, he turns and thrusts it into the groin of the other Greek warrior. I draw my *xiphos* and attempt to cover the fallen warrior and to allow him to recover, but he just lies there, as he had stood, motionless.

I can tell by the squinting of his eyes and the raising of his chin that the center Greek is now smiling at me from beneath his helmet. I cannot tell if he approves of me or if he mocks me. He takes advantage of the vulnerability my contemplation created and thrusts his spear quickly toward my face. I bend my knees, arch my back, and jerk my head back, barely avoiding spear point that passes beneath my chin. The suddenness of the moment causes me to lose my balance and fall into the moonlit dust.

Just then, the center hoplite moves toward the fallen Greek on the ground. With a stir, the fallen warrior extends his arm up at the other hoplite. They lock arms. I look on puzzled while the center warrior helps the fallen one up, shifting their gaze in my direction for a moment before making a rush at me. I try to regain my footing, but it is too late. In an attempt to finish me, one of the Greeks drives his spear down toward my chest. I quickly roll out of its path, allowing it to plunge into the dirt. With one motion, I grab the grounded shaft and use it to propel myself to my feet, thrusting my *xiphos* into his stomach, just below the breastplate. At the same moment, the other Greek's spear passes harmlessly just beyond my left shoulder as I rip my *xiphos* free from his dying comrade. He misjudged the speed of my recovery, but as I swing around to face him, he appears to have lost interest in me. Instead, he turns to face the Persians who have now begun fighting one another. The Greek runs toward both, looking as if he favors one over the other. However, the Persian he seeks to preserve falls at the hand of his kinsman, and the Eastern barbarian swings his curved blade at the unsuspecting Greek's leg, slicing his hamstring, causing him to fall upon the body of his ally.

I run at the Persian, feeling somehow compelled to aid my fellow Greek with total disregard for his attempt to kill me only moments ago. I slam my body into the Persian, knocking him off his feet and then swinging around to parry a heavy blow from the barbarian. Frantically, with my free hand, I reach for the Greek and drag him toward the edge of the clearing in a desperate attempt to remove him from the fray. The Persian and barbarian turn and charge toward us, convincing me that I will be meeting my end. I did not notice, but the Thracian has maneuvered around behind us, and he is now grabbing me and the Greek, trying to pull us back into the shrubs. In the scramble, my heel catches a root, and I fall back, slamming my head back into the earth.

My eyes open slowly, only to see Stout standing over me, chuckling.

"You okay? The way you were tossing about in your sleep, would have thought you were fighting the battle all over again."

"Not the same," I respond, rubbing my pounding head as it tries to determine what is real and what isn't.

"What?"

"Different battle, now pass me that water," I say impatiently while blankly staring into the distance.

"Hmmm, the gods must have shown you something important," he responds sarcastically, waving his hand in front of my transfixed eyes. "Come on, sir, really, time to suit up."

"Ah, hold on...Let me piss first."

I pull myself to my feet, grab a fig to gnaw on, and do a quick scan of the camp before walking into the bushes to relieve myself. Some men are just getting up, while others, already dressed in their armor, look as if they have not slept at all. I have often heard other Greeks joke about how, to Spartans, war is actually easier than our training for it. It appears so. Lack of sleep never bothers us much because during our years in the *agoge*, we never get enough of it. We treat it more like a mild discomfort rather than a debilitating condition.

The bushes are thick and coarse as I try to put some distance between my piss and the place I had just slept. Moving through their sharp branches, I unexpectedly stumble upon a clearing. Seeing the familiar ground makes me forget I am midstream, causing me to accidently piss all over my legs as I walk out into it. My heart pounds, my breath grows deep, and beads of sweat gather on my forehead as I recognize the subtle details of the terrain. No men, no blood, and no evidence of what I experienced. Still, the small little battlefield is eerily identical.

Then, movement once again, this time, it is from behind. Instinctively I pull my dagger and wheel around to face whatever might seek to take me unaware.

"Whooaa, shit! Easy, brother, battle's over. Just looking for a good spot to unload my stomach mud before we march."

"Stone! You son of a bitch, you scared me shitless."

"Why? What in Hades has you so fucking jumpy?"

The reasonable question to my inexplicable behavior and the calm way in which he continues to go about his business makes me break out into laughter. Stone catches on as he sits awkwardly in a squat, starting to shit in midlaughter, making the entire scene only more disgusting and amusing.

By the time Stone and I return, the camp is chaotic with peers and *helot* attendants scurrying about. The sun has just ascended over the mountains, and the morning rays are gleaming brilliantly off all the recently buffed shields and helmets. The orange light illuminates the deep-scarlet cloaks, making it appear much brighter, like blood just emerging from a fresh wound.

The sight of our assembly is a marvelous one. Stout helps me with my armor, and all I see around me is a sea of scarlet and bronze around us. In this moment, I can't help but be reminded just how crucial our victory had been. Seldom are the moments where the entire Spartan force protecting our city is called into action at once. Most often, we are deployed with our allies in separate occupations, engagements, or forays into enemy territory. We had all mustered to answer the aggressive advance of Argos and Athens, and had the battle been lost, this would have been the day our city died.

Sparta has no walls to protect her, so there would have been no siege. These men are Sparta's walls, and their shields and spears are her only defenses. A feeling of mixed emotions overcomes me, each representing a part of my journey that has led me to this point. This is what I was raised for. I trained, I bled, I killed, and I survived. Sparta survived.

In this churn of emotion, I find myself having visions of the night's previous dream, and it weighs heavily on me. The dream was too intentional to be insignificant.

"What could it all mean?" I whisper to myself as a small tear escapes my eyelid and gently slides down my cheek, concealed beneath my bronze helmet. Did I see Sparta's doom despite this victory? Or was it the doom of Athens? Perhaps it was all of Greece.

"Wolves!" I hear Edge yell. "Today we march home victorious! The gods blessed us with *andreia*, and we honored them with our virtue! Glory is yours, and we paid for it in blood!"

Our regiment erupts with a deafening roar. Beside us, other regiments erupt in similar displays of pride as their commanders acknowledge them. The noise, the roars, the flutes of war, they all rescue me from my emotions and snap me back into the glory of this moment. This is just another brief moment of vanity that we Spartans enjoy.

This is how we reward ourselves, in pieces, with our comrades, when it is necessary. Whether by the fires of camp, in our mess, or before entering our city victorious, we give each other these little moments to revel in the success of our trade. Of course, we will feast tomorrow night with our messes after the funeral ceremonies, but when we enter the city, we will do so in silence. This is out of honor for our fallen comrades and their families and to remind us of humility and the obligations we have to the *polis*. We do not march into our city hooting and hollering like feckless Athenians after the games at Olympia. War and victory are expected of us. Celebrations are for the gods. We are men just following their laws. We are not entitled praise for that.

Still, the march home is a pleasant one. The rain has passed and left the day feeling a little bit cooler than those previous, adding to the jovial mood throughout the army. All the men can speak of is fucking their wives and/or *helot* mistresses. Of course, laughs follow as comrades counter with the same old jokes about their friend being just as likely to go home and fuck their livestock.

Before we know it, word travels down the line to be silent as we crest the hill and our city comes into view. Our pace slows slightly as men frantically adjust their armor and cloaks and pull their shields off their backs to shoulder them. *Helot* attendants and squires are scrambling to pass men their spears. The subtle clamor of bronze and wood is the only noise as the peers tighten their marching formation. Everyone is silent in reverence of the procession and their part in it.

After cresting the hill, we can see the first elements of the procession entering the city. The road itself is invisible as the entire army weaves through the landscape like a scarlet serpent. The slow pace of the march, combined with the recent rain, make the sights and the smells exceptionally pleasant. Without the feet in front of us kicking up dust, my nostrils fill with the familiar scents of home and the fresh air off the Tegean Mountains. With much of home in view, memories flood the mind. Everything from festivals as a child, intimate moments with Gorga, and grueling training sessions beneath the sun, every inch of terrain is recognizable. Each hill, field, and tree tell a different story. When our commanders speak of home, we often dismiss such references due to the frequency they are used in attempts to motivate the men. However, in truth, this is what we train and fight for, and I suppose it takes moments like this one to appreciate it.

The women and children line the road as we enter, followed by the boys of the *agoge*. All stand in silence except for the occasional smiles passing between lovers or a few unruly daughters sprinting into the formation to greet their fathers. The little boys know better; for them, such a move will only result in lashes. We all look for family and loved ones. For us, it is but a small comfort that comes with the homecoming. For them, seeing a face is the final confirmation that that person truly lives or was not maimed in battle.

This part of the homecoming starts to feel a bit bitter as I recall the moments before I left, Gorga leaving Sparta with her husband and young son, and my would-be bride stolen away by another. No woman other than my mother awaits my face. I am mistaken, however. While no wife awaits my face, I feel a pair of eyes from the crowd on me as I pass. They are that of the *helot* servant girl who tends to Kallias. I hardly even notice Kallias standing in front of her because of the seductive smile the *helot* girl is passing me.

Before we arrive to the Temples of Artemis and Nike, we pay our respects with silent prayers, and the choir girls chant songs of victory and death. Following the formalities, men disperse either to wives and children in the crowd or back toward the barracks. No feasting tonight. Tonight we reflect on those lost, and all will mourn together with the families of the fallen. The thoughts of battle, the dead, and the gods run through my mind, and I can't help but recall my strange dream. I contemplate what I had seen and feel a cool breeze brush against my neck. Nothing about it appeared random or incoherent. There was an element of certainty and purpose woven into the vision. Whatever the reason the gods have for bestowing this upon me, I hope they are mistaken. I don't want any part of it.

While everyone slowly departs, I am in no mood to retire to the barracks, nor do I have any desire to be alone with my thoughts. Instead, I want to lock eyes once more with the *helot* girl and possibly suggest some sort of rendezvous this evening. If not, perhaps I will join my brother at my father's house so that Mother can prepare a meal, and we can enjoy some wine.

I continue to make my way through the crowd and look for the last position of the girl. So fixated on this pursuit, I lose sight of my steps as I make my way back up the road, finally walking straight into a stationary man. Our chests hit one another with a thud.

"Walking like a man that is being led not by the head above his chest but rather the one between his legs," the familiar voice states jokingly.

"Ah, Gylippus," I respond as we lock arms in greeting.

"Yes, my boy. Come, let us take a walk briefly."

We walk up the road for a while until we reach the crest of the hill that overlooks Sparta. The same spot he had taken after Gorga and I faked her rape in her father's house.

"I am sorry I did not come join you and our friends after the battle. There was much controversy in the king's tent regarding the behavior of some commanders and many among the bodyguard. Once I found out you were alive, I was content and had to attend to these political matters.

"Still, I feared for your regiment during the battle, and I am sorry my band of *helots* that I trained with Brasidas did not live up to their reputation."

"They fought well, your *helot* regiment. As you probably know, the Argive doubled their ranks on their right. They were outnumbered two to one, against our enemies' finest warriors. None but a full Spartan contingent would have been able to hold the left against that front."

"As you say." He nods his head and smiles softly in acknowledgment.

"We did just achieve a great victory for Sparta, and I am proud of the part you played in it. Yet I fear this war is far from a conclusion. Spartans feel strong once again. Many have a renewed sense of purpose and superiority, but such arrogance can be dangerous. Some followers of the Agiads desire the return of Pleistoanax and a fresh attempt at peace with Athens. While Lysander and the young allies of King Agis II will want to press the advantage as they seek to reshape Greece in Sparta's image, Agis, however, is a bit more cautious. He is more concerned with the survival of Sparta and not bringing shame or dishonor to the Eurypontid line of kings.

"I sense dangerous political rifts are developing within Sparta. Do not let the thoughts of Gorga and Kallias make you blind to the war or its influences on our people. And that is what I am truly here to discuss, Gorga. That is her name, yes? The *helot* girl you love."

"I did love her…and I guess I still do," I respond quizzically, wondering how he knew of my love for her and why he was shifting my thoughts away from the other *helot* girl.

"Obviously not the young wench you were seeking within the crowd when I found you," he states with a sinister grin.

"Gorga has left with her husband and boy," I respond dryly.

"So they have, and it was I who sent them away."

I pause, not out of disdain or anger, but to insinuate that I understand that this is some sort of instruction and that he may continue so I can try to discern the meaning of this.

"Did you think I did not know, that I somehow overlooked this little affair?"

"I was not trying to hide it from you. Really, I was more concerned about avoiding the flog. And if I may speak, I believe I already know the reason behind this instruction."

"Oh?" he responds with an eagerly sarcastic smile.

"I know I was never fated to marry her," I tell him as he plants his ass beneath the fig tree.

"Sit, my friend. You are correct," he states before I take my place on the ground beside him. "I know you appreciate the fragility of our relationship with the *helots*. It is a delicate balance of pure hate that can manifest itself into mutual respect, and sometimes even love. Those who serve you can also please you. Sometimes they are the comrade-in-arms that preserves you, dragging you from the fray or supplying you with a fresh spear when all you have in your hand is a splinter.

"Often, they are loyal, worthy of our respect. And we must grant them this, but selectively. While few among them may use their place beneath us as an opportunity to prove themselves worthy, the majority of them look to procure our downfall and death. The rest are caught up in the middle." He pauses for a second in thought.

"Hmph hmmph," he laughs to himself, holding the small chuckle behind his closed lips. "It can be like marriage to a woman. We want to murder one another. We feed one another. We fight one another. Sometimes we fight to preserve one another. At its worst, sometimes it is only held together by a sense of duty, other times, by fear. Their loyalty can come and go like the seasons."

"I understand."

"Do you? Gods forbid you would have married that girl or planted a son in her belly. It would have ruined you both. Her life would have been one of solitude and misery. Her kin would have disowned her, and your family would have to live with the disgrace. The wives of Sparta would ostracize and scorn her, and while the peers would not question your loyalty, they would question your sanity for neglecting the delicate balance on which our survival depends.

"The reason I tell you all this is to remind you that I am the spawn of such a relationship. My father was in the position that you faced, and he chose to put his lust ahead of his duty to the *polis*. His duty was to produce Spartan sons, not half-breeds.

"Only because of a friend of my father and superior fighting skills as a child did I get sponsored and granted the opportunity to enter the *agoge*," he concludes softly as he discards a chewed fig by tossing it into the grass.

"I never faced your father's quandary."

"What?"

"The choice, I never had it, for you removed my ability to choose."

"Ha ha, I am your mentor and your superior. It is my responsibility to rob you of just that. What did you think, you had hit your head and awoken in Athens?"

We both begin to laugh, and then he starts again to try to bring a conclusion to the instruction.

"In all seriousness, you know of my father. A great Spartan but overcome by that beast that causes the unquenchable thirst of want, the beast of greed.

"He fought and was honored many times, but he disgraced himself and his family by marrying a *helot*, and then he disgraced himself again in old age by disappearing with gold that was not his. So you see, this is what I am a product of."

"But you are—"

"Silence, boy! I am not finished. Sorry, I did not mean to make this about me. In truth, this is about my mother and Gorga," he bellows, but he gathers himself, and his frustrated tone turns gentle once again. "My mother was a fine woman. While my physical strength I got from my father, it is my philosophy and mental toughness that came from her. She lived that life of misery I speak of, and on the day I came back from my first campaign, I did not see her face in the crowd. A week later, one of our servants returned to tell us that she had followed my mother on an errand south with no knowledge of her purpose. When they reached the cliffs, she thanked the servant for her loyal service, gave her a few instructions, meaningless things about feeding the goats and tending to her garden. She then threw herself into the sea. The *helot* servant said she was not overcome with grief, and she had not lost any of her wit. She appeared as strong, calm, and virtuous as ever, before deciding to take the journey to the other side.

"My first campaign was in Messenia. An errand to put down a *helot* insurrection, and I did so, not as a *helot* serving a Spartan peer. I was a peer. You see, she did not throw herself onto the rocks because she had succumbed to the misery of her life. She was stronger than that, more disciplined, more deliberate. Instead, she moved on to the next life because she had reared a killer of her people. I was coming home from that campaign either dead, being carried in the bowl of a Spartan shield, or victorious, having quenched my thirst for glory on the blood of her kin.

"If you truly love this girl, Gorga, you will never seek her out, even if your road one day leads you to the place where she resides. But you won't have to worry about that for much longer anyway. Another peer, a good man, just inquired about your relationship status. I was a guest at his home before we departed to Mantinea, and I assure you, his daughter is quite the beauty. Now, go hunt down that other little *helot* doe and have yourself a good romping. Tomorrow, we will plan your next little excursion to steal a young woman from her bed and make her your bride."

I brush away the soft tinder that was the result of my graffiti. My name looks good here, but I doubt the shipmaster would agree. I peer over my shoulder less than inconspicuously to see if he seems suspicious. Men who work the ship often leave their mark on it, but it is deemed disrespectful for those paying for passage. However, I have a strange feeling that I won't be returning home after this journey. This is my way of leaving something behind. I don't know who might follow, but at this point in my life, I am not sure that I care. If some man or woman is seeking me for vengeance, let them find this and see it as an invitation. I doubt there are many who are seeking me out of love or loyalty, but perhaps, some old comrade or honorable adversary will come by this road and smile when they recall the name Andronikos etched in the bench.

When I recall Mantinea, I do so with fondness. Oh, what a glorious day that was, and what a battle. Looking back, I think all those who were present were relieved to finally meet one another in battle. Not only was it a great battle, but a proper one. A ferocious encounter like those in the tales of old. Sparta's very existence was on the line that day. There, in that field, on that day, the Argives sought to finish the war with one final stroke. Too long had the conflict between Athens and Sparta brought nothing but starvation, treachery, and disease. A physical and moral decay of Greece.

The Argives had no choice but to oppose us. They are an old and proper enemy, and the hatred between our cities will always run deep. Oh, but how fortunate we are to have them. That ancient rivalry was destined. What a great and noble gift the gods bestowed upon us. Every day, I give thanks to the gods for those sons of whores, for we Spartans would be no better than the helots who serve us if it weren't for them.

That year following the peace, it was the Argives who recognized the need for battle. Not only was it an attempt to secure total victory, but an attempt to secure it properly. A reminder to all Greeks about how we used to resolve our differences and what war was supposed to look like. When I have passed to the other side, I hope somehow that all who were *present there can meet again to fight and feast together in honor of that noble day.*

I should not say that life was downhill after Mantinea, but it was certainly different. You cannot change life; you can only experience it. It springs forth from its source and flows downhill like a stream. Water has no choice but to move in the path that's laid before it, which is why I have no pity for those who live with regret. Every experience, good or ill, is an opportunity to gain knowledge about yourself and the world around you. While Mantinea is a grand memory, I find it useless to wish that it had served as some kind of example or to ask the gods why the war became more vicious and cruel following that day. Of course, there were many moments of honor and glory to come, but unlike Mantinea, they were not on display for all of Greece. These moments were destined only to be glimpses of virtue shared by the few, who, while in the midst of one hell or another, were fortunate enough to witness them.

For all the pain, the gods give you just as many opportunities to experience joy and observe greatness. I do not look back on my time and wonder why the gods took this person from me, or why they sent me to that shithole. I know why. We are refined by our experiences. Like a blacksmith forging a blade from a block of bronze, I was hammered and beaten. I was dipped in fire and ash and beaten again until I became a fine tool, worthy of use by the gods. And while I have not yet had a chance to pass knowledge and instruction along to kin, there are still those who share my blood.

With all I have witnessed in this life, I have come to believe that there is an unspoken language between kin that is articulated and interpreted by blood. The blood shared between kin acts as a conduit for communication with those who came before us. How do I know this? I don't, but too often have I seen the spawn of great men act as if they had already learned the lessons of their fathers. Men who have the feel of destiny about them bear children of the same thread. Even if they never achieve anything exceptional in their own life, the trained eye can recognize that their line has been chosen for great things. They act as if given direction, orders in the form of whispers by gods and ancestors that they discern instinctively.

For me, it began with dreams. That is how the gods introduced themselves to me. They operate within our reality, sometimes bestowing little hints to their presence that most discard as mere coincidence. I think this is how the gods maintain the anonymity, making men keep these communications to themselves or else be labeled mad by their peers. For knowledge and madness are like the tip of the sharp knife I hold in my hand, so fine is the edge between one and the other.

The battle of Mantinea was over, and I thought that I would live as most Spartans before me, survive battle, settle down in my new home, have a family, and either die in battles to come, or watch my children grow as I start the steady decay of old age.

What fools we mortals are, pretending to know our destiny just because we have seen others live in such ways. I too was a fool. The gods had shown me a vision, and I had discarded it as merely a dream. I should have known better. The gods don't give mortals who lead such simple lives a glimpse of their awareness; these are only for the bloodline the gods intend to utilize for some purpose.

My first vision was prattle, impossible for the mind to interpret. I judge that this is intentional, an influence and preparation only for body, blood, and soul. An awakening of the bloodline and an activation of the conduit, calling on the ancestors to prepare a mortal's soul for the presence of the god and guide him on the necessary path to achieve whatever end. I had been called upon, and for me, the war was far from over. What part did I have to play? For the gods are beholden to no authority or reason but their own.

Glossary

agoge. The *agoge* is the distinctive system of upbringing and training.

andreia. A Greek virtue meaning manly spirit, courage. Aristotle believed *andreia* represented the ideal balance of courage, between too little (cowardliness) and too much (reckless or rash).

aspis. Hoplon shield.

chiton. Or exomis was the wool or linen tunic worn by Greek males. The right shoulder seam could be loosened, freeing the right arm and shoulder for labor. Spartans wore crimson *exomis*.

enōmotarche. Commander of an *enōmotiai*.

enōmotiai. Unit of Spartan military often consisting of between 30 and 50 men depending on size and organization of the army in the field.

ephors. Five magistrates elected annually from among all Spartiates (without the possibility of reelection). This board possessed sweeping powers—even over the kings—and took a leading role in the state's affairs.

equals. Also referred to as Spartiates, *homoioi*, and/or peers. These were the terms the Spartan warrior class used to refer to themselves.

gerousia. Council of elders: Sparta's supreme administrative, legislative, and judicial body.

helots. Local inhabitants of Laconia and Messenia, owned by the Spartan state (often associated with or assigned to but not owned by individual Spartans) and required to work for the citizens of Sparta in total subjection. Individual helots or communities of them were freed on occasion for service in the Spartan army.

katalepsis. Possession. The word also refers to a Stoic philosophy that the mind is constantly contemplating what is true and what is false.

kryptea. A secret body of Spartans, comprised mostly of older teens and answering directly to the ephors, who were charged with rooting out hidden enemies of the state. Their most notorious duty was to spy upon the helots, listening and ferreting out potential troublemakers, whom they were empowered to assassinate at will. Membership in the *kryptea* was awarded to the most promising of Spartan youths enrolled in the *agoge* (see *agoge*), and only Spartans who were so "honored" by membership in the *kryptea* could expect to later rise to the highest offices in the Spartan government.

lochagus. The officer or commander assigned to a *lochoi*.

lochoi. Segment of the Spartan army half the size of a *mora*.

mora. Regiment: one of the six largest units of the Spartan army.

mothax. Term meaning "half-breed," commonly used to reference the offspring of a Spartan and non-Spartan.

oikos. Household.

paidiskoi. Referring to the age class of Spartan youths/trainees in their late teens. Once in this age class, you are eligible for recruitment into a *sussitia*.

pentēkontēr. The officer or commander assigned to a *pentēkostyes*.

pentekostyes. One of four segments of the *lochoi* within a Spartan regiment often consisting of between 50 and 128 men depending on size and organization of the army in the field.

phobos. Fear.

perioikoi. Or *perioeci*, "the dwellers round about," communities of free people occupying land in Laconia and Messenia granted them by the Spartan state in exchange for military service.

polemarchs. The six Spartan army officers immediately subordinate to whichever king was in command in the field; they also attended the king's mess on campaign.

polis. Political community or society.

proxeni. Or *proxenus.* referring to a type of foreign dignitary, military representative, or "guest friend." These individuals were not

Spartan but were occasionally allowed or invited by Sparta to participate in various aspects of the social, political, religious and military affairs of the state. Most commonly associated with the offspring of prominent figures throughout Greece who have received special permission to be educated in the Spartan *agoge*.

skiritai. Light-armed skirmishers from the Laconian-Arcadian border, employed by the Spartans as specialty troops.

stade. Greek unit of measurement about 600 feet or 180 meters.

sussitia. Or syssition. Was a dining club or mess. After graduating from the *agoge*, all Spartan equals (*homoioi*) had to be inducted into a mess. They usually consisted of ten to fifteen individuals that they would dine with and fight with for their entire lives.

xiphos. The Spartan variation of a bronze short sword.

zomos. Also known as black soup, the soup was a combination of boiled pig's blood, the pig's legs, vinegar, and salt.

About the Author

William Austin Lamon grew up in Atlanta, Georgia, where he currently resides. However, his professional and academic career have taken him to many places throughout the United States, Europe, and the Middle East. After being exposed to the epic poems of Homer at an early age, he developed a fascination with classical history. He was able to explore this passion later while completing degrees in political science, history, and international relations from Southern Methodist University in Dallas, Texas, and the American University in Cairo, Egypt.

Over the course of his academic and professional career, he has had the opportunity to travel to Greece on several occasions, as well as many other parts of the Mediterranean that are relevant to this manuscript. Having studied the cultures and observed firsthand many of the ancient ruins and battlefields, his depth of knowledge and attention to detail provide the reader with a unique window into antiquity. Please enjoy *The Last Shades of Scarlet: Wolves of Laconia*, and prepare yourself for an epic journey into a conflict that changed the course of history and still influences the world we live in today.

CPSIA information can be obtained
at www.ICGtesting.com
Printed in the USA
BVHW071310141019
561050BV00002B/169/P

9 781684 565368